a Web too Tight

To Susan,
Stay faithful to God.

a Web too Tight

Barbara Eubanks

BARBARA EUBANKS

TATE PUBLISHING
AND **ENTERPRISES**, LLC

Published by Tate Publishing & Enterprises, LLC
127 E. Trade Center Terrace | Mustang, Oklahoma 73064 USA
1.888.361.9473 | www.tatepublishing.com

Tate Publishing is committed to excellence in the publishing industry. The company reflects the philosophy established by the founders, based on Psalm 68:11,
"The Lord gave the word and great was the company of those who published it."

Book design copyright © 2012 by Tate Publishing, LLC. All rights reserved.
Cover design by Ronnel Luspoc
Interior design by Ronnel Luspoc

Published in the United States of America

ISBN: 978-1-62295-539-8
1. Fiction / Christian / General
12.10.26

Dedication

First and foremost, this novel is dedicated to my husband of fifty-four years, Steve Eubanks, who has remained faithful, loving, and true to me and to his marriage vows. He has made being a pastor's wife a pleasant journey for me.

Next, it goes to all the men of God who have stood firm, resisted temptation, kept the faith, and honored God with their lives and ministry.

Finally, to my friend Kaye, who is the best Christian lady I know, one of God's paramount forgivers, who has shown others how to forgive, I dedicate this work.

Preface

Although this is a work of fiction, which does not intend to represent any literal person, situation or place, it does compile the common characteristics of the many ministers who have been trapped in the web of sin and adultery. Hopefully, the work is realistic to the point that any man of God who has had similar situations in his life will think I have written it about him.

Most people have someone in their lives whom they have respected and held in high esteem, often a man of God, one who has fallen to temptation and taken a moral tumble that has disappointed and affected friends and churches enormously. One cannot think of this scenario without reflecting on King David's fall, his adulterous affair with Bathsheba, his repentance and forgiveness. In his case, as with people today, one sin led on to another. Although forgiven, David lived with the consequences of his sin for the rest of his days.

This is, not only a saga of a fall, but it also shows that, although sinners may repent and be forgiven, sin still exacts a great price in the form of its built-in consequences. This also chronicles how, by the grace of God, a hurt wife can demonstrate Hosea-type forgiveness and lead others to forgive.

Contents

Foreword

In order to truly understand the dynamics of Barbara Eubanks' book title, *A Web Too Tight*, a reader should research the incredible strength of a spider's web. The composition of a web can withstand tears and winds that exceed hurricane speeds. The construction of the web, as well as the individual silk strands, responds to stresses and damages. Even when a part of the web is disturbed, the web returns to stability after repairing that portion of the design.

A Web Too Tight shows how families are affected when the web of trust is damaged. In this instance, Barbara shows the effects on Molly, her family, the church family, and the town of Smythville when her husband, Jack, has an affair with a church member he is counseling as Senior Pastor of their church. Molly also learns that Darcy is not the first attraction that has been caught in Jack's web.

Molly shows strength, courage, and the model of forgiveness. The Bible has given guidelines for handling stresses and forgiveness in Ephesians 4:30 – 31, "And do not grieve the Holy Spirit of God, with whom you were sealed for the day of redemption. Get rid of all bitterness, rage and anger, brawling and slander, along with every form of malice."

For those of us who have experienced traumas in our lives similar to Molly's, we are given hope and courage by her faithfulness to God's Word as she exhibits forgiveness. Her family, church family, and town draw strength in her willingness to fight to keep God first in her life even when her world was being drawn into Satan's web.

Barbara Eubanks has written about a subject that is often taboo in denominational circles. Statistics have shown that four out of seven ministers who have 'failed' will rekindle romances even after restoration with their family and church family. Once a minister has been trapped and has lost his ministry, there is a greater risk to again fall into Satan's trap.

A Web Too Tight shows the design that God has given us for repentance and forgiveness just as the spider has shown us the engineering structure of its web. A web is designed to withstand large loads with very little damage because the web allows a 'sacrificial member' to be given up under extreme loads. In a minister's 'fall,' the family or the church may feel they are the 'sacrificial member;' however, Satan has trapped the minister into a web that has squeezed tighter and tighter. Generally, a minister is trapped into a web when his ministry is at its peak, God is being glorified, and souls are being saved!

Read Barbara's book with a sense of urgency to PRAY for ministers and their families without ceasing. Pray that Satan will NOT be allowed to use the trap of an adulterous affair to tear ministers, families, and churches apart. Take away a resolve to live a 'Molly-type' of life that glorifies HIM in all we do!

—Marsha Beavers Smith
New Albany, Mississippi

—Katy, Texas
Al-Khobar, Saudi Arabia
Educational Diagnostician working in Al-Khobar,
Saudi Arabia with International Schools Group.
President of Metochai for seminary wives at Southwestern
Baptist Theological Seminary (SWBTS) in Fort Worth, Texas
Pastor's Wife for twenty-five years in
Texas, Florida, and Mississippi
Conference Speaker

Prologue

He sat, legs outstretched, under the indifferent oak with a deer rifle across his lap. Jack Pate, shoulders slumped, glared transfixed into some unknown world. The towering trees accentuated his sense of worthlessness. The polished butt of his Remington 30-30 rifle rested in one hand; his other gripped its icy barrel. In the wrinkles of his camouflage jacket, puddles of shed tears mingled with the drizzle and ran down as rivulets of sorrow.

Slowly, with trembling hands, Jack angled the barrel of his rifle under his chin with the butt braced on the ground. Mesmerized, he released the safety, reached forward to position his thumb on the trigger, and started the steady pressure.

Molly

Sorrow engulfed Molly as she lay face down across the very bed where she and Jack had slept just two nights before. His words, like a branding iron, burned their imprint on her heart and still rang in her ears. "If only you could have been more...more expressive, more daring. I needed more. I *deserved* more."

In troubled times, Molly had always been able to see the bright side or, at least, to have faith that something good could come from bad situations. In her forty-three years, she had experienced many hard times without losing hope. But now only despair clothed her; self-deprecation became her mantle.

Jack has always been my idol, she thought. *Since we were teens he has been my everything. He was my savior, helping me escape from a life doomed to failure and poverty. Haven't I told him often, shown him how much I adore him? How could I have been so wrong for so long about the love of my life? How blind could I have been not to have seen the signs of betrayal, immorality, deception? How could he spit in the face of the unfaltering faith I always had in him? How could he degrade me and the love I have shown him?*

For once Molly had been assertive. She had rushed to the foyer as soon as she heard the door open. Jack looked haggard. As he came through the door, in addition to the distinctive perspiration odor produced by stress, Molly detected the stale perfume of a woman on him. The scent both aroused fresh anger in her and strengthened her to stand her ground as she confronted her husband.

"Jack, you're finally here. We've got to talk. I want to know what is going on. The phone hasn't stopped ringing with people wanting to make sure I've seen the article in the newspaper. The paper's account is so different from what you told me and what you told the church. Who is this other woman? Don't walk away from me! For once in our marriage, I demand an explanation."

"Where do you come off demanding anything of me, woman? I've got to make a call. We'll talk after that, so just shut up for now and quit your nagging."

Jack slammed the door and took the stairs two at a time. Fear of making him angrier would normally have quieted Molly, but this time she was determined to get a believable explanation, even though she sensed she wouldn't like the truth. However, she knew him well enough to give him time to calm down.

While Molly paced in the living room, Jack was upstairs on the phone. "You can tell the church I won't be back," Jack almost shouted. "All they want to do is tear down a pastor with gossip. Furthermore, I don't have to defend my actions to you, the other deacons, or the church. Just make your own error-ridden assumptions. God will punish all of you for mistreating a man of God."

As he had done so often in the past, Jack tried to transfer blame to others. As he said the words, he almost convinced himself that he was the victim. He had to get away. He didn't know where he would go, but he couldn't take any more inquisitions. He couldn't face the shame ahead, and he had no idea how he could untangle this mess. His idyllic ride as one of the most admired and respected men in Smythville, Georgia, was now ended. No longer would he be known as the most dynamic pastor in the area, the one responsible for leading Pleasant Valley Community Church to be the largest, fastest growing church in all of North Georgia. Instead, people would remember the disgrace he had brought on his family and the church. He grabbed his Remington 30–30, his hunting jacket, and boots from the closet then went downstairs and rushed to the door.

But Molly was waiting for him. She placed herself between Jack and the door. "You're not leaving this house again until I get some answers. Where are you going?"

Then she noticed the rifle in his hand. "Where are you going with that? This just doesn't make any sense. None of it does."

"Okay, we'll talk," he said with a bitter tone she had never heard before. "I've been miserable with you for the last twenty-five years. You think cleaning the house and taking care of the children make you a perfect wife. You have ignored my needs—sexually, emotionally, and spiritually. You have never measured up as a wife. Everyone thinks you are so perfect—the perfect little pastor's wife. Well, they are wrong. I've never loved you. You trapped me by letting yourself get pregnant. I've had enough. I won't be back. I'm leaving you." Tears welled up in Molly's eyes. Shock and fear replaced her anger. Weeping bitterly she begged, "Wait, Jack, wait. You can't leave. Please don't do anything drastic. We can work out any problems we face—with the Lord's help."

Jack pushed her out of his way. As he opened the door, he turned back to her and said, "If only you could have been more... more expressive, more daring. I needed more. I *deserved* more." Then he slammed the door. By the time she caught her balance and managed to get out the door, he was speeding away. Torrents of tears blinded Molly as she stumbled up the stairs and fell across her bed.

She wasn't sure how much time passed before the ringing phone got her attention. At first she was going to ignore it, but she noticed on the Caller ID that it was her daughter Caitlin. Although Caitlin and Bob had moved several hours away to Atlanta soon after their wedding, she never missed a day talking to Molly. Usually Molly called around 10:00 a.m., but today Caitlin's phone didn't ring. It was Tuesday and Caitlin knew her mother worked only Wednesdays and Thursdays at the hospital. Molly had cut back to two twelve-hour-night nursing shifts in the emergency room when Caitlin and her brother were small because she refused to delegate their care to someone else every day. Caitlin held the phone impatiently as it rang the fourth and fifth times. During the sixth ring, she heard the click at the other end signaling someone had picked up. No hello came. "Mom?"

Still no greeting. "Mom, is that you? Answer me." All Caitlin heard was the sound of her mother's sobs. "What in the world is wrong? Tell me, please."

As Molly answered she knew she couldn't hide her grief, but neither did she have the voice to offer any explanation. "I just can't talk right now," Molly managed.

"Mom, are you hurt or sick? Has something happened to Dad or Benji?"

"No, no, no!" She cried. "Your dad… He… It's too much. I just can't say it." Molly's voice dissolved into sobs, and she dropped the receiver. Caitlin could still hear her mom's moans as the line went dead.

Caitlin was stunned and for a moment sat thinking about what she should do. She had always received love and support from her mom as she was growing up. Now that she was married and had a baby of her own, Molly was her go-to person for advice on everything from how to make formula to how to cook chicken casserole. Molly had always served as her role model but now had become her best friend since she married.

Although she didn't know what the problem was, it was evident it concerned her father. Caitlin had been constantly rebuffed by her dad. He showed no confidence that she would or could make good decisions about anything. Jack made his daughter feel she was a second-class citizen simply because she was female. Jack had repeatedly cautioned her, "If you're not careful, you are going to mess around and get yourself pregnant and shame our family. You seem to date any Tom, Dick, or Harry who will ask you. You're going to end up being their backseat 'Dolly' if you're not careful."

This hadn't been the case, but his remarks sunk deeply into Caitlin's psyche. She never felt she measured up to his expectations. The negative effect of her father's words outweighed the positive input her mother always provided. She sometimes wondered if that was why she so readily accepted Bob's proposal while she was a high school senior. Already having graduated from college and having a great position with a prominent engineering firm, Bob had impressed Caitlin. He gave her support and approval in anything she attempted. He filled a void in her heart that her father never filled.

She came back to the realization that she must do something to help her mother, even if it meant confronting her father. Picking up her cell phone again, she called her dad's office. "Kim, I need to speak to Dad."

Hesitantly the pastor's assistant answered, "I'm sorry, Caitlin, your dad hasn't been in the office since the convention. I haven't seen him since he returned. I really don't know where he is. As a matter of fact, he called to cancel his appointments here at the office but said nothing of his plans."

Caitlin called information and got the number of Smytheville High School. Within a few minutes, she had her brother on the phone. "Benji, something is terribly wrong with Mother. I called and she couldn't even tell me what's wrong, she was crying so hard. I tried to reach Dad at the office, but they don't know where he is. Can you go see about Mom? I'll come but I'm over two hours away, and I have to pack. I can't get there as quickly as you can."

"Sure, Sis. If I can't get permission, this is one time I'll leave without being checked out." After telling the principal he had a family emergency, Benji bounded out the door, ran across the parking lot to his car, and sped toward home. As he drove, he thought about how his mother had quietly encouraged him as he left for school. "Benji, I'll be praying for God to bring to your mind all the things you have studied and that you will do well on your biology mid-term. You know how proud I am of you."

It was always his mother who praised Benji for his academic and athletic accomplishments. She understood the pressure of being a pastor's son, and she had helped him learn to live a Christian life based on his own commitment and convictions.

Molly had never been too busy to attend his football games and other school functions. She was the one who always helped him pray through any difficult situation. Benji felt comfortable sharing his worries, needs, and joys with his mom.

His father usually got to his games when he was in town but rarely complimented him. He always played the part of the sports critic, telling Benji what he should have done and how he could have played more effectively. Having been a great athlete himself, he had a feeling of superiority. Somehow his father never found the good in his children. Or at least he wasn't able to express it as his mother always could.

He parked in the driveway and ran through the back door. "Mom, Mom, where are you? Answer me, Mom," Benji yelled. "Caitlin called me at school and told me something was wrong. There you are," he said as he reached her bedroom.

She looked up with a tear-stained face, which seemed to have aged twenty years since he had seen her just a few hours before. Jerking sobs replaced words when she opened her mouth to try to speak. Benji took her into his arms to try to console her. "I don't know what's wrong, Mom, but it surely can't be this bad. Whatever it is, I will do what I can. You know God can help any situation. Lean on Him. Lean on me this time, too."

Benji felt a sudden reversal of roles. Molly had always made things better for him, regardless of the situation; she had soothed skinned knees; she had fixed his broken heart when he had to leave his best friend to move to Smytheville. He sat holding his disconsolate mother for what seemed like an hour. As he sat there not knowing the problem or how to fix it, he silently prayed,

"God, please help my mom as she has helped so many others in the past. Heal her hurt, I pray. Give me wisdom and strength for the moment."

Eventually Molly lifted her face to her son's. This time she managed to verbalize a weak sentence. "Your daddy has left me."

"I don't understand.

"He said he didn't love me any more…that he had lost interest in me. He said our marriage had been sheer drudgery for him."

"Something's very wrong. That doesn't sound like Dad. He's the one always preaching the importance of family. Just last Sunday he preached about breaking promises made before a holy God. He even used marriage vows as one of those promises."

"I know. I know. I must have failed him terribly," she sobbed. "I've tried to be a good wife and mother, but I know I've let the romance and excitement of our marriage fade."

"Mother, whatever has happened, I can assure you, it's not your fault. I've never seen a more dedicated wife and mother. You have followed Dad around, seeing after his every need like a paid servant. You always put his needs and ours before yours. This must just be some big mistake. Maybe Dad is having some sort of midlife crisis or a mental breakdown of some kind," Benji said as he tried to convince himself as much as his mother.

"I don't know. He just took his rifle and walked out the door. I tried to stop him, but he wouldn't listen. Benji, I would change. I would do anything to make life better for him."

"How could he do this to you? I hate that hypocrite."

His typically calm demeanor was gone. His love and respect for his dad turned to something Molly didn't even recognize in her son.

"Benji, Benji, you don't mean that. Please don't say anything like that. You are probably right. He can't help this. He's having some kind of breakdown."

"When I find him, I'm going to break him of ever treating you this way again. I'm calling Janice Baugh to come stay with you while I go find Dad. You can trust her; she will keep this in confidence. We don't need this news out in Smytheville yet. Caitlin will be here soon. She had to make a few arrangements."

"Oh, I can't bear for anyone to know this. You go find your dad, and leave me by myself. I've got to try to get some of this worked out in my mind. I'll just stay here to think and try to pray. This may be one of those times where Jesus will have to take my groaning and intercede for me. I don't know how, but God will help us work this out some way."

For the first time in his young life, Benji assumed the role of the parent. He realized his mother wasn't capable of thinking clearly. Putting his arm around her shoulders once again, he overrode her decision. "Mom, I'm not leaving you here alone all afternoon. That's that!"

As soon as Janice arrived, Benji gave her a partial explanation. "I just didn't know who else to call. I knew you would come without having to know every detail. All I can say for now is Dad is having a problem of some kind. Mother is in a terrible state—near hysteria—and doesn't need to be alone. I've got to see if I can help straighten this out. Please stay with her until Caitlin can get here."

"You know I will. I can't imagine what kind of disaster has occurred, but I don't have to know. I'll just stay here and pray for you, your dad, and Molly."

"Mother has gone to the bathroom to try to pull herself together. If she doesn't come out soon, please check on her."

"I will take care of your mom. You go. Do what you can and be careful."

Benji had an idea where his search would lead him. He and Jack had hunted the north woods not many miles away. If Jack was determined to be alone, he might go there. Driving his old VW up the interstate, Benji's thoughts vacillated from a desire to cause his dad great pain to a concern his dad was in trouble and needed help of some kind. His thoughts of possible scenarios in the event he found Jack fed the rage and fear Benji felt. The secure world he left that morning had suddenly turned to chaos.

Caitlin

At dusk Caitlin turned into the driveway of the home where she had lived until she married. The place, which seemed to hold out welcoming arms when she would come home each day, now looked dismal. She dreaded what she might find there. She opened the back door of her Escort and took out baby Emily. Not waiting to take time to gather the other baby essentials from the car, she dashed into the house to be greeted by Janice Baugh instead of her mother.

"Caitlin, I am so sorry you are coming home to trouble. I can't tell you what's going on because I don't know myself. All I know is your dad is gone, and when your mother has been able to say anything, all she says is, 'It must be my fault. It must be my fault.' I did something your mother didn't want me to do, but I thought it was necessary."

"What did you do? Where is Mom? I need to see her."

"Molly had wept for so long and had the symptoms of someone going into shock, so I called Dr. Simmons. You remember him from church, don't you? He came over from his office and gave Molly a shot—a sedative. She has been asleep for a while, if you can call it sleep. Even asleep she moans constantly."

"I won't wake her, but I'm going to look in on her." Caitlin quickly climbed the stairs and peeked into the bedroom. She couldn't believe the curled-up, disheveled woman on the bed could be her mother. After quietly pulling the bedroom door closed, she returned to the living room to try to find out what was going on.

The shot Dr. Simmons gave her had taken effect quickly. Molly had at first protested but then found herself desperately wanting to drift into nothingness. As the drug entered her system, thoughts she usually kept deep within washed over her—memories of what her life once was like and how Jack Pate had changed everything so long ago.

Every good memory she had of her youth involved Jack. He had been kind to her when many others shunned her because of her simple-minded mother and alcoholic father. James, her dad, did the most menial farm tasks like shoveling manure and burying dead calves. He did those jobs on days he was sober enough to work. Poss, the farm's owner, drove his Ford pick-up to the tenant farm house to get him when the stables needed mucking or when a cow had gotten stuck in the pond. Other farmers also used James for any dirty work they didn't want to do themselves. Her father always came home covered in dried manure on his rancid-smelling, seldom-washed work clothes. He had little pride or reason for it.

All Sue, Molly's mother, was concerned about was candy. "Did you get to go to the store with Poss? Did you bring me some peppermint sugar sticks?" No one knew why her mind had stayed like a small child's while her body had fully developed. Sue spent her days wandering in the yard, picking flowers or walking down the highway kicking tin cans. Some days she found Molly's lipstick and painted her lips in clown fashion and stood by the road waving at men as they drove by.

When Molly started school, she heard some of her classmates talking about the good things they had eaten for supper the night before. She soon realized everybody didn't live on bread and cereal. Molly learned to cook early. The only time a decent meal appeared on their old chrome-topped table was when James earned enough to buy groceries and she cooked.

One day her home economics teacher, Mrs. Owens announced, "I will be checking on the home improvement project each of you girls have committed to do. I will make it a point to visit in every student's home sometime during the term."

Molly cringed at the thought of this refined, impeccably dressed teacher sitting in her filthy kitchen. Grease coated the raw-wood floor; it smelled of stale lard. That was a result of Sue deciding one day she could make her floors shine like Mrs. Johnson's beautiful linoleums. She had seen her neighbor's house only one time—the day she had gone to get the discarded clothes Mrs. Johnson had for her. In one of her few attempts at housekeeping, Sue took a handful of rancid lard and smeared it on her boarded floors. The fat failed to bring a shine; it merely made dirt and filth stick like nails to a magnet and served as a feast for roaches.

Molly realized Mrs. Owens's visit was inevitable, but she also knew she would be one of the last visited because she lived away from town. This would buy her some time. She resolved that day to do something about the squalor her family lived in. After she got in from school, Molly began by taking one of their four rooms a day to clean. She heated a bucket of water on the old wood stove and stirred in the Tide washing powders her dad had brought home. There was no mop in the house, so Molly took the straw broom and scrubbed the grimy floors with the sudsy water. Eventually, the fresh soap scent replaced the stench of the stale lard and the filth which had collected for months. Once again, the grain of the wood showed.

In that home Molly was an anomaly. Fortunately, she had inherited her grandfather's bright mind and her grandmother's sense of pride. Molly had decent hand-me-down clothes, thanks to the women from the little country church she had attended since they had moved to the community ten years before. With each change of season, one of the ladies brought a grocery bag of clothes for Molly. By watching Dorothy's mother do their family's laundry, Molly learned to properly wash and iron her own clothes.

Dorothy was the closest thing Molly had to a friend. On a few occasions, Dorothy had invited Molly to come over, but it was obvious to Molly she was only an at-home friend to Dorothy; she wasn't a welcomed member of the clique of town kids Dorothy hung with at school.

One day when the bus stopped to let her and her little brother Homer off, Molly's eyes filled with tears as she saw Sue at the clothesline with scissors, cutting to shreds the dresses Molly had hung that morning before school. So distressed by what she saw, Molly was barely aware of the pointing and snickering of the students left on the bus. She knew her mother was just as jealous of her clothes and appearance as a young sister might be, but she never imagined her mother would do something like this. Seven-year-old Homer seemed totally oblivious to the spectacle. The next morning as Molly boarded the bus, head down to avoid the stares of the others there, she started for her regular seat near the back. Midway back, Jack Pate's hand reached toward her. "Molly, why don't you sit here with me?"

Jack Pate was one of the best basketball players at SHS. She saw him at church every Sunday, but nothing more than a casual hello had been exchanged between them.

"Are you sure Joel won't sit here when he gets on the bus? He usually does."

"He'll find another seat today. Come on. Sit down."

Molly then held her head high as she took her seat. Jack's acceptance and affirmation of her hushed the giggles and stopped the ridicule. This was the way Jack was. He always seemed to have a place in his heart for the underdog or the needy. She had observed his compassion being offered to others, both at church and at school. When a need for encouragement or comfort arose, Jack supplied it.

From that day on, her permanent seat was beside Jack. He also sought her out at break. He would stand with his long left arm propped on her locker door, casually clasping his books in his right hand. With Jack's attention, Molly was soon accepted by his friends. She no longer felt ostracized by the stigma of her home life.

Being elected class beauty her junior year was a surprise only to Molly. She had spent her life trying to make herself simply acceptable; she hadn't realized she was blessed with beautiful hair, a powdery complexion, and eyes that were like blue magnets. Her quiet demeanor and sweet smile had gradually endeared her to her classmates. In her unassuming manner, she befriended them in inconspicuous ways. Others enjoyed basking in the admiration and sincere compliments Molly offered them.

Soon after she finished high school, Jack asked her to marry him. By then, he was playing basketball for Trinity State University, a college about sixty miles away, but after the season ended, he started coming home most weekends. After taking his laundry home and answering his mom's countless questions about school, he rushed to see Molly. Jack rarely came in. Molly grabbed her sweater and rushed out the door to prevent the embarrassment of her parents' presence.

Often they drove down a pothole-filled dirt road, winding down a steep hill to the peaceful lake. Jack put his arm around Molly and pulled her close; they chatted about the last week's events. Although Jack always treated Molly like a lady in public, in private their petting and necking became more passionate.

Late one spring, Molly and Jack made their usual trek to the lake. On the blanket by the shoreline, Jack's advances became more demanding. She tensed for a moment but barely resisted. "It's okay, Molly. You know I would never do anything to hurt you. You are mine and always will be. You're the only one I have ever wanted."

Experiencing desires she had never known before, and accepting Jack's assurance that everything would be okay, Molly allowed him to go beyond the limits she had set in her mind. She desperately wanted him to love and accept her. Before the afternoon ended, passion had consumed the two. She could never call back her state of purity. Although Molly had given up her innocence, she knew from whispers among the girls at school that Jack was far from innocent. There had been many girls before her. But she told herself that it didn't matter. He loved her, not them. Late in June Molly broke the news to Jack about her pregnancy. She remembered apologizing to him as though it was totally her fault. She waited for his reaction, fearing the worst.

Jack had quickly decided they would get married. Molly had always been grateful for that. For the first time in her life, with this new knowledge she had of him, she wondered if he had married her out of love or because his family might have otherwise been disgraced and he would have had to face his father's scorn.

What has happened to you, Jack? she thought as she sank into unconsciousness. *Is this the end of everything we've known?*

Caitlin took baby Emily from Janice. "Thank you so much for coming to see after her. You did the right thing by calling the doctor. But I just wish I could understand what's taking place. Where is Benji?"

"He went to look for your father. You will get the full story in time, sweetie. I really don't know anything about it. I put on a pot of soup, and I will leave for now. Molly will feel freer talking to you if I'm not here. I am just a phone call away if you need anything at all. Maybe you can get some soup or juice down Molly when she wakes up. Dr. Simmons said she must drink some fluids. She will dehydrate if we don't insist on her drinking something. I know you can handle this."

"Mrs. Baugh, thanks for all you've done. Mother has always loved and trusted you. I'm not sure I am strong enough to face whatever Mother is going through."

"Let me pray for you before I leave. Remember, God's strength is perfect. He does his best work when we are our weakest." Janice put a loving arm around Caitlin and prayed. "Dear heavenly Father, we know your mercies and grace are with each of us when we need them most. Right now I ask that you give Molly, Caitlin, and the rest of the family what they need in this hour of uncertainty. Help sort out these difficulties. We don't know all the circumstances, nor do we need to know them because we trust them to you. You have each of these sweet people in your loving hands. Do your work in this place just now. We thank you for what you will do. Amen."

A holy peace immediately washed over Caitlin. She felt strengthened by an unseen force. The Holy Spirit gave Caitlin assurance in an unsure situation. Even Emily, who had been crying in Caitlin's arms, quieted.

Caitlin used the time between Janice's leaving and Molly's awakening to bring in their things from the car, feed Emily, and get her ready for bed. Just as she was about to lay Emily in the travel crib, she heard her mother stirring in the bedroom. She wanted Molly to see Emily before she put her down, so she eased the bedroom door opened. Molly was standing by the bed, straightening the comforter in a zombie-like state. "Mom," Caitlin said in a hushed voice, "Emily and I have come to be with you. Whatever has happened, we will get through it together."

"Oh Caitlin, I don't know if I can even talk about it."

Janice's prayer had brought soothing results for Caitlin. Instead of displaying her normal impatience and inquisitive nature, she gently hugged her mom and handed the baby over to her. "Why don't you hold Emily before I put her down, and you can tell me what you feel if you're able to after she goes to sleep."

This brought a slight smile to Molly's tear-streaked face. "Sweet Emily, you've grown since Gran has seen you. Caitlin, I can't believe you made the drive without Bob. You told me last week he was going to be in Philadelphia on business this week, but I am so glad you're here." The tears broke loose once again, this time startling the sleepy child. Emily started fussing, so Caitlin took her.

"Mom, while I get Emily settled in, I want you to go to the bathroom, wash your face, and come to the kitchen. Janice left us some corn and potato chowder she made. You need to eat some."

"I don't think I could swallow—-"

"Listen to me. Regardless of what has happened, I'm not allowing you to dehydrate and starve."

Like an obedient child, Molly complied. As they sat at the table, Molly slowly took a few spoonfuls of soup. Putting her spoon down and pushing back her bowl, she looked at her daughter and began. "Sweetie, I'll tell you what I know, which isn't too much. For months now, things have been strained between your dad and me. He has distanced himself for some unknown reason. Everything I did irritated him. When I would ask him what was wrong, he'd brush me off. I just accepted the fact that he was under some great stress with church matters and gave him his space. But his space kept getting broader and broader. Maybe I should have insisted he talk to me about it, but instead, I've just been praying about the situation. I prayed God would ease his stress and help me be the wife I should be.

"Then he came through last night and told me he wouldn't be home. He would be sleeping somewhere else. When I questioned him, 'Why? Where?' he just ignored me. Again I mentally excused him. I thought he might be having an early morning meeting down in Augusta or somewhere. He came back this morning after Benji left for school and announced he was leaving—that he just didn't love me anymore." Molly barely got the last part out before burying her face in her arms on the table. She wept and wept. All Caitlin's efforts to console her failed.

"Mom, there must be some explanation. I know Dad not only loves you, he worships the ground you walk on. He has affirmed you so many times from the pulpit. He may be experiencing some sort of breakdown. I think he'll come to his senses."

"You just didn't see the entire picture, sweetie. That emotion was expressed more as a public image thing than a private, heartfelt love. That same esteem didn't extend to home or our private life. I realize that now. I failed miserably at measuring up to what he wanted, but if he would just come back, I would try harder. I really would."

"Mom, don't beat yourself up like this. You are more than any man could ask for. It's not you. Something's wrong with him." Molly realized, in hindsight, she should have warned Jack to be careful where Darcy was concerned. Intuition and other signs told her if there was another woman, it must be Darcy. She remembered a conversation Darcy had initiated a few months before.

"Do you know just how lucky you are? You've got it all: a husband who adores you; he's a master preacher, a wonderful counselor, and your children are smart and handsome. What I wouldn't give to be in your shoes!"

Darcy and the Preacher

"Darcy, you must realize no one falls beyond God's reach. He still cares for you, and so do I. Why don't you just go back to where you believe the beginning might be? We don't have to feel rushed. I can meet with you as often and as many times necessary to get the entire story out. You will get relief just by telling it, and I'm a good listener."

"Preacher, I'm not sure you're ready to hear the dreadful conditions of my life. Your ears have never heard such degradation."

"Try me, hon. I've heard more than you can imagine."

"Okay, here goes. I believe this all started when I was just four-years-old. My mom was a weak woman—always sickly. She could barely get through the daily tasks of cooking and washing to keep us five kids taken care of. She would go to bed by dark every night, totally used up. Papa took solace in the bottle and the companionship of his poker buddies. They would gather around our old, red and gray chrome and Formica table with their cards and beer. Sometimes their laughter and bawdy jokes would awaken me.

"One night I eased out of bed and went in the kitchen where they were. 'Git yourself back in that bed,' Papa barked at me. I cowered back and began my retreat just as our neighbor Paul intervened.

"Paul weighed at least three hundred pounds and seemed to always have a trickle of tobacco streaming down the corner of his mouth, but he was a jolly man who always had time for the neighborhood children. Maybe it was because he and his wife Sophie never had any of their own. 'Ah Lucas, let that child be. She can come here and sit with me a few minutes. Maybe she'll help my luck.' Paul opened his bulky arms for me to run to him. He pulled me up on his fat leg and let me look at his cards. 'Now, Missy, you think we oughta play this hand or fold?' he asked not really expecting an answer. I knew to sit quietly or Papa would make me leave. As the night wore on and the beer bottles accumulated, I began to relax against Paul's chest and was about to drift to sleep when Paul started rubbing my leg ever so gently while the cards were being dealt. I liked his soothing touch and felt such comfort as I snuggled against him. This began a ritual that continued for many poker nights. As his touches became more intimate, I felt an uneasiness, an inkling that something wasn't right about this, but I trusted him. After all, he was an adult. I didn't resist because I wanted to remain his special pet. He always came through the door asking where his 'little poker charm' was. If I had already gone to bed, I would wait for his loud voice and quietly go in the room and crawl up in his lap.

"One morning I awoke in a strange bed. Paul was snoring to my right, and Sophie lay to my left. Later that morning, Paul laughed and told me he won me in the poker game the night before. I looked a bit puzzled, and he explained, 'Nah, honey, your daddy got a little behind, so I told him if he would let you come stay with me and Sophie for a while, I'd forgive his debt. You know we don't have any younguns so we'll enjoy having you here. Is that all right with you?'

"Knowing I didn't have a say in the matter anyway, I nodded in agreement. In fact, I liked the idea of being the only child around and not just one in a hill. Sophie fed me a good breakfast and seemed pleased I was there. Paul took me with him to milk the cow and see after the other things on the farm.

"That night, Sophie took me to a tiny room off the kitchen where there was a single bed sitting on worn linoleum. 'I put you some extra quilts on the bed so I think you'll be warm enough here. Your mamma sent over your flannel nightgown with your other clothes. You can put it on by the kitchen stove where you'll stay warm.'

"I noticed Paul's gleaming eyes as he sat at the table and watched my every move as I took off my dirty dress and slipped on the ragged gown. Sophie led me to my room, and Paul said, 'I'll come in and tuck you in good after a little bit.' He sat relaxed as he sipped his bottle of home brew.

"Sophie told me she was tired and was going to bed also. It took me some time to get comfortable on the knotty, musty-smelling mattress, but just as my eyelids began getting heavy, I heard the door creak open. 'Baby Girl, move over a little and old Paul will lay down beside you and get you good and warm.' I innocently did as he told me."

Darcy continued recounting to Jack the details of the sexual abuse that began that night and continued for years that followed as Paul stole her innocence and replaced it with nothing but pain and shame.

"I guess you could say that's where my story began."

"Oh Darcy, I'm so sorry you had to endure such exploitation and maltreatment, but I understand you much better after hearing this," Jack said as he rubbed the top of Darcy's hand. Just this fatherly touch ignited unexpected electricity that they both felt. "Why don't you come back this time next week after work, and you can tell me more. I want you to know God can take away your pain and your shame."

As Darcy left the office, Jack was very much aware of her well-proportioned body. Her story had strangely aroused him for which he felt a fleeting bit of guilt. *She needs to tell her story, and I can't help this involuntary reaction,* he rationalized. But this arousal prompted him to want more. He turned to his computer and clicked on one of his favorite sites. Jack thought of his wife as his helpmate and the mother of his children, not as his lover. Oh, she was forever the dutiful wife, never denying him, but she never initiated intimacy. He knew her well enough to know she would be appalled at the thought of trying some of the things he saw on this porn site. An unexpected thought came to his mind: *Darcy would try anything.* He knew with her past experiences and her present needs, she would be more daring and exciting.

Sunday morning Jack preached a stern sermon on the sexual perversions that were destroying the society. "You men are doing your families a grave injustice when you spend time watching pornographic movies and making computer porn sites your mistress. I know what some of you are doing. You say you're not hurting anyone, but you are. You are committing a form of adultery against your wife and stealing family time from your children." His altar call centered on confession and repentance. Five young men with tears streaming down their faces rushed to the altar and fell to their knees in repentance. This wasn't the first time Jack's sermon took the form of transference of his own sin.

Smytheville's Good Ol' Boys

Smoke from the paper mill hung over the bank that Tuesday morning like a dirty blanket the way it always did when the humidity was high. The smut and gossip provided a different kind of pollution in the basement of the bank. Jack drove up and parked in his usual spot, ignoring the H signifying the handicap parking space. He enjoyed joining in the joking and ribbing of the group. There he was just one of the guys. They treated him like an average Joe, not as a pastor or some religious icon. He needed this camaraderie, and it helped his standing in the community. Here the leading businessmen of Smytheville met. Most of Jack's men friends attended his church, so the good ol' boys' club broadened his popularity with men from different denominations. Most all of the men affiliated themselves with some church; that was the expected thing to do in Smytheville.

Sawyer Thomas, a ruggedly handsome bachelor, was an exception. He made no pretense of any religious involvement and made it clear he simply had no use for church. He had commented several times there were too many hypocrites in the churches already. Sawyer had a keen discerning instinct about people and seemed to see through sinners' veneers.

The Colonial Bank included an activities room in the basement when it was built a few years back. Many of the civic clubs used it for their regular meetings, and the good ol' boys met there every Tuesday at 9:00 a.m. That time was never announced nor was it posted on the wall as were the meeting times for the Rotary Club and the Civitans. A couple of the men started going down for coffee when they made their morning trip to deposit the money taken in the day before. Soon two or three others started meeting up about the same time until the number had grown to ten. Although Jack wasn't a businessman, he managed to insinuate himself into the group. The men made it clear from the beginning his righteous ears would not be shielded from their usual bawdiness. The meetings were marked by scurrilous chatter and behavior. This was fine with Jack. He needed a little spice in his bland life. Anyway, meeting with them didn't necessarily put his stamp of approval on their goings-on.

He entered last the day after Darcy's first visit to his office. Carl Fincher was telling his traveling salesman joke of the day about a large-breasted farmer's daughter.

"Speaking of large breasts," Logan Sims interjected, "have you guys ever seen a nicer pair than those hung on Darcy Sims? No wonder Dr. Martin keeps her on in spite of the gossip about her and old Perry. Jackson may be getting old, but he still enjoys sneaking a peek." The room roared with laughter. Logan continued, "Why do you think I have so many cavities? I just lay back in the chair, feigning sleep from the sedative Dr. Martin always gives me and enjoy her brushing up against me. Occasionally I'll 'accidentally' let my hand flop over to get a feel. I don't think she minds at all." The men hooted, Logan louder than anyone

Several of the others told of encounters with Darcy—some true and others, as the group knew, were fabricated just to get a laugh, each one getting a little coarser. Jack laughed as loud as the others. Ben Franks said, "Preacher, I guess the deacons down at your church just enjoy passing the offering plate by her too much to confront her about her affair. Why, that's probably the only time old Deacon Jones ever gets close to anything like that." Whooping and snorting filled the space where Jack otherwise might have been expected to have given a reply. He just nodded and laughed along with them. Sawyer Thomas also remained unusually quiet. Occasionally Jack would catch him staring at him over the edge of his coffee cup with a quizzical look.

Jack was aware that jokes about Darcy were exchanged throughout town—in barbershops, cafes, and clubs—not just at the bank. Darcy provided a great conversation piece among the men of Smytheville.

Jack was the first to leave that day. He had an appointment to get his hair trimmed and dared not miss it. He carefully maintained his professional image. He knew there would be many photo ops tomorrow when he went to the League of Community Churches conference in Atlanta where it was a given he would be elected president. He had served as vice president for the past two years. In the normal order of things, the vice president was always elected president when his time came around.

After Jack drove away, Sawyer shuddered and shook his head. "There's just something sleazy about that preacher. I don't trust him," he uttered.

"You better not let any of that bunch down at the Community Church hear you say that. Some of those folks would knock your block off. They think he can do no wrong," teased Logan.

"I know, I know, but I can't believe he's as perfect as most folks believe."

"Ah, you just don't like any preacher, Sawyer. You're afraid they'll try to convert you," inserted Carl.

"Okay, but one day you'll say Sawyer was right. I'll see you guys later. I've got to get back to the office."

When Jack returned to church later that morning, he found a stack of messages on his desk. Among them was a memo saying Darcy had called. He tossed the others aside and dialed Darcy's work number.

"Dr. Martin's office. Darcy speaking."

"Darcy, what are you doing answering the phone? I thought you would be assisting Dr. Martin."

"I'm the only one left in the office. Both Dr. Martin and Becky, the receptionist, have already gone to lunch. I had the instruments from the morning to get in the autoclave before I left."

"I have a message saying you called while I was out. I'm returning your call, but actually, I had planned to phone you later on today to see how you were after our last session. I know telling your story must have been emotionally draining."

"I feel so much better just knowing someone else knows the truth. I was calling to ask when I can see you again. I have so much more to tell you. I also wanted to just let you know how much I admire and appreciate you. Your sermons are always right on the mark, and your leadership skills reign supreme. As I sit in church listening to you, I find myself thinking of you not only as a preacher but also as a man. I know there must be times when you need to slip out of your minister role. It must be difficult to live up to the expectations of everyone. Do you ever have the urge to just let your hair down, so to speak?"

"Darcy, you have such a keen perception of me. Most people forget that I have needs and passions like any other ordinary man. And, yes, I often fantasize about putting off this 'pioustity' and just to be a normal man. About our next meeting, I'm driving to Atlanta tomorrow for the conference. I have to be there a day early for some committee meetings. If you can take off work a bit early and drive down, I'll buy your dinner, and we can talk in private. You know how people would start rumors if your car was seen in the church parking lot after hours too often."

Darcy's heart fluttered with excitement. "That would be great. You are so thoughtful. Dr. Martin closes the office on Wednesday afternoons anyway. Where shall I meet you?"

"There is an excellent steak restaurant, The Angus Shop, on top of the Sun Trust Bank building on Peachtree Street. It usually doesn't attract the preacher crowd because it is a little pricey, but it has a great view of downtown. You know what they say about preachers: 'They come to town with a twenty dollar bill and a copy of the Ten Commandments and don't break either one.'" Jack laughed more than did Darcy at his tired joke. "They can't say it about me, though, because my church is more than generous with my expense account, so we can splurge. Be there about six."

About this same time, downtown at the Bluebird café where he went for lunch, Sawyer encountered an out-of-towner. "Hi, name's Sawyer Thomas," he said, sticking out his hand to greet the stranger.

"Nice to meet you. Gerald Baugh, here. I'm just in town making calls on a few of my stores in town. I work for Stover's Candies and have just taken on this area. I happened to notice Jack Pate's name on the Peaceful Valley Church sign as I came into town. I have a friend who has moved to Tennessee, Andy Moore, who will be pleased to know his whereabouts. At one time Andy served as his minister of music. Andy called me recently to see if might know where Dr. Jack might be now. I think he has some unfinished business of some kind."

Sawyer lifted his chipped white and green mug for another sip of coffee contemplatively. He gazed at the old table top and unconsciously picked at a flaw in the Formica top. "Do you know him well?" asked Sawyer. His interest piqued.

"I guess you could say that. I served as a deacon at Carter's Bluff for part of his tenure there. I probably know him a little too well."

"Mr. Baugh, why don't you sit with me? I'd like to hear what you have to say about him."

A Voice from the Past

Jack left the office eager to get home to pack for his trip to Atlanta. As he entered the house, he was aware of the aroma of comfort food wafting from the kitchen.

When she heard the front door open, Molly came to the foyer, wiping her hands on her apron. She opened her arms to hug him; Jack gave her a slight pat on the back.

Ignoring his lack of affection, Molly exclaimed, "What a great surprise! You never get home this early. In fact, I'm cooking your favorite dinner—beef stroganoff and salad. I've even fixed a coconut cream pie. It's the recipe Lisa gave me when we were at Carter's Bluff. You always raved about her pie at church suppers."

"That's nice," Jack said distractedly, as he thumbed through the mail Molly had placed on the antique hall table for him as she did every day. I'm going upstairs to pack for my trip to Atlanta. I leave early in the morning."

"You know, Jack, I was thinking of making this trip with you. We haven't gone anywhere, just the two of us, in a couple of years. Besides, I want to be there when you are elected president of the conference."

Startled at Molly's unexpected suggestion, Jack stammered, "I don't think that's a good idea."

"Why not?"

"I just wouldn't have time to spend with you," he offered. "I have meetings from early morning until late night." Putting her off he added, "Maybe soon we can make that trip to the Smoky Mountains you've mentioned."

Somewhat disappointed because she rarely volunteered to go with him on these trips, Molly simply said, "Well, okay. I guess I should stay here and go to Benji's game anyway. Will you call me as soon as the vote is in? I want to be the first to congratulate you. I know being president of the conference has been your goal for a long time."

After dinner Jack thanked Molly for the great meal, and in an attempt to ease her apparent disappointment about not accompanying him, he added, "Molly, you are a wonderful wife and mother. None of us could function without your support." He took her in his arms and kissed the top of her head.

Overwhelmed by Jack's unexpected and rare compliments, Molly leaned against him, wrapping her arms tightly around his waist. "I'm so honored to be your wife."

"Let's make it an early night," Jack said, looking at Molly with a slight smile.

They walked up the stairs, arm in arm, after telling Benji good night. Even he noticed this unusual display of affection between his parents.

After their perfunctory lovemaking, Jack's mind wandered. He fantasized what it would be like making love to someone worldlier, more experienced, and more adventurous in bed; someone like Darcy even. He couldn't imagine Molly ever bringing herself to talk sex to him like the girls on his 900 calls did.

Molly lay awake afterward feeling disappointed. Jack never concerned himself with her enjoyment, only his own release. The only pleasures she ever enjoyed during these sessions was her satisfaction in fulfilling her wifely duties and of being close to Jack for a few moments. *I wish I could enjoy sex like some women seem to. I always feel so awkward and embarrassed. I know that's not the way it should be, but Jack has never really seemed concerned with my needs.* Then she scolded herself. *Oh, I'm just being selfish to think such things.*

Jack was awakened by the alarming clock at 6:00 a.m. He quickly showered, took his bags downstairs, and went to the kitchen to grab a cup of coffee. Molly had been up for two hours already. She had her quiet time before there were any distractions in the house. That morning, she also prepared a beautiful breakfast as a special send-off for Jack. To her disappointment, though, instead of gratitude, he merely displayed impatience. "Why did you cook all of this? You know I don't have time to eat. I've got to get on the road."

"I knew you had to eat somewhere and just thought we'd have a quiet breakfast together before you left."

"Sorry, gotta go. Bye."

Jack left without even giving Molly a good-bye peck. He had more important things on his mind today.

As Jack backed out the driveway, his cell phone rang. "Hello, Jack Pate speaking."

"Hi, Jack. This is Sawyer. I know you're leaving town today but wondered if you would have time for a cup of coffee before you left."

"Sure. I'll meet you at the Bluebird in five minutes." Jack couldn't imagine what had brought on this invitation. Sawyer had always seemed so distant and skeptical. Maybe this would be a step to diffuse Sawyer's cynical attitude toward him.

"Hi, Jack. Have a seat." Sawyer motioned to the other side of the back booth, his face still as stern as it was on their last meeting.

"What a nice surprise to get your call and invitation, Sawyer! You just caught me. I was backing out the drive on my way to Atlanta when my cell phone rang."

"This really isn't a social breakfast. I just wanted to tell you I talked with a former acquaintance of yours, Gerald Baugh."

"Well, what kind of rumors might he have been spreading today?" Jack teased to try to hide his nervousness while at the same time throwing up a smoke screen.

"What can I get for you guys this morning?" interrupted Katy, who had waited tables at the Bluebird since it opened.

"Give me the daily special," Sawyer replied with a quirky smile.

"I'll just have coffee. I'm in a bit of a hurry, sweetie," answered the distracted Jack. He knew he couldn't swallow a bite of food with his cotton mouth and throat.

Sawyer continued, "Oh, he saw your name on the church sign and just asked a few questions about you. He said he was curious to know if you were still doing a lot of counseling. Actually, I didn't have much to say. He did most of the talking." Sawyer stared at Jack, checking his reaction. It seemed he could see right through Jack.

"I don't know what he told you, but you should dismiss most of it. He was nothing but a gossiping troublemaker when I was at Carter's Bluff. The other members knew better than to give credence to his farfetched ideas and rumors. In fact, he was rebuffed by so many he finally left our church. It was a blessed departure."

"Is that so?" Sawyer smirked. "He said you were a great preacher and had a strong following there. Should I dismiss that?"

Caught a bit off-guard with that, Jack got up, laid a dollar on the table and said, "Nice to have a cup with you, but I have appointments in Atlanta this morning. Gotta go."

Driving down the interstate, Jack experienced a plethora of emotions—guilt for not eating breakfast with Molly, anxiety because of a voice from the past, but even greater, anticipation to hear another of Darcy's sagas.

Atlanta

Just as Jack reached the Atlanta city limits, a deluge began. Mere rain couldn't dampen his spirits. The rain would be no problem for him, though. He'd stay dry. All he had to do was drive under the beautiful pavilion at the Ritz-Carlton, open the trunk, and leave the rest to the bellman. He would deliver his suitcases and hanging bags up to his suite, and the valet would park his car for him.

After all, he deserved the best; he put in many hours at Pleasant Valley and never failed to mention that fact from the pulpit. He had finagled an unlimited expense credit card at the last budget hearing. All he had to do was merely mention to his deacon chairman how his conference/convention budget never covered everything and how he had to pay for many expenses out of his own pocket, which wasn't completely true.

Jack signed for generous tips for all who served him, so he got prime treatment. His suite, complete with a Jacuzzi, was larger than the first house he and Molly had bought, and it outshined the accommodations of the other conference officers. As he walked in, Jack noticed the luxurious sofa in the sitting room. The furniture was not your usual basic hotel variety; instead the heavy walnut coffee table and the ceiling-to-floor, elegant burgundy brocaded drapes equaled what you might find in the most expensive homes in town. As he walked into the bedroom, the chic down-filled comforter caught his eye. Piles of decorator pillows echoed the excesses. Every extravagance imaginable filled the gigantic room. Guilt for not allowing Molly to come nagged at him for just a minute—but no more.

After eating a salad lunch in the hotel's sumptuous dining room, Jack stretched out on the oversized bed, hands behind his head, contemplating his meeting with Sawyer. *Just what had been his purpose? Why can't I feel more pleasure simply being in this mag-*

nificent place? Why this nagging feeling in my gut? Just then his reflections were interrupted by the phone. "Hello."

"Jack, this is Stephen Works. Some of the conference officers came in early to get things lined up for tomorrow. We thought you might meet us for dinner tonight. We wanted to make sure we are all on the same page about a few issues before Tipton nominates you tomorrow."

A call from the reigning president of the conference usually meant a command appearance to anyone else, but not to Jack. He wasn't anyone's puppet. Besides, he already had an appointment for tonight, one that held a much greater interest and promise than a meeting with a group of egomaniacs who thought they ruled the world. He was also aware he would be elected president the next day; he could think of nothing that would keep him from realizing this longtime ambition. He didn't need to suck up to anyone tonight.

"Sorry, Stephen, but I already have an important engagement tonight. Maybe we could do breakfast early in the morning. You know how it is. Everyone thinks they need some private time with me to bend my ear about conference politics."

Jack felt the undercurrent in Stephen's tone when he answered. "The boys aren't going to like this, but we'll see you at seven in the morning downstairs."

Despite the many voices in Jack's head, he dozed off and was in a deep sleep when the phone rang again. This time it was Darcy. "Hi Jack, I have just entered Gwinnett county. I thought you might give me the exact directions to the restaurant. I'm not sure what exit to take. I know I'm early, but I will just do a little shopping before time to meet."

"Darcy, there is a mall a block from the restaurant, but you are coming in at the high-traffic hour. I don't think there will be time for shopping before dinner. You would get soaked going from your car to the mall anyway. It will take you at least an hour to make your way in. I will just come on and meet you at the restaurant." After giving her directions, he instructed, "Park in the underground garage at the bank so you won't get wet. I've made reservations, but you can just wait for me in the lobby if you arrive before I do."

Jack parked his black Volvo and took the elevator up to the twenty-fifth floor. Darcy, looking unusually elegant in a simple black dress, which contoured to her body nicely, sat in the lobby waiting patiently. Her long blonde hair shimmered in the dim restaurant lighting. Jack's heart raced unexpectedly just seeing her there. *I haven't felt this excited since I was a school boy.*

"I made it faster than I thought I would. The traffic moved nicely, and I had no trouble finding the place. I've shopped at the mall near here several times," Darcy said as she stood up to greet Jack, "but I didn't remember exactly how to get here."

Jack reached out to give her a gentle hug. "I'm glad you made it safely. The rain makes the highways quite treacherous some-times. I was watching the weather report a few minutes ago, and the weatherman predicted freezing rain and possibly snow later tonight."

"On, no! I'll have to drive home in that."

"Not to worry," Jack comforted. "Maybe you won't. I'll figure out something." Darcy flashed him a questioning smile. "Let's just have a good meal, and then we can pick up where you left off the other day. I know you must carry a ton of baggage, and being able to tell someone about it is the only way to lighten your load." The maître de passed them off to a tuxedo-clad waiter who led them to a back corner table with a window. The view of the Atlanta's night lights added to the ambiance.

More silver and nice china than Darcy had ever seen lay on white, starched tablecloth. A fresh, white orchid rested in a small silver vase. Darcy felt somewhat like a princess as the waiter pulled out her chair for her to be seated. Then, he shook the folds out of the oversized cloth napkin and took great care as he placed it in her lap. "Wow! This extravagance overwhelms me. A Bluebird-type café would have satisfied me, but I certainly appreciate and enjoy luxury like this."

"You can't imagine what a relief it is to have a non-judgmental confidante to listen to my story," Darcy continued. "It was more than thoughtful of you to think of coming here for this session. I, too, feel uncomfortable meeting you late at the church office. I just don't think I could endure more rumors about me, and I'm sure you know how people talk. Sometimes it seems they watch my every move, and I know you are forever in the spotlight."

When the waiter came to take their drink orders, Jack surprised Darcy by ordering a bottle of fine wine. Noticing her shocked expression, alluding to her question during their last session, Jack said, "Even a preacher needs to let his hair down occasionally, and you know I could never do this in town or in Molly's presence. No one but the two of us will know." He gave her a knowing wink.

"I'm sorry my surprise showed. I think it's great for you to be able to relax and be like an ordinary man. I just would have never imagined your taking a drink the way you preach against it."

"That's different. I know I will never abuse it like others are likely to. Besides, there is a difference in pulpit talk and real life," he teased.

Jack ordered the finest filet mignons for the two of them. Then he not only enjoyed a lavish feast for the stomach, but when Darcy removed her velvet bolero jacket, he also relished the opulent banquet for his eyes. She revealed mountains of cleavage, which she had slightly dusted with iridescent powder. By the time the waiter served the dessert course - Crème Brule- Jack was feeling quite mellow from several glasses of wine. Conversation had been centered on each of their professions until then. The waiter browned the tops of the desserts with his blowtorch. Darcy didn't conceal her enchantment. She was unaccustomed to elegant dining such as this and said so. Jack reached across the table and rubbed her soft hand. "You deserve this kind of treatment more often, you know. You are worth it."

"I don't believe anybody has ever told me before I was worth anything but a hard time. You are so very kind and considerate." Darcy's heart raced with sensations more than mere gratitude.

"Why don't you continue telling me what you began the other day?" Jack urged.

"I'm not sure your ears can take it all. My story just becomes more sordid."

"Just try me. Don't leave out anything."

"I lived with Paul and Sophie until I finished high school. What began as my staying a few nights with them evolved into a permanent arrangement. My parents never asked for me to return home, and neither did Paul and Sophie suggest I go. I must confess, in some twisted way I can't explain, I reached the point where I looked forward to Paul's visits to my room. He awakened a fire in me that couldn't be extinguished and provided affection that I didn't receive from anyone else in my life.

"By the time I reached the sixth grade, the older boys on my bus must have sensed my premature and overdeveloped sexuality, and they certainly were aware I needed friends. I was ignored by most of the girls in my class, and the boys liked to point and joke about my well-developed breasts. Alan Teal was the first to ask me out on a date. I was flattered by the attention from an upperclassman, and, with the thought of going on a first date, I quickly accepted. I knew I could wait until Paul was in a drunken stupor and slip out. Sophie was always in her room by six o'clock. The date wasn't at all what I expected. I had so looked forward to Alan's taking me to a movie and then maybe to the Sonic for a burger. I knew if others saw me with him, it would give me a little status at school. Alan's idea for our night was quite different. With little ado, he drove to the field road that runs alongside the Burdock's pasture. As soon as we were out of sight of the main road, he wasted no time getting me to join him in the backseat. With little affection, he simply got what he came for. I didn't resist because I wanted him to really like me."

"Darcy, your self-esteem was so damaged by then, you couldn't help yourself."

"I know," she answered with tear-filled eyes, focusing on some invisible spot on the table. Regaining her composure after a bit, Darcy looked at Jack and continued, "News of that night must have traveled fast because I was flooded with invitations from other boys after that. I didn't realize I had become the community's boys' sexual rite of passage. I'm ashamed to say it, but I took pleasure in meeting their needs. It made me feel wanted, even needed, and I'll admit, I liked the sex as much as they did." Tears filled her eyes as she bowed her head in shame.

"Darcy, you realize your past behavior wasn't your entire fault. Girls who are sexually abused at an early age often become sexually promiscuous, according to the studies."

"But I feel so guilty about my past."

"I know, but understand, talking about this will help purge you of some of this guilt." Jack didn't bother to add that it also turned him on to hear the details of her escapades. "Go on. Is there more?"

"You just won't believe how much more. The next part is so difficult for me to talk about. I've never really told anyone the whole story of what happened when I went to college."

"Darcy, if you find telling me about it to be emotionally distressing, we may need more privacy than this place provides," Jack said in a low tone as he looked back and forth as though he was checking to see if they were being observed by others in the restaurant. "If you won't think me too forward to suggest it, why don't we go to my hotel? I have a large suite there with a nice living room. What do you think?"

"That's a wonderful idea. I'm not sure I can tell you more without totally losing it."

51

"Just ride with me, and I'll get you a taxi to come back to your car later." Jack drove cautiously, because the streets were already very slippery, and he realized the wine had slowed down his reflexes. Jack wanted to avoid any questions or signs of impropriety, so he chose the outside self-park option. He couldn't afford to be seen entering the hotel with a strange, beautiful woman. He jotted down the combination and number to his suite and instructed Darcy to wait in the car a few minutes and then come up. Even though she followed his directions to the T, her entering his room didn't go unnoticed.

Once inside, Jack noticed Darcy shivering from her rain-soaked dress. He was taken aback when he saw how the wet dress accentuated each of her beautiful curves. His appreciative glare didn't escape Darcy's notice.

"Darcy, you are freezing in those wet clothes. There is a hotel robe hanging behind the bathroom door. Why don't you get out of those things and hang them over the vent to dry? Just slip into that robe." He had already made a quick change into lounging pants and a turtle neck while he had been waiting for her to reach his suite.

Darcy was compliant and eager for some warmth. Still shaking when she came out of the bathroom, Jack snuggled her in his arms to warm her. His consideration was so welcomed.

"Let's sit over here on the sofa so you can finish what you started. I'll call down for a pot of hot coffee." Soon a knock sounded at the door, and Jack went to intercept the waiter and take the coffee from him at the door. To his dismay, Cecil Tipton's face greeted him instead of the waiter's. Jack stood stunned, unable to say anything.

"Hi, Jack. I thought I would stop by to see if we could talk about a few things before tomorrow. I can't make it for breakfast in the morning. I have an appointment for a press conference then."

Recovering quickly, Jack answered, "This really isn't a good time. I was on the phone with my wife, and then I have several other calls to make before bed time. I'm sure everything is in order for tomorrow."

Peeking around Jack, Cecil got a good look at the non-wife female sitting on the sofa. "Okay, I see," he commented with a perceptive air.

Jack, so eager to listen to the rest of Darcy's saga, brushed off the fleeting idea that Cecil had seen her. It was rude of him to stop by in the first place, after Jack had already refused the earlier meeting.

Just as Jack was about to close the door, the waiter appeared with the coffee service. "I'll take that." Jack quickly reached for the tray, brought it in, and set it on the coffee table; then he poured two cups. "Finally, we can get back to your story."

"You get the idea of what my high school days were like. They were just an exaggerated extension of what began in sixth grade. I really had only one true boyfriend in high school, one who dared to be seen in public with me—Sawyer Thomas." Jack's opened mouth revealed his surprise. "Sawyer was always kind and gentlemanly toward me. Once he even slugged a boy for making lewd remarks about me. Of course, our relationship faded when I went to college."

Still stunned to hear about that side of Sawyer, Jack sat silently trying to assimilate this new knowledge. Somehow he couldn't imagine Sawyer showing compassion for a whore.

"Sometimes having so few friends in high school can be a plus. I had plenty of time to study, so my grades were high. I scored a thirty-four on my ACT, which brought colleges throughout the South knocking on my door. I wanted to get away, so I accepted a scholarship from North Carolina. I'm embarrassed to say much of my decision rested on their powder-blue and white colors. I loved watching their basketball games because of the uniforms. Isn't that the silliest thing you've ever heard?"

"I'll have to admit, it's close to it, but North Carolina is a great school."

"I guess, but I learned to hate blue and white, and I never went back to North Carolina after my premature departure."

"Why?" What happened there?"

"Do you want the short version or the long one?"

"You need to tell it all, in full detail."

Trusting that he knew what was good for her, Darcy began. "Not long after I got on campus, Sanford Jenkins, one of the smartest guys there, invited me to a frat party. Thinking it was my chance to start over where no one knew me, I saw this as an opportunity to meet some good people. After all, only the smart guys were accepted into this fraternity.

"Sanford had told me, 'When you arrive at the fraternity house, just tell whoever is manning the door that you are my guest. They'll call for me then.'

"When I arrived, Sanford came to my rescue just as he said he would. The house, filled to capacity, roared with laughter and deafening music. The alcohol flowed like a waterfall. Even though I had never been much of a drinker, I accepted a drink just to be part of the crowd. Soon a guy I had never met walked up to where Sanford and I stood and reached out his hand for me.

"'Sanford, don't be so selfish with this babe. Let me take her for a spin on the dance floor. My name's Joey, and I'm the best dancer in the room. Come on.'"

"I looked back at Sanford to see what I should do.

"'Go ahead. I'll hold your drink for you. He's not lying. He is the best dancer at school.'

"Joey was a fun person. He laughed and joked all the time we were on the floor. He would give me an expert spin and then draw me back close to him. By the end of the song, he gave up the spins, and he just held me close. I was aware he was enjoying our nearness a little too much. I refused the next dance and hunted for Sanford. He handed my drink back to me and suggested we go upstairs so he could introduce me to some of his other friends. Thirsty from the exertion of the dance, I took a sip of my drink. By the time we reached the top of the stairs, it hit. I realized Sanford was supporting my weight. The little bit of liquor couldn't possibly incapacitate me so quickly, I thought. I had heard of the date rape drug, but now I experienced its effects.

"The next thing I was aware of was being on a bed surrounded by a group of guys making lewd comments. Then, although I was conscious enough to realize what was happening, a strange paralysis overtook me, and I lacked the ability to scream, talk, or resist."

Darcy continued her saga of that night's abuse at the hands of drunken fraternity guys. Details of that night's horrors continued to cascade like a fountain, captivating her listener.

"From what I gathered later, my grave condition sobered up the guys enough for them to realize the severity of their actions and the impending repercussions, so they rushed out of the room. Sometime later I learned Sanford called his dad, a highly respected gynecologist in town, and told him a girl at the frat house needed help, that something really bad had happened to her. His dad had little trouble getting the shaken Sanford to fess-up and admit he had taken part in the night's events. To protect both their reputations, Dr. Jenkins came with the ambulance and whisked me away to his private clinic.

"I will have to say his kindness and care over the next six weeks helped me recover both physically and emotionally. When full consciousness returned after the second day at the clinic, Dr. Jenkins told me how critical my condition had been.

"He sat on my bedside, took my hand in his, and told me, 'Darcy, I am so very sorry for what you had to endure, and I want to give you the assurance that all of your future needs will be taken care of, but I'm afraid I have to tell you something that makes the situation even worse. Your uterus was lacerated and ruptured. I repaired it the best I could, but in all likelihood, you will never be able to conceive.'

"I still had not found my voice, but tears flowed from my face and dampened my pillow, not so much because I couldn't conceive, but because the full trauma and disgrace of that night hit me full force. I thought, at the time, my sterility was the least of my worries because the thought of ever having any kind of intimacy again was so repulsive.

"Dr. Jenkins held true to his word. Although I wasn't able to return to classes at the university, not that I had any desire to, he provided an apartment in Durham and gave me the financial support to take classes there to become a dental assistant. He told me he wouldn't blame me for filing criminal charges against all involved, even against his son, but I didn't feel I could go through a trial and other court proceedings. I just wanted to put the ordeal behind me.

"I had received the news shortly after I had arrived in North Carolina that both Paul and Sophie had died within two months of each other; Paul, in one of his drunken binges, had gone around a curve too fast and drove his old Ford pickup into a ravine, and Sophie's heart simply wore out.

"I decided to go back to Smytheville, the only place I had known as home, and start a new life. I hoped my earlier reputation there would, by now, be forgotten. Acquiring a job with Dr. Martin was my first step. I made enough to live on, so I decided to cut off my financial dependency with Dr. Jenkins, but he insisted on my taking a generous settlement before I left. He told me no amount of money would compensate me for that horrid night, nor could a person put a price on a young man's reputation. He felt I spared his son's future."

Jack reached over and pulled Darcy close. "No human being should ever have to endure what you went through. I wish I could make the past go away for you." He handed Darcy a clean handkerchief on which to dry her tear-soaked eyes.

"You are helping to do just that by listening. You know most of the rest of the story. Needless to say, I eventually became interested in a man. Perry Porter and I have stirred quite a scandal in Smytheville. I do believe Perry really loves me, though, but I now realize he has so many family strings holding him down. We could never have a future together. I guess you could say I found true love a little too late."

"I'll tell you what. I can't help what's happened to you in the past, but I am going to protect you from what might happen tonight. I'm not going to let you drive back to Smytheville on these icy roads. Besides, you are emotionally spent and in no shape to be driving. You can stay here with me, and no one will know. I'll sleep on the couch,"

"Dr. Pate, you undoubtedly are the kindest, most considerate man I have ever known. Does Molly realize just how blessed she is to have you as her husband?"

Even though it was meant as a rhetorical question, Jack answered with a faraway look. "I'm afraid she doesn't. She takes me for granted. You've been honest with me, so I will be with you. My marriage to Molly has lost any pizzazz it ever had, which was never much. She takes care of the household and children. She does accommodate me with obligatory sex. Of course, she is naïve. I was her first and only lover. She won't even watch R-rated movies on HBO. I've encouraged her to so she would learn a few tricks to spice up things, but she thinks it's sinful to watch them. There is just no other way to say it, she's a prude and simply boring in bed. Sometimes I think she is just too holy for her own good—and for mine."

"I'm so sorry to know that. I always thought you must have a perfect marriage. I think I will take you up on the offer to stay the night, but I won't have you giving up your bed. I may need to borrow one of your T-shirts to sleep in. The bed is huge, and since no one knows anyway, what harm would there be in sharing it?"

"I think you are right. We might even enjoy a movie while we relax."

"If you will get me one of your T-shirts, I'll go in the bathroom and change."

Jack was teeming with anticipation, for an innocent sleepover wasn't in the cards for that night, he knew. He hurried to the dresser where his clothes had been neatly unpacked and pulled out a Jockey V-neck, realizing the neckline would come down far enough on Darcy to reveal the right amount of temptation. He would soon partake of the forbidden fruit.

Darcy felt honored to share a bed with the most respected man in Smytheville, and she knew only one way to show her gratitude for all his help. The web, which had already been woven, tightened that night.

The Officers

Cecil Tipton wasted no time in contacting the other officers. "Am I just being a suspicious busybody, or is a young woman entering Jack's suite grounds for question?"

Stephen Works spoke up immediately. "It would be inexcusable and unjust for us to accuse a brother falsely, but, on the other hand, we would be derelict in our duty if we didn't check it out."

"What do you propose we do?" inserted Clay Sartain, the officer with the longest tenure. Clay had served as registration secretary for the past fifteen years. "I can only remember one other situation where an officer's morality was questioned. You all know what I'm talking about. When Dr. Samuels was serving as president and his wife accused him of both physical and emotional abuse, we easily made it her problem, not his. If you recall, 'the powers-that-be' realized it would be too great a scandal to let him take the fall, so we brought out her past mental and emotional conditions and claimed he was falsely accused. The conference whole-heartedly supported Samuel's then. I think that even worked to his advantage because of the sympathy he got."

"We're not dealing with a Dr. Samuels here, though. Pate is just an 'up and comer'. I think we've got to check this out. We need to know our facts. Does the woman stay the night? Who is she? And so on. We can take shifts watching the room for the remainder of the night. I'll take the first watch," offered Stephen.

In turn, each of the men volunteered for a couple of hours. Everything was quiet until 5:00 a.m. Clay, being an early riser anyway, had volunteered for the 4:00 to 6:00 a.m. shift. He had pulled one of the beautiful brocaded Queen Anne chairs from the sitting area in front of the elevators to the end of the hall where Jack's suite could easily be watched. He had brought his Bible so he could have his devotional time while he watched. The sound of soft whispers interrupted his meditation. He observed Darcy saying her good-byes to Jack, who was standing at the door. Clay quickly moved around the corner as not to be seen. He could still hear most of the whispered conversation.

"Jack, thank you so much for letting me stay. Everything was absolutely perfect."

"I'm the one who should be saying thanks." Jack's sensuous tone suggested much more as his gaze traveled up and down Darcy's curvaceous body. "We will have to do this more often."

Darcy stood on her tiptoes and gave Jack a passionate good-bye kiss. As she walked to the elevator, Clay simply went and stood as though he was waiting for the elevator also. "Morning, Ma'am," he greeted Darcy with calculated casualness.

"Good morning," she replied as they stepped on the elevator together. I see you have your Bible. You must be here for the conference."

"Yes, I am. I usually get up early to do my daily Bible reading. I thought I would read over coffee this morning."

When the elevator arrived at the lobby level, Darcy took the main exit and hailed a cab to take her to her car. Disheveled and disturbed, Clay went to the restaurant and quickly called Tipton. "Call the others and get down here. We've got things to discuss before Jack comes down for our breakfast meeting with him."

When Jack arrived promptly at 7:00 a.m., the waiting group greeted him. Jack noticed the somber atmosphere. "What's up?" he asked in a chipper mood.

"Sit down, Jack." Looking to the others, Tipton said, "We've got some questions for you."

Immediately on the defensive, Jack assumed they were upset because he didn't agree to meet them for dinner the night before. "Guys, I'm sorry, but I just couldn't meet with you last night. I already had scheduled a very important meeting."

"That's not the problem we want to discuss," inserted distressed Clay.

Not letting him off easily, the group told him what had been witnessed. "Now, what do you have to say about this situation, Jack?" inquired Tipton.

Thinking quickly, Jack excused the whole matter. "You thought I had a gal on the side?" He feigned amusement. "Molly's cousin was coming to the city on business, so Molly called and asked if I would have room for her in my room. The girl has just started a new sales job and has to foot her own expenses. Molly thought she could sleep on my sofa and save a few bucks. I was glad to accommodate the poor girl. Don't you think that was the Christian thing to do?"

Still having some doubt, Tipton apologized for the group's wrong assumptions. After a strained breakfast, each returned to his room to get ready for the first day's session. The phone was ringing as Tipton entered his room.

"Cecil, I think you should think again about nominating Jack today. I observed doubt in the eyes of everyone at the table," Stephen offered.

"I'm in total agreement. I had already reconsidered nominating him. With so much turmoil in the conference already, we can't risk another scandal. The accusations wouldn't roll off Jack as they did 'Teflon' Samuels."

Time for the nominations for president came about 11:00 a.m. that morning. The convention center was packed as each delegate was eager to cast a vote, most expecting to vote for Jack Pate and others for his pre-announced opponent, Kevin Rogers.

When Tipton went to the microphone and nominated Clay Sartain, the hall buzzed with shock over this unexpected nomination. "Many of you were expecting me to nominate Jack Pate, as has been presumed and indicated by our Community Church newspapers." He continued with a "holy" lie. "The other officers and I, including Jack Pate himself, held a prayer vigil last night and agreed the Lord was leading in another direction. Clay Sartain has served the conference well for the past fifteen years as registration secretary, a very stressful and unrecognized position. It is the consensus of the officers and Dr. Pate that Clay Sartain's day has come to be president of this body."

The shock and dejection, which was obvious in Jack's face, defied Tipton's assertion that he was in agreement with the decision. As the session broke for lunch, Jack exited through the back curtains just off the stage. He had to go through the press room, where several reporters tried to stop him to get a quote from him. He rudely brushed them off and found a freight exit. He couldn't leave this place fast enough. A photographer who followed him out captured it all as Jack jumped down from the ramp. Jack, deep in thought, was oblivious to the eager photographer.

The anticipation that filled Jack as he drove to Atlanta was usurped now by great dejection, anger, and disappointment. A troublesome foreboding feeling about the future engulfed him. *How will I explain this to my congregation? I had already told them how honored the church would be in the conference for having their pastor serve as president,* Jack mused. The grayish-brown landscape filled with the straw-colored grass and bare oaks mocked his dismal mood. This bleak winter scenery flying by his window as he drove down the interstate matched the miserable angst inside of Jack as he headed home.

Andy Moore

"Jack, what a pleasant surprise! I didn't think you would be home for another couple of days. Tell me about the election. Was the convention hall filled with cheering supporters?" Molly rushed on without waiting for a reply, "Oh, how I would have liked to have been there for that experience!"

"You would have been sorely disappointed then," Jack snarled. "We put up Clay Sartain," he said, lying about the "we" part, "and he was elected." Without even a perfunctory hello kiss or an offer of more explanation, Jack pushed past her. "I have a headache. I'm going to bed."

Molly stood stunned. She wished Jack had been more forthcoming with details. So many questions raced through her mind, but she knew Jack's moods well enough to leave it alone at the time. His demeanor indicated there had been some sort of trouble. She would let the matter go for now and not be the nagging wife.

Jack didn't bother to undress before he stretched out on the bed. He had so many thoughts dancing in his head. *How will I skirt this issue with the church? Molly will be easy; she'll accept any explanation I give. She's just too trusting for her own good. Why am I so tormented and torn by the pleasures I enjoyed with Darcy? Don't I deserve some happiness? Surely God would understand because He wants me to be happy.*

He then tried to pray. "God, forgive me for any indiscretions I may have committed. You forgave King David of so much more, so I know you will forgive me, too."

Since he wasn't expected back in the office until Thursday, Jack didn't go the next day. Instead, he cocooned in the bedroom, still not ready to give Molly the full particulars. He didn't feel like facing anybody. He simply curled into the fetal position and stayed in bed.'

Thursday morning, Jack awoke with resolve to face the world again. He went down for breakfast with Molly. Benji had already left for school. "What's for breakfast?" he asked with artificial enthusiasm.

"I have bacon and eggs cooked. Do you feel like eating that, or do you want me to fix you something else?"

"No, I don't want you to go to any extra trouble. Bacon and eggs will do."

Before he sat down, he surprised Molly by reaching out and taking her into his arms. "Molly, I love you more than anything. Do you know that? Regardless of what we might face in the future, just remember that."

This unusual affection caught her off guard. "Yes, I know that. I love you, too—until the end of the world, and then some," she replied as she unconsciously twirled a loose curl with her finger.

While Jack nibbled at his breakfast, he explained his concocted version of the circumstances of the election to Molly. "After I got to Atlanta, I realized Clay had served the conference faithfully in his unappreciated office for so many years. I just felt God leading me to suggest he be nominated this year instead of me. Besides, I have so much going on at church, I didn't think I needed to be away as much as the position required."

"Maybe that's why I love you so," answered Molly. She looked at Jack with great admiration and love. "That was the most unselfish thing I've ever heard. God will bless you for that. That makes me prouder of you than if you had come home as president."

Her response made his lie burn deep in his heart. "I really wasn't very hungry, but thanks for the breakfast anyway. You know how these headaches take my appetite. I think I'll go on to the office. I'll have a ton of things to catch up on."

When he arrived, the secretaries greeted him tentatively. They had been discussing what they had heard on the morning news.

The networks always did a piece on the goings-on at the conference. Without giving any clarification, the news reported that, to the surprise of the conventioneers, Clay Sartain had been elected president of the League of Community Churches Conference. "More to come later on that story," said the newsman.

Jack greeted them all briefly and announced a called staff meeting at 10:00 a.m. When the staff, including the secretaries, gathered, Jack thought his explanation went so well with Molly, that would be his answer for the staff and the church. The staff accepted his story with more reservations than did Molly, but they asked no questions.

Not long after Jack had gone back to his office, he heard a commotion outside his door. Kim, the receptionist, had followed Andy Moore down the hall. "I've already told you. Dr. Pate isn't to be disturbed. This is his study time. You mustn't go in there."

Andy Moore, Jack's former minister of music and once friend, ignored the receptionist and doggedly burst through the door. "I just have one thing for you, Dr. Pate," he snarled. With that, Andy drew back a fist and pelted Jack right in the nose.

Jack lay on the floor stunned. Holding his bleeding nose, he asked, "What was that about?" At first, neither of the men noticed the secretaries gathered at the door observing the scene.

Jack then became aware of hearing Kim say, "I'll go call the police." He maintained enough presence of mind to stop her. He didn't want this spread all over town right now. He had to invent a way to explain this confrontation away.

Looking down on Jack with total disgust, Andy answered. "I've wanted to do that for some time now. You almost destroyed my marriage to Lisa. She was ready to take your unchristian counsel to divorce me. You knew that would ruin my ministry, as well as my entire life." Andy reached down with a hand and jerked Jack to his feet. He wanted to face his adversary nose-to-nose. "The Lord foiled your plan, though. I realized I had neglected Lisa while trying to do all you expected of me at church. You kept giving me more and more assignments, things you should have been doing yourself.

"But nonetheless, I confess that I didn't treat her right, and a barrier grew between us. I volunteered to go for marriage counseling if she would stay with me and try to work things out. Since that time, we have strived diligently to repair the brokenness, and finally we have found happiness together. That is until yesterday. Yesterday, in our counseling session, Dr. Cross addressed the topic of honesty and trust in marriage. When we got home, Lisa felt the need to be too honest about what had taken place between you two. She told me what I had already expected, that you took advantage of her when she went to you for counseling when you were our pastor at Carter's Bluff. She also took her share of the blame but told how you two became involved and of your trysts at the beauty shop. No wonder you kept me so busy with church duties!"

Andy paused for a moment and stared at the splattered blood on the floor. "I don't know what that's going to do to our efforts now. Although I admit I wasn't all I should have been to her, I was never unfaithful. I just don't know if I will be able to forgive her for allowing you to woo her into a relationship.

"Regardless of what these fine people here at Pleasant Valley have thought of you in the past, your reputation with them is about to change when I spread the word about who and what you really are." Andy almost ran over two secretaries as he bolted out the door.

Jack faced the puzzled staff at the door. "Not a word about what you heard is to leave this office. Do you all understand me?" he instructed sternly. He continued, "There is a reasonable explanation for this. Andy has been prone to mental episodes like this from time-to-time. He is paranoid and suffers from a manic-depressive disorder. I just caught the brunt of this particular episode," Jack said as he held the bloody handkerchief to his nose. "Let's say a prayer for him right now."

"Kim, now you can call the police. I want you to tell them I want to sign a restraining order to keep this maniac away before he destroys me and the church with his delusional tirades."

"Demons come in many forms to attack God's church and his servants," began Jack on Sunday morning. He had decided his best defense would be a strong offense. He had to circumvent fallout from any rumors resulting from the horrible events of this last week, and he realized he wielded great influence when he stood behind the pulpit.

"When God's servant is at his best trying to fulfill His plans and do His work, Satan attacks the most viciously. In an attempt to follow God's leadership, I humbled myself this week and gave up a place of honor in the conference to a man I felt more deserving of the office of president. I got back in town, and that's when Satan's darts assailed me. After staff meeting on Thursday, a former staff member, who suffers from mental illness, burst into my office making terrible false accusations and even attacking me physically. This swollen face you see testifies to that. But as God's people, we can't be deterred from our mission by Satan's attempts to stop us. Most men would have stayed home in embarrassment, but I am here to face the devil head-on today," Jack shouted and pounded the pulpit for emphasis.

"Today I will base my sermon on God's promise, not only to men of old, but to us today. Genesis 12:3, 'And I will bless them that bless thee, and curse him that curseth thee.'"

Jack proceeded to preach a dynamic sermon that not only sent up a smoke screen to shield him from any forthcoming gossip about the week's happenings, but also as a continued warning against anyone who contemplated saying negative things about him. He felt quite smug about his success in his endeavors as members filed out the door, praising him for the wonderful sermon and sympathizing with him over his injuries. But, he only noticed the positive reactions. Therefore, he remained oblivious to many who chose to exit through other doors or to those who bypassed the backdoor greeting. There were many. He hugged Darcy slightly longer than he had the other ladies, and as Jack pulled her closely, she whispered in a seductive tone, "That was magnificent. Your talents never cease to amaze me. Call me this afternoon."

After the service, Donald Brooks waited around until Jack had finished greeting the parishioners and asked if he and his family had lunch plans. "We were planning to stop by the cafeteria for a bite," Jack replied.

"Sharon and I would like for your family to be our guests for lunch at the club today, if this isn't too short a notice."

Jack realized he needed to keep his supporters close, so he accepted the invitation, although he was eager to get with Darcy. "Molly and I would love to go, but it will be just the two of us. Benji has to be at practice in a few minutes. He has already said he would just grab a burger on his way." Jack's preoccupation was evident as they sat down for lunch.

"I know this has been a tough week for you, Pastor, and thought this would give you an opportunity to talk more about it if you want to."

Appreciative of Donald's sympathy and understanding, Jack replied, "Donald, you are always such a great friend and good listener, but I pretty well explained the week's events from the pulpit. If it's okay with you, I'd just as soon we find something else to talk about. I need to get all that off my mind while we eat."

Quickly changing the subject, Sharon interjected, "By the way, I had the most unusual experience this week. I went to Atlanta shopping, and just as I came out of Cold's Casuals, I saw a young lady, who was the spitting image of Caitlin, walk by. I called out 'Hey, Caitlin,' and she looked my direction and just kept walking. I was so sure it was Caitlin, I ran her down. I'm telling you she was Caitlin's size, had her hair color, and could have been her twin. When I got closer, I realized her nose was slightly different, but she had lips just like Caitlin and Jack. Jack, you really marked Caitlin with your chin dimple and eyes. I was so embarrassed. I had to explain my mistake to the young girl. She was very nice about it and told me her name was Celeste Downs.

I've heard that everybody has a twin somewhere," offered Molly, "and maybe that was Caitlin's."

Shortly after lunch, Jack excused himself and Molly. "I'm sorry to eat and run, but I have so much to catch up on this afternoon. Being out of the office a few days has me so far behind on everything. The lunch was a real treat. Molly and I will have to get you two over soon and grill a steak or something," Jack offered, while knowing full well that would never happen.

Standing to say good-bye, Donald replied, "We understand completely, but, Jack, you look like you need to go home and rest instead of working in the office all afternoon. You know, even preachers need to rest on the Lord's Day."

Knowing he never really intended to go back to the office to work, Jack, quick to make his exit, replied, "I might just do that."

Instead of going in the house to rest, when Jack and Molly arrived home, he told her, "I think I'll just let you out, and I'll go on back to the office. I need to catch up on some communications."

"I understand, but I am concerned about you. You look so very tired. Couldn't the office work wait until tomorrow?"

"Molly, discussing this is just taking up more of my time. I told you I need to go."

He sped away and drove directly to Darcy's house. By this time, his need to be with her overshadowed his fear someone might see his car there. Just as he had suspected, when he arrived, Darcy offered him support and understanding in the way she knew best. As Jack left later that afternoon to go home and freshen up for the evening service, he was plagued with guilt. *What I'm doing is wrong, but God knows I need Darcy. Maybe he is allowing this affair to be sure I get what I need. He knows Molly certainly doesn't satisfy me."* he rationalized. *If no one else knows about what I'm doing, who could I possibly be hurting?* His defense continued in his thoughts.

Rather than going home to answer Molly's questions, he went back to Darcy's for the night. After spending the night with Darcy, Jack awoke early Monday morning. As he was leaving her house, he picked up the *Atlanta Constitution* lying on her doorstep. He stood aghast as he opened the paper and saw a picture of himself jumping off the loading dock at the at the back of the convention hall. He was shockingly aware of the anger and tears revealed in the close-up. The headline spanned the width of the front page. It read "Is there trouble in the fast-growing League of Community Churches?"

The article told the story. "An unnamed source reveals disgrace and disappointment resulting in a surprise and sudden change in presidential election at the Conference of the League of Community Churches." The article went on to disclose the whole story about a strange woman spending the night in Jack Pate's hotel suite the night before he was to be nominated for president. Jack felt like a fly trapped in a spider's web.

Celeste Downs

About the time Jack saw the paper, over in Atlanta, Celeste Downs saw hers, too. She went to the front door of her apartment and retrieved her daily paper, as was her normal routine. She laid the paper on the kitchen table and took her bagel from the toaster, poured herself a cup of coffee, and then sat down to read the paper as she ate her breakfast. At first she simply glanced at the front page picture and then perused the headlines. The picture drew her attention back for some reason. "That face! There's something about that face," she said to herself. Then it hit her. "That looks like me!"

She quickly read the caption to find a name. Jack Pate. Although Celeste's morning schedule left little extra time before she had to leave for work, this morning she took the time. After five rings, a sleepy, hungover voice answered.

"Hello, who's calling at this ungodly hour?" Gloria mumbled, her irritation evident.

"Mother, this is Celeste, and it's not an ungodly hour; it's almost 7:30 a.m. Wake up! I've got to ask you something important. Do we have any relatives named Pate?"

"No, and if we did, they would still be our relatives after noon. Why is our family tree suddenly so urgent that you had to call this early? I need to go back to sleep, and you need to go to work."

"Don't hang up, Mother. This is important. There is a picture of a man on the front page of the Atlanta Constitution who has my face. His name is Jack Pate."

The mere sound of Jack Pate's name served as a glass of cold water in Gloria's face. With the portable phone still to her ear, she immediately got out of bed and started to the door to get her paper.

Gloria lied, "I've never heard of a Jack Pate. This must just be your imagination, but I'll look at my paper in a little while to see if I note a resemblance. She had found the picture before she could get the denial out of her mouth. You go to work, and have a good day."

Suddenly the details of her tryst with Jack, which she had tried to suppress for so long, filled her mind. They were as fresh and clear as they had been years back. Gloria had been excited when lab partners had been assigned when she was a student at TSU. Jack Pate, handsome and well-known around campus, was to be by her side for the entire semester. Her classmates had warned her to be careful and not be lured into his trap. He had the reputation of being a stud, a reputation he perpetuated; he never remained silent about the women he seduced. She had not heeded their warnings. Gloria found Jack to be compassionate and kind, not sleazy as some had described him.

Gloria had enjoyed the party life at school, something that had been forbidden in her conservative home. After of one of the parties where there had been too much alcohol and pot circulating, Gloria found herself in a situation that became too heated, one where her "nos" were ignored. What happened amounted to date rape.

Afterward Jack became her comforter and confidant. She couldn't tell her parents or anyone but Jack. Her parents didn't have a clue that she would be at a beer bash, and she knew they would believe she had gotten what she deserved if she had been a participant in that kind of debauchery. Only Jack listened. During their "counseling sessions," Gloria gave in to Jack's advances, and they became lovers.

A couple of months after that fated night, Gloria confirmed what she suspected; she was pregnant. Although Jack was not Gloria's first, she strongly suspected him to be the father because of the timing, but she couldn't be absolutely sure of the paternity of her baby without going through expensive testing. Now, Gloria knew she had been an easy target for Jack. She was already spoiled goods, but she had trusted Jack with her secret and with her body. She had believed him when he said he loved her.

In late June when Gloria called Jack at home and broke the news to him, his compassion and love evaporated like rain on a summer day. "You can't possibly expect me to marry you," he told her by phone. "Gloria, you know that baby is probably not mine anyway. Remember all those guys you've been with? Besides, Molly and I are about to be married. Good luck. I'll be thinking about you, though. You find the right guy, you hear."

There really hadn't been "all those guys" as Jack had said, only the boy who had raped her and Jack. Gloria felt disillusioned and disappointed. She came to the realization she had been used by Jack as much as she had by the rapist, but she couldn't argue that point because she had no proof and certainly wouldn't go through the embarrassment of trying to be sure. Gloria had endured the pregnancy and delivery without the father's help. Those had been the toughest days of her life, both physically and emotionally.

"Mom, please don't drink so much today. You know I love you and worry about you. I'm seventy miles away and can't come to check on you every day. Are you eating right? Have you had your liver enzymes checked recently?" Celeste fussed over her mom's condition every week.

"I'm okay, sweetie. Don't you worry about me. You've got your own life to live. Have a good day."

Celeste wasn't satisfied with her mother's answer. She heard something in her voice that belied her words. She determined to make the drive to Athens that afternoon when she got home from work. She had much more to ask her mother face to face.

On those occasions when she inquired about her birth dad, Gloria always told Celeste the same story—that her dad walked off before she was born. That part was true, because Jack Pate never knew the child was his. When pressed for more details, Gloria would explain she and Jack Smith were married for only three months before he left. She had told Celeste, "I never tried to locate him because he was nothing but trouble anyway. If he didn't want to be with us, I didn't want him anyway."

A few times when she was in college, Celeste's efforts to locate her biological father failed because she didn't have enough details about him, and what she had was incorrect. There were just too many Jack Smiths. Besides, her stepfather, Clark Downs, had been a daddy to her since she could remember, and he was a good one. He even adopted her and gave her his name. He treated her like his own.

When he was killed in a car accident two years ago, Gloria began her major affair with the bottle. Whiskey was her lover and comforter. Since that time, Celeste felt as though she had lost her mother also, at least the mother she had always known. Clark had left Gloria comfortable financially, so it wasn't necessary for her to work to survive. This financial security was not the blessing it seemed, because it allowed Gloria the opportunity to spend her days and nights numbed by alcohol's sedation.

Hoping her mother would refrain from drinking to the passing out stage before she could get there, Celeste called Gloria later that morning to tell her she would be to Athens by 7:30 p.m. to take her to dinner.

Good to her promise, Gloria was in good shape when Celeste arrived. In fact, she looked the best she had in a while. Although her drinking had taken a toll on her, her shapeliness still turned heads wherever she went. She had taken great care in applying makeup—something she hadn't done in quite a while. Careful to cover the dark circles under her eyes, Gloria appeared ten years younger than she had a few minutes before. Of course, this was the first time in months that Celeste had seen her mother dressed and with makeup on. It was also the most sober she had been. She had forgotten how beautiful her mother was.

Although her heart pounded and her tongue longed for the burn of just one drink, Gloria liked the idea of going out to dinner with her daughter. Gloria thought perhaps being in a public place would discourage Celeste's probing. This proved to be so wrong.

Soon after they placed their orders, Celeste began. "Are you positive we aren't related to any Pates, Mother? Just look at this picture, and tell me this man and I don't share genetic features." Celeste placed the picture on the table between them. That morning she had cut it out, and throughout the day, she examined each visible feature of this stranger.

Gloria tried diligently to mask her shock and feelings as she recognized her lover of long ago. "I don't know the man," Gloria denied. Seeing Celeste was not to be deterred, Gloria offered, "I didn't know your father's family very well. Maybe they are related."

"I think this deserves more attention. I'll spend the night here and call the office in the morning to tell them I'm taking a personal day to attend to some pressing business. I'm going down to Smytheville and check this out. I don't think I can rest until I do."

Gloria lowered her voice and pleaded, "Drop this, Celeste, please just drop it. Don't set yourself up for hurt. If the Smith family didn't want anything to do with us earlier, why do you think they would now?"

"I don't intend to go plan a family reunion or anything like that. I just have to satisfy my curiosity. Just this past week, a lady from Smytheville mistook me for a person named Caitlin, her pastor's daughter. She said I looked just like her. All I want to do is see if I have relatives there. Surely that can't do any harm."

"I can't stop you, but I beg you not to stir this up," Gloria pleaded with tears filling her eyes.

Celeste knew by her mother's reaction there was much more than she was telling. "Mom, I don't want to do anything to upset you, but you must understand why I've got to explore this for myself. I need to know who I am."

Celeste left Athens early the next morning before her mother awoke. As the morning sun rose in the distance, the sky began to brighten on the horizon. Celeste hoped light would shine that day on her search for any possible relatives. She pulled into the drive-thru at McDonald's to get her morning java. The girl at the window recognized her. "Hi, Celeste, do you remember me? I'm Sandra Meadows. I was three years behind you in high school. I always admired you so much. I see you are just as pretty as you were then. I can remember how fascinated I was by that slight dimple in your chin. Here's your coffee. Have a good one."

As she drove away, Celeste's mind drifted to her high school days. They had been good ones. Gloria succeeded in her determination to make Celeste's life easier and better than hers had been. She provided her with the best of everything money could buy. She and Clark endowed her with love and security. They went to church as a family every Sunday. Celeste's only complaint was her mother's overprotection. She hardly allowed her to date, her only explanation being, "I don't want you to make the same mistakes I did."

At that time, Celeste thought her mother was referring to her first disastrous marriage. Now, she wondered if there was more. Seeing Jack Pate's photograph and recognizing her notable resemblance to him raised many questions. She felt certain by now that her mother had kept some things secret. The not-knowing set Celeste's imagination on high speed. She thought of every possible scenario; she knew some questions would be answered when she got to Smytheville.

When she got to Americus, Celeste decided to get a bite of lunch before she continued. As she drove through town, she spotted a quaint hometown-type diner. She found a parking place and went in. The waitress greeted her with a friendly smile. "Can I take your order, Ma'am? We've got homemade chicken pot pie for our special today. It's sure enough good. I've already had some of it. You'd like it."

With a gentle smile, Celeste replied, "With a commercial like that, how could I refuse it?" While she sipped her iced tea and waited for her meal, she pulled the newspaper clipping from her purse. She spread it out on the red-checkered oil cloth and smoothed it with her hand, trying to get every wrinkle out. Examining each feature once again, she spotted the slightly dimpled chin. "How have I missed that before?" she pondered.

Sally, the overly friendly waitress, broke Celeste's concentration. "Here's your lunch, hon. You look like you could use a few stick-to-your-ribs meals. You can tell by looking at me I've had my share of them." Then noticing the picture on the table, she exclaimed, "That's it. I knew you looked familiar. You must be Dr. Pate's daughter. You look just like him."

"No, I don't even know him," answered Celeste a little too quickly. She picked up the clipping and put it back in her purse. "Could I have some more tea, please?" she asked eager to change the subject.

Sally may not have been the brightest crayon in the box, but she knew when a customer didn't want to talk. "Sure thing, Ma'am. I'll be right back."

Celeste ate a few bites and then asked for her ticket. She was anxious to leave. It was as though she had been found out. When she cranked her car and drove off, her mother's words resounded in her head. "Drop it. Drop it, Celeste. Don't set yourself up for hurt."

These thoughts somewhat weakened her resolve to solve her mystery. When she came to the exit for a rest area, Celeste pulled off the highway. She went to the restroom, came out, and walked to the picnic area instead of returning to the car. A battle raged in her mind. The struggle between curiosity, a need to know, and fear of the unknown troubled Celeste. She was in no hurry to continue. An hour passed before she made up her mind to continue her quest.

Celeste set her speed control at fifty-five mph instead of her normal seventy-five. Apprehension had replaced urgency. Although eager, she was afraid of what she might discover. *What if my mother has lied to me all these years? What will that do to our relationship?*

She noticed sights she normally overlooked. Off to the side in the bare trees, she spotted a doe and her little one. She reflected on God's amazing order. That doe knew how to care for her young and how to teach it to survive.

As she entered the city limits, she was impressed with the old but well-cared-for Victorian houses that lined Main Street before she got to the business district. Celeste's mind seemed to race in many different directions. Celeste slowed to turn around and give it up, but as soon as she did, she heard a distinctive but inaudible voice. *I am with you always, even to the ends of the earth, daughter. Keep going.*

Celeste then knew what she was supposed to do. She would leave the results in His hands.

She then focused her search on finding the church that was mentioned in the newspaper. As soon as she made her decision, two white steeples appeared over the businesses. *Just follow the cross*, she thought, reflecting on an illustration her pastor had used in a recent sermon. In the story, a man came to town searching for a certain pastor of a local church. The man saw a little girl on the sidewalk. He stopped and asked a little girl if she could tell him where the church was.

"You see that cross. Just follow the cross, and you will find what you are looking for," the little girl told him.

Celeste pulled her car to the curb, bowed her head, and prayed, "Dear God, is that illustration prophetic for me? If so, what does it mean? Show me what you want me to do. Please, pave the way. Help me, Father."

When Celeste raised her head, she knew she was doing the right thing.

Celeste kept the steeples' crosses in her sight and drove directly to the street where the three churches stood—the Baptist Church on one corner, the Community Church by it, and the Methodist Church across the street on the next. She turned into the parking lot of the huge, modern Community Church and parked. Butterflies fluttered rapidly in her stomach as she looked into the car mirror to arrange her hair with her fingers and to check her lipstick. Her eyes locked on the slight dimple in her chin. Her finger touched the spot.

Mustering up what courage she could find, Celeste held her head high and walked into the church office, which had been chaotic all morning. The phone lines had been jammed with reporters trying to schedule interviews with Dr. Pate and with church members seeking more information about what had happened in Atlanta.

Celeste told the flustered receptionist, "My name is Celeste Downs. May I see Dr. Pate?" Kim couldn't keep from staring. This young woman could almost be Caitlin's twin.

"Excuse my staring, but you are the spitting image Dr. Pate's daughter. You must be a relative."

Celeste hesitated longer than she realized. "Oh, no...I mean...I don't know, but that is what I'm trying to find out for sure. Other people have commented on my having a strong resemblance to him and his daughter. I just needed to ask Dr. Pate a few questions."

Maintaining her professional demeanor, she answered, "I'm so sorry. He called this morning to say he had to make an emergency out-of-town trip. This isn't unusual; he is on so many state committees."

"Could you tell me where he lives? His wife might be able to help me."

"Sure," Kim answered. "Go back to Main Street, travel south until you reach the Sweet Waters subdivision. There is a bricked entrance with a waterfall built into it. It will be about a half-mile past the Citgo station on the right. Turn in and go to the second street, it is Concord Street. Take a right and go to the cul-de-sac. The Pates live in the middle house in the cul-de-sac, number 248. Mrs. Pate should be there. This isn't her regular work day. I'll call and tell her you are coming."

"Oh, thanks. I would appreciate that. You have been more than helpful."

As Celeste left the office, Kim rushed to the other secretaries to tell them about her encounter with this Caitlin look-alike.

Celeste Meets Molly

When she arrived at the beautiful French-modern two-story, Celeste had hardly touched the doorbell when the door opened. Molly's sweet smile and greeting immediately set Celeste at ease. Although she covered it well, she was shocked to see this young lady who looked like her own daughter and who had a strong resemblance to Jack.

"Hello, my name is Celeste Downs."

"Please come in. I'm Molly Pate." Molly received this uninvited guest as she did others—with graciousness and a smile. It was a God thing.

No one could have guessed Molly had just spent a sleepless night. Jack had dashed in this morning, not offering an explanation of where he had slept the night before. He had run upstairs and then rushed out without even taking time to shave. He had grabbed his dirty jeans from the clothes hamper and pulled on an old sweatshirt. He clasped the paper under his arm as he went out the door.

Molly had pleaded, "Jack, please talk to me. I know something is wrong. You have behaved strangely since you came home from Atlanta. Where were you last night?"

"Quit badgering me. I've got to go." Jack didn't offer answers or explanations. He brushed passed Molly. She had never before seen his brow so furrowed and his appearance so disheveled.

Although Molly hadn't seen the morning paper, she had received several strange calls—one from a reporter from the *Smytheville Gazette*, who expressed an urgent need to talk with Dr. Pate and several from church members who insisted on knowing where Jack was. To add to these strange occurrences, there had been a call from Kim telling her a young lady—maybe a relative—was on her way to see her. Molly was struggling with unexplainable uneasiness when the doorbell brought her out of her musings.

She invited Celeste in and led her to the spacious, well-decorated family room. "Kim called to say you were coming. How might I be of help?" Molly couldn't keep from staring at this Caitlin-like creature. This attractive young lady, dressed in a classic gray pants suit, was stunning. Her beautiful hair glistened like sunlight. Although Molly didn't comment on this immediately, Celeste realized Molly's eyes were examining each of her features.

Celeste said, "I really don't know how to begin, but I had to come to Smytheville to see if I had family I never knew about. When I saw Dr. Pate's picture in the *Atlanta Constitution*, I realized he and I share many physical features, and I wonder if we might be related."

"What picture was that?" Molly was already perplexed by the other events of the day. Not the least was this meeting with a girl who looked as though she could have been her daughter. Celeste handed her the picture and article she had been carrying around.

Molly silently read the article and couldn't hide the astonishment that shook her very being. "I hadn't seen this," she muttered distracted by this unexpected news. Lost in her thoughts and with tears welling up, Molly kept staring at the article.

"I'm so sorry, Mrs. Pate, I didn't mean to upset you like this. I thought you would have already known about it. I could come back later if—"

Molly interrupted. "No, no. I want to hear what you have to say."

As Celeste related her story to Molly, Molly's eyes fixed on an inconspicuous, almond-shaped birthmark just under Celeste's right jawbone. She knew at that moment, this had to be Jack Pate's daughter. It was not mere coincidence. Not only did this girl possess Jack's facial features, including the slight dimple in the chin, but also this birthmark was tell-tell proof. Jack had marked each of his children with this mark, which matched his. *Can this day possibly become more bizarre? God, I know you won't put more on me than I can bear, but you are coming awfully close to maxing me out today.*

For the next hour, Celeste related to Molly her history, including the story her mother had perpetuated about her real dad being Jack Smith. Molly listened with great interest. Suddenly, Benji burst through the front door with three of his teammates—Dog Hair, Tadpole, and T-Winy. With their typical teenage exuberance, they were oblivious to the fact they were interrupting such a serious discussion or to the fact there was a visitor in the house. "We're starved. Is there anything to eat in the kitchen?" Benji asked. Seeing the young lady on the sofa, Benji stopped. "Oh, I'm so sorry. I didn't know we had a guest," he said politely, never looking at anything but Celeste's face. When he realized he was staring rudely, he reached out his hand and introduced himself and his buddies.

Easily transitioning from the serious conversation with Molly, Celeste greeted the group without letting on. "I'm glad to meet you. I'd be pleased to discover if I'm related to a young man like you, but I'm not sure," she answered. Looking to Dog Hair, Tadpole, and T-winy, she added, "I'm glad to meet you guys, too," she said with a smile. "Somehow I can't believe those are your mother-given names."

Molly, masking her troubled emotions, interjected, "Every kid in school seems to go by a nickname."

"Nice to meet you," each of the boys said in turn before they went to raid the refrigerator.

The interlude with these guys made Celeste even more comfortable in that house. It was almost as if she belonged there.

All her life she had yearned to be part of a real family, one with siblings and a home bustling with activity. The interruption gave both her and Molly a break from the intensity of their conversation. Celeste's eyes traveled to the photographs displayed on the piano. She recognized Benji's and then saw one that could have been her own picture. "That must be Caitlin," she commented to Molly.

"Yes, that was her senior portrait." Molly couldn't help but notice how much that picture resembled the young lady in her living room. Molly felt her knees were close to crumbling beneath her, just like the world she'd known with Jack.

Finally, Celeste had done all she could do for that day and stood to make her exit. "You have been so very kind to listen to me. I can't thank you enough," said Celeste. "It would please me so much to find we are connected in some way. Both you and your son are such warm, gracious people, but I guess I will need to talk with your husband later to really know. Would you tell him I came by and that I would like to talk with him at his convenience?"

"You can rest assured I will tell him. I would like some answers also. I'm sorry I couldn't be more help. I know Jack was never married before, but there must be some explanation. This is more than coincidence. I agree you have reason to continue this research, and I have questions for Jack.

She said, "Jack has been so preoccupied lately with other matters, he hasn't been in town much. But when he returns, I'll see if he will set up a meeting with you. In the meantime, I would like to come to Atlanta and get you and Caitlin together for lunch sometime. I'd like to make your picture together." Molly knew this couldn't be her last encounter with Celeste.

"That would be great. Do you think we might be able to arrange that for Saturday? I'm anxious to meet my 'twin.'"

"I'll call Caitlin to see and call you later," Molly replied. Molly had no idea what state her marriage and family would be in by Saturday.

Celeste had come this far with this matter and wasn't about to slow down now. She said her good-byes satisfied she had made some progress. She only regretted she didn't get to meet this Jack Pate face-to-face.

The Deacons

Donald Brooks picked up the paper Monday morning after another sleepless night. Ever since the conference—actually before it—the church rumbled with gossip, questions, and doubts. In some members' eyes, Jack Pate's crown had begun to tarnish. If there had been only a few hints of indiscretion, Donald could continue defending his beloved pastor and friend, but his last episode had changed the church rumble to a roar. Donald's phone rang with regularity, both at home and at the office, with members wanting answers to what was going on with their pastor. He had made excuses for Jack as long as he could. In the past, he spent many hours trying to pacify both laymen and staff. He had spent his dark hours asking God to guide him, to direct his actions, and to keep his motives pure. He felt God would judge him harshly if he did anything to harm a man of God.

As he walked back up the sidewalk, he opened the paper to check out the day's headlines. His unshaven jaw dropped when Jack Pate's tear-streaked face stared back at him. He stood like a statue reading every word of the article with tears streaming down his own face. "This is the straw that will break Jack's back," grieved Donald. He had God's answer sooner than he expected. Knowing what he had to do, he rushed into the house and started making phone calls. "Troy, this is Donald. We've got to get the other deacons together this morning for an emergency meeting."

"I was just about to call you myself. I've just seen our pastor's picture plastered on the front page. Are we meeting in the conference room at church as usual?"

"I don't think that's a good idea under the circumstances. We can meet in the activities room at my bank. Can we meet by 9:00 a.m. this morning?"

"The earlier the better. We've got to take action before more damage is done to the church. Once everybody sees the paper, all of our phones will be ringing. I'll help you call the other deacons. I'll take the first half alphabetically, and you can call the others," Troy volunteered.

"Thanks, Troy. Let's encourage the others to refrain from discussing this with anybody until we know what we are going to do. By the way, pray in the meantime. Pray we will have God's guidance in whatever action we take. Pray for Jack also. Something has gone really wrong."

Since he served as president of the Colonial Bank, Donald had no problem acquiring the room for the meeting. Fortunately, no club was scheduled to meet that morning. He told his assistant to keep the regular coffee drinkers out and to tell them the room was closed for a private meeting. He knew it certainly wouldn't be a secret meeting since people in Smytheville knew what just about everybody in town drove. The collection of deacon's cars in the parking lot was a dead giveaway.

The twelve wide-eyed, tense men were all there and seated by 9:00 a.m. No one was in the dark about why they were there. They all had seen the morning paper. Shock and sadness was apparent in each face.

"I think we all are aware of why this meeting has been called," began Donald. The situation we are facing with our pastor is very grave. I think I understand more fully Jesus's prayer in the garden of Gethsemane. Along with Him, I've prayed 'If it is your will, let this cup pass from me.' None of us want to be in the position we are in right now, but God hasn't removed this cup from us. This morning we must determine how we are going to handle the situation with our pastor. It is apparent by a preponderance of evidence Dr. Jack has had a moral fall. But before we are hasty in our actions, I believe we need to get on our knees before almighty God and plead for his help and direction in our decisions."

After each man had prayed, Donald addressed the group again. "You guys know I love Jack Pate like a brother and have defended him to a fault, but we must face this situation head-on. I am convinced our preacher is having an affair with Darcy Price. For quite some time I accepted his explanation for things, but there is substantial evidence that he has been untruthful. Yesterday, we took Jack and Molly to the club for lunch. I thought he might open up about last week's episode with Andy Moore, but he didn't want to talk about it. He left soon after we ate to go get some rest, or so I thought. In about thirty minutes, I had to go check on Mother. I passed Darcy's house on my way. Just as I approached her house, I saw Dr. Jack at her door. She greeted him with more than an innocent, Christian kiss. Then, when today's paper contradicted his account of the convention scenario, I realized he had duped us all.

"The Bible teaches we should go to a brother taken in a sin and try to restore him. Listen to this passage from the sixth chapter of Galatians 6:1. 'Brothers and sisters, if someone is caught in a sin, you who live by the Spirit should restore that person gently. But watch yourselves, or you also may be tempted.' Do you agree that should be our first step?"

John Wright spoke up first. "I'm not sure he wants to be restored, but I agree we should handle this in a biblical way. I would be glad to make the visit if two more of you will go with me."

"Because I'm the chairman of the deacons," volunteered Donald, "I think I should go also. We need one more. Is there someone else who feels they should be a part of this committee?"

"It's not that I'm so eager to make this visit, but maybe I should go with you since I'm the chairman of the personnel committee," said Cory Colvin. "I don't think we should put this off. If we are going to do it, let's go now before the whole town is abuzz with the news."

xxxxx

When the trio arrived at church, they commented on the absence of Jack's Volvo. "Kim, is Dr. Pate in?"

"No, Donald. He called from his cell phone this morning, saying he wouldn't be in, and he wanted me to cancel his appointments for the day. He didn't say where he was."

"Thanks anyway, Kim." When the men got back to the car, Donald said, "I have an idea where he might be. Let's go by Darcy's house."

His car was just where Donald expected—in Darcy's driveway. The men got out of the car and went to the door. Each man mentally rehearsed what he might say when someone came to the door. No one did, though. Darcy's car was gone, but the men surmised she had driven it to the office. Next, they drove to Dr. Martin's office. Her car wasn't there. Cory Colvin went to inquire of Darcy's whereabouts.

"Darcy called me and asked me to tell Dr. Martin she had to go out of town unexpectedly. She refused to give me more details than that," reported the receptionist. "Needless to say, Dr. Martin was chapped about her unexpected absence. I don't know how much longer he's going to put up with her," she whispered.

Outside the office, Cory reported to the others, "Well, we're back to square one. They don't know where she might be. Why don't we see if Molly knows his whereabouts?"

"I don't think we are ready to discuss details with Molly yet. I don't know how much she knows about this situation," answered Donald. I'll just call and tell her to have him call me when he gets home. I think that might be more discreet than the three of us appearing unexpectedly on her doorstep."

"He will return by tomorrow. That's when the staff gets their checks. He'll be the first in line." Cory's sarcasm didn't go unnoticed by the others.

"Cory, we all feel anger and disappointment, but let's make an effort to guard our attitudes until we try to restore him. We can't take back bitter words, you know," encouraged Donald. "How can we set a forgiving example if we burn bridges too soon?"

"You're right, I know, but I thought that man hung the moon. I'd do anything he asked me. He was the one who encouraged me to accept the office of deacon last year. I felt I was too young for the responsibility, but he said he needed me, whatever that meant."

Jack

Earlier that morning, Jack had arrived at Darcy's just as she was leaving for work. What's wrong with you? I've never seen you so scruffy."

"Darcy, we've got to talk. We've got major trouble." Jack knew with certainty people, especially the deacons, would seek him out today with questions he wasn't ready to answer.

"Okay, but can it wait until I get off at lunch? I'm already running late for work."

"No. I've got to get away. Let's go somewhere away from here. Now."

"I'll have to call the office and tell them I won't be in. Dr. Martin's not going to like this. He doesn't like surprises, nor does he appreciate the employees calling in at the last minute."

"Hurry! Can we go in your car? Mine is almost out of gas, and I certainly don't want to stop in Smytheville to get any today."

"Sure. I filled up yesterday."

Minutes later, with Jack driving Darcy's eight-year-old Fiero, they were speeding south toward Albany. "Darcy, what have you got me into? My life is in shambles. You trapped me. The wheels are coming off. We are being found out. I am ruined. The church, my family…" Words rushed from Jack's mouth before he could finish a complete thought.

"Woe, Jack. Where do you come off blaming me for your troubles? I believe you initiated much of this! What are you talking about? You sound like a crazy man. Slow down and explain what has happened."

"Apparently you haven't seen the morning paper. It has my picture on the front page. Here, read it for yourself," he said shoving the paper toward her.

"Jack, you can handle this. You always convince people so easily." Darcy's emotions ran the gamut. Part of her wanted to comfort Jack, but the dig about what she had done to him lingered in her mind. She was seeing a different side of Jack. He had traded the compassionate Jack for some strange accuser. But for now, she had to put her petty feelings aside to try to help him find a solution.

Soon after passing the Albany city limits sign, Jack whirled in at a Motel 6. This time he wasn't spending the church's money. A cheap hotel seemed appropriate at the moment—cheap and dirty.

Jack fell face-down across the bed as soon as he got in the room. He cried for the first time in years. He couldn't clarify why, exactly. Was it remorse, or was it fear of humiliation? He was giving up everything for a tramp and was in deeper trouble than he had ever known.

Darcy lay by him, trying to soothe him with her touch. She massaged his back, rubbed his neck to relieve the tension, and finally tousled his hair. "You know I love you, regardless of what happens, don't you? I'll be with you."

Somehow these words temporarily alleviated his agony. For the next hour, he buried his troubles in their lovemaking. Darcy always could make things better for him this way. He needed her.

Reality came back like a boomerang and hit him in the face. He knew he would resign at the church before he was asked to. He couldn't fix this with mere words. Thoughts of the way he had trampled God's precepts and of the commandments he had broken raced around in his mind like cars at the Talladega Speedway. *Thou shalt not commit adultery; thou shalt not bear false witness; and how about loving God above all else?*

What about Molly, though? He vacillated between making her a villain and realizing he wasn't worthy of her unquenchable love. He thought his troubles revolved around their intimacy. *If she had been the lover that Darcy is, I would have never been caught in this trap in the first place, but she is the mother of my children and has always been a great helpmate.* But, at some level, he knew she was much more to him than that. *I've wronged her, but I can't go back and undo the damage now.*

"Darcy, I think I will have to make a clean break with everything I know—Molly, the church. My children will hate me, so I will lose them, too. What am I going to do?"

Darcy realized this was her chance to have the one she wanted. "Marry me, and we can make it together."

"That's ludicrous. I won't even have an income, Darcy. I can't support us." Her offer tempted him, though. Fear of facing this situation alone paralyzed him. He didn't want to be left with nothing. At the same time he couldn't imagine giving up what he had for a tramp.

"I will have a modest income, Jack. It is nothing to compare with your salary, but we can get by until you find another church."

Shocked by her naiveté of church politics, he shouted, "You really don't get it, do you? I'm through. I'm washed up as a minister. No church will have a pastor who's been caught in adultery."

His attitude surprised Darcy. Although she admired everything else about Jack, she didn't like his tone and manner toward her sometimes. But after they were married, that would change, she knew.

"I have some savings that will get us by until you find a new niche, and you will. I know," Darcy assured Jack. "I know I can make you happier than you've ever been before."

Just as he tried to untie his knotted mind, his cell phone rang. Seeing his home number appear on the phone, he answered, not masking the disgust he felt at the interruption. "What do you want, Molly?"

"Jack, I know you don't like for me to bother you on your cell phone, but this is urgent. Donald called and is anxious to get in touch with you. He said it was very important. Where are you? I was embarrassed to tell him I didn't know where you are, that I couldn't find my own husband." Molly's voice dropped to an unusual stern tone. "Besides that, I have a lot of questions for you about another matter. You had an out-of-town visitor who is the spitting image of you. Jack, I'm beginning to think you're not the person I've always believed you to be. Why have you deceived me?"

"I'll be home after awhile. I'll wait until then to call Donald." He hung up the phone without responding to Molly's question.

Jack turned to Darcy. "I've got to go, Darcy. I've got so much to work out."

"Why? What's going on? What's more important than discussing our future?"

Gruffly, Jack replied, "That will just have to wait. We've got to get back to Smytheville. The wheels have come off at church and at home. I just can't think about anything else right now."

Darcy drove back to Smytheville in silence. Jack laid his head back and feigned sleep while his mind swirled with decisions.

I just can't handle this. It's too much, Jack contemplated. The little poem from his childhood resounded in his mind, *Humpty-Dumpty sat on the wall. Humpty-Dumpty had a great fall. All the king's horses and all the king's men couldn't put Humpty back together again.* He knew at that moment he was Humpty.

The Woods

How had things gone this far? Just last Sunday he had stood in the pulpit of the Peaceful Valley Community Church, dynamically preaching the Word before some fifteen hundred members and visitors. This conservative church had grown by three hundred members in the mere twelve months he had been its pastor. Until two nights ago, he had never been any place where he felt more loved and appreciated. Was that his Achilles's heel, an overwhelming need to be loved, admired, and respected? But now that opportunity was lost forever. He was exposed.

His musings transported him to his childhood home nestled in the mountains of north Georgia. There he had been nurtured by his soft-hearted, loving mother and prodded to do more, to reach higher and higher by his hardworking father. Though it appeared an idyllic home, something had been missing; a void permeated their relationship that could never be filled, a pinnacle the son could never reach.

Thoughts of how he left Molly then began flooding his mind. Jack couldn't erase his last image of his childhood sweetheart, his wife of twenty-five years, weeping inconsolably, moaning in unbearable emotional pain. This image was especially troubling for this was one of the few times he had ever seen her distraught. Occasionally, he had seen her tears at church when she was touched by a song or a special service; mission programs seemed to always have triggered her emotions. Molly was the most emotionally even person he had ever known. She rarely guffawed, even at the most hilarious situations, nor did she exhibit anger. She was steady—a rock. *If only*, he despaired, *she could have been more expressive when it came to her devotion for me.*

There was no way to put his life back together, even if he had the will to do so. Uncertain of how God would judge his decision, Jack believed there was only one way out. Although he knew his conservative doctrine taught, "Once saved, always saved," he even questioned that now. What if committing suicide doomed him to an eternity in hell? He realized that would not be punishment enough for hurting so many people.

Poised, ready to end it all, Jack saw no other way but to end it with one shot.

Benji parked in a little trail road where he had several times before on those memorable occasions when Jack afforded him enough of his precious time to take him hunting. The cold drizzle hitting his face as he tromped through the woods did little to cool his temper. Adrenaline had fueled Benji to the point he thought he could kill a lion with his bare hands.

After thirty minutes of following one trail after another in search of his dad, he finally spotted a path of fresh footprints in the wet leaves and recently broken sticks. His heart pounded as he felt he was nearing his prey. He had planned in his mind how he would waylay his dad with one solid punch and then ask him questions later. He wanted to make his dad suffer physically more than his mother had suffered emotionally because of what he had done. With fists clinched ready for fight, he climbed over fallen trees and plowed through briars as he followed what he believed to be his father's trail. His eyes focused on the rugged path. A soft click sounded a few feet away causing Benji to look up.

Seeing his dad sit under an old oak with his rifle under his chin ready to pull the trigger caused Benji's anger to dissolve into fear in an instant. The thought of this disastrous day ending this way was more than he could bear. He feared making any sudden move would cause his dad to jump and finish what he was set to do. A plethora of emotions flooded Benji's mind. Just minutes before he had wished his dad dead; now he was desperate to prevent this tragic ending.

A slight rustle made Jack pause for just a moment. He involuntarily glanced in the direction of the noise. The sight of his son standing a few feet away with his dark hair plastered to his head and forehead and his eyes bugged out with disbelief made Jack forget his mission, if only for a moment.

Seeing his dad look up provided Benji his cue to speak. In an instant, he assumed an authoritative stance. "Put that gun down, Dad. Whatever has happened doesn't call for this drastic end. Let me help you," Benji pleaded with his dad. "I know we can work things out."

"You can't say that because you don't know what all I've done," replied Jack.

"I know more than you think, Dad, and part of me wants to come over there and pull the trigger for you, but I know that's not the solution, not God's anyway."

"Just leave, Benji, please. I've got to do this, and you don't need to witness it." Jack's voice jerked with tears. "I am giving up my right to live. I can't face the shame. Go on, now."

Jack had slackened his grip on the rifle. It dropped a little and was no longer aimed his head. Benji took advantage of this moment, made three long strides, and yanked it from Jack's hands. "You're not ending it this way, not today," Benji said through clenched teeth. When he realized the imminent danger had passed, more kindly Benji added, "Let's just go home, Dad."

"I can't do that, Benji. I've given up my right to be a part of the family forever."

"Don't say that, Dad. God will help us get over this. You've always told others when things were too complicated for them to work out, God could handle them." Benji spoke with more confidence than he really felt. *How could God ever make things right in his family again?* Benji sat down by his dad. His desire to punish him had morphed into a new desire, a desire to help him get through this.

For the next hour, Jack told all. He confessed his sins to Benji like a parishioner to a priest. This confession and the profuse weeping served as a catharsis. But the disgusting particulars of Jack's confession refueled his son's anger.

"You're right, Dad. You don't deserve to live or to be part of our family, but by Job, you're not killing yourself today. You're going back to face the music. Death is too easy. You deserve the humiliation. The rest of us aren't going to experience the shame and disgrace in Smytheville while you take the coward's way out. Now get up off your sorry butt, and let's go."

Mechanically, Jack followed his son like a whipped, obedient dog. He couldn't imagine a positive outcome, but he found some solace in someone else doing the thinking, if for just a few minutes.

"Let's go home, Dad, and try to sort this out with Mom. You know she can always come up with solutions to problems when the rest of us come up dry."

"I can't do that, son. I burned my bridges with her when I walked out the door. I said some unforgivable things to her as I left. I'll have to face the consequences of my actions alone this time. I'll come by tomorrow and gather my things while she's at work."

"Dad, you know Mom. She's got a heart the size of a number 2 wash tub. She'll forgive you."

"Not this time, son. I can't even ask her to. I can't face her now. Besides, you know I'm not good at apologizing and groveling."

"Where will you go then?"

"I don't know, but I'll find a place."

After listening the past hour to his dad's tale of infidelity, Benji had a good idea where that place would be.

All afternoon, Benji's emotions had bounced back and forth like a Super Ball thrown in a concrete hallway. His dad's last comment about not groveling made his protective instincts for his mother surface. Although much more than material possessions was on Benji's mind, that came out at the moment.

"If that's the way it's going to be, be sure you leave the Volvo at the house when you go. Mom needs better transportation than that old Pathfinder you passed down to her. It's worn out."

His selfishness resurfacing, Jack asked, "But what will I do for transportation then?"

"That's your problem—just one of the problems you've created. I'll tell you right now, you aren't going to shaft Mom anymore. She may be too gentle for her own good, but, trust me, I'm not that good. If you hurt her in any way again, I may forget I'm a Christian for a couple of minutes and give you what you deserve. You can take your clothes and personal belongings when you come tomorrow, but nothing else."

Friends

Few secrets exist in a small town like Smytheville. Jack's downfall, including his walking out on the family, certainly wasn't kept quiet. It was the hottest news that had hit the streets of Smytheville since the story of an escaped convict being found in Mr. Sokel's barn. Talk of this scandal could be heard in any store in town. How people knew so quickly mystified the family.

When Benji returned home, he sat down to recount the events of the afternoon with, Molly. She was still angry, worried, and confused, but less hysterical than when he had left. Caitlin sat with Molly and listened intently. The anguish still showing on all their faces revealed a kind of grief that even superseded the grief of facing the death of loved ones. Caitlin expressed what Benji had thought. "Dad's death would have been easier to have accepted than this kind of distress. At least a funeral would have provided closure. As things stand now, we three will face shame and sympathy for a long time."

The trauma of the day had caught up with Benji. He started second-guessing himself. "Maybe I shouldn't have stopped Dad. If he had killed himself, life might have proved simpler for all of us."

"Benji, you don't mean that. Never doubt the fact that you did the right thing, regardless of what hardships we might face," Molly asserted.

"I know how Benji feels, Mom. I know it's wrong, but I wish he were dead, too."

"Caitlin, that's just your shock and disappointment talking," inserted Molly. "Whatever we three face, you can rest assured we won't be facing it alone. Just remember all the fear-nots in the Bible. God will hold us in the palm of his hand."

After the three spent hours scrutinizing the situation and trying to fathom how Satan got such a hold on this man of God, they went to bed. Molly's night was spent alternating between crying and praying.

When the doorbell woke her at 8:00 a.m., Molly hadn't been asleep more than an hour.

"Molly, I hope I didn't awaken you, but I felt I must come by and do something. I really don't know what to do or say, but I want you to know I love you, and my thoughts are with you. I hurt, too. I baked you a cake to try to sweeten the day." Sara Finch, a quiet unassuming lady from Molly's Sunday school class, handed her a homemade yellow cake topped with thick, crusty caramel icing. She knew this was Molly's favorite. Sara had no clue as to what to say to comfort Molly. This was the best way she knew to bring her condolences.

Molly had just showered and was drying her hair when the doorbell rang again. Caitlin answered the door this time to receive similar words of love and encouragement along with a casserole. This process continued throughout the morning with Caitlin answering the door one time and Molly the next.

Benji dreaded going to school that day more than anything he had ever done, but he knew he had to face people sooner or later. He had gotten up, after sleeping very little, and slipped out without disturbing his mom or Caitlin.

The other students who had heard the news really didn't know how to react toward Benji. Some just diverted their eyes when they met him in the hall to avoid an awkward conversation. His buddies just gave him a pat on the back as a silent show of support. Others huddled in gossip and stared as he walked by.

Mrs. Mashburn, his first-period teacher and a member of Pleasant Valley, asked him to stay back when class was over under the pretense of discussing his term paper topic with him. "Benji, I just wanted you to know how much I admire the way you are handling yourself under these difficult circumstances. It must have been really difficult for you to come to school today. A lesser man would have stayed home. I wanted you to know I will be praying for you throughout the day. If I can be of help any other way, just let me know. I'm giving you an open pass to come back to my room if you find you need to talk or to just get away for a few minutes. If need be, we can go in my office and shed a few tears together."

Mrs. Mashburn, normally a stern, no-nonsense English teacher, would never comprehend what this show of kindness did to bolster Benji throughout the day. When he would feel tears welling up in his eyes, he would reach in his pocket and touch the pass she had given him. The fact that he did have an outlet helped him remain strong and stay in his other classes.

Throughout the day, he had determined what action he must take. He was aware his dad's income would stop and his mom's two days a week at the hospital wouldn't cover expenses. He would drop basketball and get an afternoon job to help out.

Benji trudged to his locker to gather his uniform, barely nodding to the few who spoke to him in the hall. Hating having to give up the sport he loved and regretting the effect his quitting would have on the team, he handed it to Coach Sloan.

"What's this?" asked the bewildered coach.

"Coach, I'm going to drop basketball and get a job. Circumstances at home have changed drastically, and I need to bring in some money to help Mom out."

"Benji, I've already heard about your situation, and I'm not going to let you do this. Is your mother aware of what you're trying to do?"

"No. If I told her, she would try to stop me, but I've already decided this is what I must do." He laid down his uniform and walked out the gym. Although class time wasn't officially over, he overlooked Benji's leaving before the bell rang.

The coach didn't try to stop Benji after his determined response. He knew Benji's mom well enough to know she wouldn't let him do this. He immediately went to his office and called Molly.

"I'll talk to him," Molly assured. "I'm not going to allow him to do this. I've already called the hospital and told them I want to go on full-time status. The nursing supervisor has tried to get me to for years. Keep his uniform for him. He will be back tomorrow. Thank you for understanding his situation and for calling me."

The stream of friends coming by and the phone calls continued until it was time for Molly to put on her uniform and go in for her second-shift duties. She dreaded facing sympathetic coworkers and patients more than anything, but she had told many people before that one of the best ways to cope with major problems is to get back to normal activities as soon as possible. Now she needed to take her own counsel. She silently prayed, "God, give me strength for today. I can't face people alone, but with your help, I can. Help me be a witness of your grace through this most difficult time in my life." *If Benji can face people today, so can I*, she reasoned.

By this time the table and refrigerator were loaded with food church members and other friends had brought in. "Do they think we will starve without dad here or something?" asked Caitlin as she examined the many dishes. "If we eat all this food, not only will we be a family deserted by a dad and husband, but we will be the fattest three in town." This comment served as a moment of comic relief. Molly and Caitlin laughed for a moment for the first time since the catastrophe had surfaced.

"This is the only way many people have of showing their love and support." Before she hardly had the sentence out, the doorbell rang again. This time Molly went to the door expecting yet another dish. Instead she was surprised by Sawyer Thomas's face staring at her. She knew who he was but had never had any one-on-one dealings with him. His name had been on the prayer list at church many times before revivals. Many who knew him were concerned for his soul's salvation. Someone had expressed,

"Sawyer is a morally good man but just will have nothing to do with church or spiritual matters." This sentiment had been repeated by other members of Pleasant Valley. The two just stood and stared at each other for a minute, not knowing what to say, before Molly invited him in. "Please come in. I'm somewhat distracted today. Excuse my manners, but just for a minute, I was surprised to see you," Molly offered.

"No, I won't detain you. I see you have your uniform on. I guess you must be going in to work." Looking at some imaginary object on the ground, Sawyer said, "I just had to come by to tell you I know a little about what you and your family must be going through. I experienced something similar years ago. I just wanted you to know I'll be here for you and your kids. I'm going to let you get to work now, but could I come back and talk with you later?"

"Sure. You don't know how much your coming by means to me, Sawyer. I wasn't too surprised by the outpouring of support from my church friends, but your visit is something special. I would like to hear more about your situation."

"I don't know," Sawyer mumbled, "but sometimes when people have suffered similar problems and pain, they can better identify with the situation. Maybe I can help you. I'll see you again in a few days when all this 'splutterment' dies down a bit. I'd tell you I'd pray for you, but I gave up on prayer a long time ago. It never solved my problems or situation."

Molly's selfless nature surfaced, and for a moment she became more concerned for Sawyer's spiritual wellbeing than she was for her own problems. "I'm sorry you feel that way about prayer, Sawyer. I don't think I could get through this without it. Sometimes, when words elude me, I know Jesus is interceding for me. I have to lean on Him. But you may be right about our helping each other. Don't wait long to come back."

xxxxx

Benji came up the sidewalk just as Molly was leaving to go to work. Even though she was running later than usual, she stopped long enough to confront her son about his decision to give up the one extracurricular activity he adored. "Benji, Coach called and told me you turned in your uniform. I'll not have it. You will *not* quit basketball and take a job. I've already called Mrs. Nichols, my supervisor, and told her I would take the fulltime job offer she has been trying to get me to accept. Actually, with the twelve-hour schedule, I won't be away from home but one or two more days. She even said I could start on first shift next week. We will be okay financially. I'm still your mom and am responsible for you. You've shouldered enough already. There is no debate on this issue. See you in the morning. Try to study, and do your homework. By the way, you'll find *plenty* of food on the table. Call Tadpole and T-Winy to come eat some of it up. Caitlin and the baby are still here."

Benji stood stunned, listening to this woman who had just experienced the worst disaster of her life give orders like a drill sergeant. She seemed strengthened and renewed by some unseen force. *There must really be something to this intercessory prayer thing. I made it today better than I thought I could. I guess quitting basketball and working is totally out of the question after Mom's speech.* Watching his mother drive off, Benji shook his head in disbelief at the determination of his mother. Most women would still be curled into a fetal position, licking their wounds. How would she endure the questions, the gossip, and looks of pity she would face tonight?

Molly got to the emergency department in plenty of time for the shift-change patient report, but not her normal one-hour early arrival.

Niva was the hospital cut-up. She faced the most serious situations with humor. "You're late. You just got here fifteen minutes before shift time today," Niva teased. Grinning, she added, "You're just getting sorry and good-for-nothing." The others appreciated the relief from what otherwise would have been an awkward moment, for they all had heard the news and had been surprised when they heard Molly would be making her shift today.

Molly appreciated her humor more than anybody. Niva set the example for the others at the desk to treat Molly, at least for today, like nothing abnormal had happened. This made Molly's segue from domestic problems into her work shift some easier. She realized emotional encounters and distractions would hinder her proficiency in this place where other lives were dependent on her performance. She determined to put on her game face and think about patients' problems rather than her own for a few hours.

Soon Molly had settled into her normal shift, handling everything from a child with the sniffles to car wreck injuries. Molly suited her role as an ER nurse perfectly. Each case received the attention it demanded as Molly automatically prioritized her actions according to the severity of situations. She moved with speed and efficiency, but also took time to show compassion to every patient and family.

About 7:00 p.m., Dr. Simmons, a long-time family friend, came in to see one of his patients. After checking the man out thoroughly, he jokingly told the man he didn't think he would die that day. The patient's heart attack was simply an overdose of peanuts he had eaten earlier that afternoon at a ballgame. Thad Simmons had treated this man in the emergency room before and knew his proclivity for overeating and then panicking at the first sign of indigestion.

When Dr. Simmons came out of the treatment room, he went behind the desk to finish writing on the patient's chart. He saw Molly taking orders over the phone from another doctor for one of his regular ER patients. "I understand, Doctor. I'll tell him to take his medicine as usual and to call your office tomorrow," she repeated his orders with her normal professional manner.

"Hi, Molly. You must be feeling better today. To tell you the truth, I'm surprised you came in today."

"I'm much better than the way you found me yesterday. I scolded my friend Janice for bothering you. She found your number on the refrigerator with my list of emergency numbers. But I'll confess, I guess if ever I needed a sedative, it was yesterday. That, along with the prayers and visits from friends, has helped me go on."

"I understand that all too well. I didn't get on my feet quite as fast as you have after Margaret died last year. You know, after you've been married to someone for thirty years and suddenly they're gone, there is unspeakable trauma. Even though she had fought lymphoma for a year, it still tore my heart out to give her up. I guess a person is never ready for that. I know your situation is different from mine, but you can know you have both my sympathy and support. Lean on me whenever you need to, and you will need to from time to time, trust me."

Molly received his sympathy and condolences better than she would have from anyone else. She realized he did understand better than most. Molly had watched him suffer, both at home and at work, through Margaret's illness. Molly had been the first to sign the list for volunteer sitters that had been passed around at church. She took the early morning hours, from midnight to 6:00 a.m., two days a week. Many of those nights, Dr. Simmons would get up because he couldn't sleep and would come sit in the room with his moaning wife. Toward the end when the lymphoma had attacked her bones, no amount of pain medicine completely eased her. Molly watched him suffer just as Margaret did. He would sit with his face in his hands, pleading aloud to God to relieve his wife.

One night, he confided in Molly his vulnerability. "I treat so many patients and help most of them. Why am I so helpless when it comes to giving my wife comfort?"

"You do bring her more comfort than you realize simply by sitting with her. She calms down when you enter the room. Her vital signs always improve. Usually, she dozes off and seems to be in less pain for a little while when you sit with her."

Molly had always seemed special as a strong Christian and an outstanding pastor's wife, but the way she gave of herself to both Margaret and him had endeared her to Thad Simmons in a very special way. He hoped he could comfort her in the coming days as she had him through his wife's illness and death.

Thad Simmons talked with Molly easier than he did with most of the nurses. Since his wife's death, he found it necessary to keep up a strong professional guard with both patients and nurses. He had been shocked and overwhelmed by the forwardness of many of them. From the day he returned to work after he buried his wife until the present, he was approached with offers that made him blush. Some of the women invited him to their homes for meals, while others made propositions much more directly. He had not been interested in any of these women, nor what they had to offer. As a matter of fact, he didn't think he would ever be interested in another woman. He had had the best and that was enough for him. He still enjoyed the memories he and Margaret had made together. Thad knew Molly wasn't like those women who took every opportunity to come on to him or to engage him just to flirt. Molly's coworkers who observed his relaxed conversations with her recognized the difference, also. Molly, even though she could talk easily with any man or woman, gave off an invisible signal that said, "I'm not available. I'm a happily married woman."

Molly had overheard her coworkers discussing Thad just a few days before. "He is such an attractive man, not only because of his neat physical appearance, but also because of his gentle, pleasant nature," commented one nurse.

"I know," replied another, "he never acts like a mini-god as a few of the doctors do. He speaks respectfully to all the staff, from RNs to custodians."

"I know. If all Christians treated people like Dr. Thad does, I might consider becoming one. No one ever hears him bark orders."

Behind his back, some of the nurses called him Smytheville's own Robert Redford. In the mornings, his reddish-blonde hair would be carefully styled, but by afternoon it had a slightly tousled look, which, along with his smoky blue eyes, accented his sexiness. His well-fitted dark suits couldn't hide his athletic build.

Perhaps by focusing on Molly's needs at this time, Thad could feel some relief from his own grief. "Molly, you are handling this situation like a real trooper, but you have to allow yourself to grieve, though. Just as when a family member dies, there are stages of grief one must go through. When you are home, don't fight it. Cry when you need to. Please call me if you feel the need to talk with someone. It would also help me to feel I was repaying you somewhat for the way you came to my rescue when Margaret was so sick."

"I'll do that. You are the one here who would understand." Molly reflected on the many who had expressed love and support throughout the day. *God truly does work in mysterious ways,* she thought.

The Church

The following Sunday, an unusual pall rested on the congregation at Pleasant Valley. Most had some idea what was coming when a solemn Donald Brooks made his way to the podium. After enduring the hardest week of his life, he now had to publicly deliver the news most already knew.

Donald and the other deacons finally tracked Jack down. Through several phone calls, they discovered he had taken a room at Mrs. Sisco's boarding house. It was the only rooming house in Smytheville, and, although it wasn't luxurious, it was clean and respectable. The uninvited deacons were met with less than graciousness. "What do you want?" They hardly recognized the unkempt Jack who seemed to have transformed from the handsome, well-dressed pastor into a much older creature—a bum.

Donald began, "Jack, the other deacons and I would like to talk to you a few minutes if you will let us come in."

"I don't guess I have much choice in the matter. Sooner or later I'll have to face you."

When he gestured for the group to enter, they tried to find places to sit. The sparsely furnished living room had only a well-worn sofa resting against the wall. Some sat there while others perched on the hearth of the fireplace. Jack offered no help in helping them find seats. He stood in front of them assuming the posture of a trapped wild animal, not knowing which way to turn.

"Go ahead and speak your piece. I know I have it coming. Just say what you've got to say so we can get this over." Jack stood ready for his upbraiding.

"Jack, we didn't come to condemn you or to even chastise you. That job belongs to the Lord. We came to see if we can help you work this situation out with your heavenly Father." In a kind, Christian manner, Donald made his best effort in trying to offer restoration. "As you have preached so many times, 'If we will confess our sins, he is faithful and just to forgive us.' We love you, brother, and beg you to give it up to God."

"I guess you perfect men have come to redeem me then. You seem to have already tried and convicted me. How would you like for me to stand here and name all your sins? You all have them, too, you know." Transference of the guilt he felt seemed to be Jack's only recourse at the moment. "The Bible also says, 'He without sin, cast the first stone.' Which one of you will it be then?"

After a few more minutes of useless bantering with Jack, the deacons realized their trying to bring him to repentance and restoration was pointless. Donald finally said, "Nonetheless, could we have a word of prayer before we leave?"

"If you feel you must," answered a sarcastic Jack.

As they drove back to the church, Cory Colvin matched Jack's sarcasm. "Well, that went very well, don't you think? I've never seen a colder fish than the one we've just dealt with. I hope he gets his just desserts."

"Cory," John, the older deacon, scolded, "check that attitude right now. As a deacon body, we've got to set the example and tone for the rest of the congregation. Yes, Jack has sinned, but he is still God's child, and God saved him from hell long ago. We're all angry and hurt, but we must control our tongues and attitudes. If we don't, Satan will win a victory by bringing us all down."

"You're right, I know, but when I think of what he's done to his family and what this is going to do to our church, I just want to punch his lights out. You all are going to have to pray for me. I don't always handle things with the same Christian attitude you do."

"You are just younger in the faith, and perhaps you haven't had to deal with as many situations as we older ones have, but we will pray for you and ourselves as well," offered John. "May none of us compound the sin by projecting holier-than-thou attitudes. Jack was right about one thing: 'We are all sinners saved by God's grace.' Let's not forget that."

Donald approached the pulpit with his head hanging and shoulders slumped. It was not until he stood behind the holy lectern that he raised up with confidence and support, which could only come from the Holy Spirit.

"Today, our faith is being tried. Satan attempts to shake our faith in God when our faith in one of our Christian brothers has been destroyed. It is my sad duty to report the resignation of our pastor, Dr. Jack Pate. I will read the short note he gave me this week:

> *To those at Pleasant Valley Community Church who have looked to me for divine guidance over the past months and to those who have supported my endeavors here, I tender my resignation. I am only human, not God. Therefore, I falter from time-to-time, just as you do. May God continue to bless Pleasant Valley Community Church.*

"May we spend some time in a season of prayer for our fallen pastor, and may we use this time for our own soul-searching. Let's pray for God's guidance as we face this very difficult time in our lives and in the life of our church. After this time for silent, individual prayer, our youngest deacon, Cory Colvin, will come and lead in a congregational prayer. Then, our director of missions for the association, Dr. Norris Phillips, will come and deliver the message for the day."

Sounds of weeping were heard throughout the congregation. Some prayers were heard as groans.

This juncture in the life of Pleasant Valley served as a sifter of the people. It separated the strong from the weak. Nowhere was this more evident than it was in the recovery group.

On Monday night, this group, lovingly called the "Hallelujah Boys" by some, met in the upstairs corner room of the education building at Pleasant Valley as it had for the past three months. All of the members were present with the exception of two regulars whose absences stood out prominently.

Jack Pate had seen the need for a Christian recovery group in Smytheville. Many of the church families were affected by the addiction of a child, father, mother, or some other family member. Addiction in Smytheville, as in most cities, came in many forms—drugs, gambling, alcohol, abusive behavior, and adultery. Jack had a passion for reaching out to these people and bringing them into the church. This group had become the most active outreach arm of the church. Not only were the charter members a spiritually changed group, but with their newfound faith, they had become super evangelistic in nature. They had brought in many of their friends. To those who much had been forgiven, God expected great things. The eight charter members were obvious in every service. They always sat together about a third of the way back in the center section. At the beginning, some other church members were slightly offended by the vocal support this group gave the pastor when he preached. "Amen, amen, praise the Lord, preach it, brother" resounded during every church service forthwith giving the group the title of the Hallelujah Boys. After Jack, from the pulpit, had praised the fervor with which they worshiped, their style was accepted more readily by the other members. No one could deny the good results for the community. These guys, who had come from varied backgrounds and problems, had been great witnesses to others like themselves and had brought many to church with them.

PeeWee led the group that night. "Guys, the devil is at it again. Dr. Jack's fall just proves Satan will attack anyone. As some of you have already heard through the grapevine, he isn't the only one of our regulars who has fallen. Josh Howard was taken to jail Saturday night. He got into a scrape with some out-of-towner down at the County Line Bar. When the cops came, they found a stash of marijuana on him. I made my accountability call to him Thursday and sensed then he was headed for trouble. I guess I should have called some of you to go with me to intervene, but I failed to do that. He was bitter about Dr. Jack. He told me, 'I guess there was nothing to this religion stuff but a bunch of propaganda. Dr. Jack just hoodwinked all of us. We just shined as stars in his religious cap. That's all. He didn't care about us. He just wanted to look good as a pastor. If he can't stay straight, why should we even try?'

"We all may have a test of our faith through Dr. Jack's fall. To be honest, I have had my doubts about a lot of things; I even had to ask myself if Benji is as good as he has always acted. Maybe when he led me to Christ, he just did it to put another notch in his holy belt," confessed PeeWee.

One by one, they began drifting away.

Conversations expressing shock and disgust ran through the church and town like water off a rooftop during a monsoon. "I've lived to the ripe old age of ninety-one and have suffered much pain and great disappointments of all kinds, but Dr. Pate has caused the greatest yet. I just wish I had gone on to meet my maker before this happened," Mrs. Morris, Pleasant Valley's oldest member told a friend.

"Mom, when will you and daddy get a divorce? Who will I live with when it happens?" asked one of the children.

The mother was shocked. "Baby, why would you ever ask such a thing? You know your dad and I love each other very much, and we both love you too much to ever let that happen."

"Dr. Pate left Mrs. Molly and he loved her, too, so I'm afraid the same thing will happen to our family."

One child asked her mother, "Am I still a Christian? Dr. Pate baptized me, and you said he wasn't real."

From the oldest to the youngest, each life suffered its own kind of pain from Dr. Pate's fall. Some expressed gentler spirits than others, but the one who stood as a monument to Christ-like love was Molly.

Sawyer Thomas

Sawyer Thomas held true to his promise to come back and talk with Molly. Soon after the initial shock of Jack's leaving had subsided, Molly received a call from him. "Molly, I'd like to talk with you at your convenience. I might be able to help you."

Thinking it strange that this anti-church, near stranger could offer any solace, Molly told him to come by about five that afternoon. Although she had little expectation of his being able to help her in any way, she didn't want to offend him, and she also was curious about what he might have to say.

Prompt to the minute, Sawyer arrived. Molly invited him in and escorted him to the sun porch. There she had a pitcher of iced tea awaiting them. Molly remained the perfect hostess, even though her red, swollen eyes and general appearance revealed that she hadn't slept in many nights.

His efforts were a strain to his shyness, but Sawyer began, "Mrs. Pate—"

"Why don't you just call me Molly?"

"Okay, Molly, as I told you when I stopped by before, I know some of what you are going through. I'd like to explain what I mean by that."

"I wish you would. I can't imagine how you could know. I've been puzzled by that remark since you were here before."

"Since you and Jack moved to Smytheville, I've closely observed you both. From your first week here, something about Jack Pate haunted me. From the first, I had a strange sense about him. While everyone in town thought he was the best thing since sliced bread, I saw ingeniousness in him that reminded me of my father. I grew up in a minister's home near Gatlinburg, Tennessee. My father, like Jack, was admired and praised throughout the town, but I saw a totally different side of him at home. All the praise and adulation convinced him he was God's gift to the world. When he would come home to face reality, he resented any action of our family that didn't directly exalt him and keep him on his holy pedestal. He became abusive."

"Sawyer, although Jack wasn't all he should have been at home, he certainly wasn't abusive."

"Pardon me, Ma'am, but he was. I've watched him. Maybe he didn't knock you around physically like my dad did Mom, but he did his own number on you. I see it in your eyes. There is so much more to you than this little meek, obedient wife he has tried to make you be.

"My father wore five hundred dollar suits, drove the most expensive cars, and tipped waitresses fifty dollars for bringing him coffee while his wife and children nearly starved at home. Just getting school lunch money from him was like getting orange juice from a lemon. I don't think he would have ever provided for even our most basic needs had it not been for the fact it would have been a strike against him in the community if he hadn't. The stain-glassed ministerial tones he used from the pulpit and with his congregation became crude curses and railings to his family. None of the church people would have ever believed the man he became once he entered the four walls at home."

"Sawyer, I didn't know. I'm so sorry you had to endure a childhood like that. I'm beginning to understand why you are so bitter toward the church."

"Oh, you haven't heard the half of it yet. My dear mother feared for her life if she made even the slightest misstep at church or with any of the members. My daddy, the sorry hypocrite, would even go shopping for her church clothes, and he made all the decisions. Her clothes had to be in style, but not flashy in any way. He said that would detract from him. He wanted to strut like a peacock and be seen. She was to be an inconspicuous sidepiece. In public, he showed her every kindness and consideration, but when he got her home, he flew into rages, telling her how worthless she was and how much help she could be to him if she would just look, talk, and be like Mrs. So-and-so.

He saw my sister and me as inconveniences and burdens and never failed to tell us as much. We grew to hate him. We learned we were going to get it from him whether we did things right or not. As you can imagine, we soon gave up on pleasing him. If he was going to berate us and beat us anyway, what was the use? So instead of being pleasing to him, we went in the other direction. Embarrassing him in public soon became our favorite pastime. One of our favorite pranks, after he had scolded us for not participating in the song service, was to take our hymnal and intentionally sing off key as loud as we possibly could and stay about three notes behind everybody else. We smiled like angels so people would think we were innocently praising God."

Molly laughed. "No, you didn't."

"Oh, yes. We did that and more." Sawyer, enjoying the humor of the moment, continued, "Melba, my sister, acquired skills with a needle at an early age. Mom insisted she learn to sew. We decided to put her talents to good use. I sneaked Daddy's expensive suits from his closet while Mom was at the ladies' missions meeting. Melba carefully removed the fine stitching from underneath the arms of one of his suits and replaced them with loose basting stitches. On Sunday when the old goat raised his arms to emphasize a point, the stitching came loose, just as she had planned. The congregation couldn't stifle their laughs. As you can imagine, my daddy didn't enjoy being the object of their humor.

"That worked so well, and since he was none the wiser that we had done it, we did the same thing to the fly of another of his suits.

"'You're just falling apart at the seams,' joked one of the deacons after Dad inadvertently exposed his underwear while he was delivering another of his 'hellfire and brimstone' sermons.

"With that embarrassment, he flew down to the men's store where he always bought his suits and attacked them about their shoddy workmanship. On close examination of the garments, they found the problem and explained to him that someone had sabotaged his wardrobe."

Sawyer again became serious. "It was not until he blamed our mother and physically assaulted her over the incident that we confessed. He then continued beating her because she couldn't control us, and then he started in on us."

"You would think we would have learned our lesson from that, wouldn't you? Wrong. That just made us meaner. I put Atomic Bomb, a strong sports liniment, in his under shorts soon after that. Of course Melba and I stayed close by so we could watch him gyrate and yell. That time it wasn't hard for him to guess I was the villain. For the first time in my life, I ran from him. I knew he was still more interested in relieving his burning crotch than he was catching me. Of course, I got more than my 'just desserts' later.

"He made Melba fix the damage she had done to his suits. She did, but intentionally left a needle in the very seat of his pants." This tale brought laughter from both of them.

Looking at his watch, Sawyer realized he had been there over an hour. "I'm so sorry I've stayed so long. I meant to come by for just a few minutes. Even with all this time, I never really got to tell you all I came to say."

"Sawyer, this has meant more to me than a dose of medicine. You know how the saying goes about laughter being the best medicine, don't you? Will you come back soon?"

"You just tell me when, and I'll be here. I got side-tracked today and didn't say what I meant to."

"Why don't you come at this time every Tuesday until you've told me everything? I want to hear more about your antics."

Sawyer kept his regular date at Molly's every Tuesday at five o'clock. The next Tuesday, he got to the point more directly, though.

"I told you I saw some similarities in your situation and mine, but I never really explained. Not only was my dad a revered pastor, he also was known throughout the county as a great counselor. As you are well aware, women come for counseling much more often than men. Daddy saw the need for many return visits if the counselee was young and attractive. As a teenager, I soon saw through much of what he was doing. I suspected he was doing more than counseling when he and Margaret Davis continued staying well past office hours. I knew there was an outside window to his office, but the blinds always stayed down, covering it. One day when he had left the church to visit members in the hospital, I made some excuse to his secretary to get her to let me in his office. I knew if I opened the blinds, he would just close them back when he came in, so instead, I bent a couple of slats in the corner where I could peek in from the outside. Thinking I would be overjoyed to catch him in his adultery, I positioned myself where I could get a good view when Miss Margaret came visiting the next day. To my surprise, what I observed brought me no pleasure. Instead, it turned my stomach. I witnessed my father participating in the most depraved sexual acts imaginable. I knew how wrong what he was doing was but could tell no one, not even my mother. His actions were unspeakable.

"That night I handled my disgust by going out with friends and getting sot drunk. I didn't care who saw me in that condition either. I wanted to bring as much disgrace to my father as he had to me. He couldn't possibly hurt me more than he already had. That began my path to alcoholism, which I didn't escape until years later.

"Little did I know at the time, others in the church had gained knowledge of his sin. Without fanfare or warning, he was fired. At the time we didn't know why he immediately left town without any explanation to our family, but later we heard he got a very direct message from the local KKK to "leave town or else."

If his hypocrisy had not been enough to drive me away from the church, the way the church responded to his penniless, deserted family certainly was. The day after he left, we received a letter from the finance committee demanding the full amount of money they had loaned my dad for our house. The agreement had been the church would forgive $5,000 of the debt for each year he served as their pastor. Suddenly they showed their 'Christian love' by putting my already distraught mother in this insurmountable financial crisis. We had no choice but to vacate the house immediately. No kindness was offered to our family at all. As a matter of fact, some there blamed us for my father's downfall. I overheard rumblings like, 'If his wife had taken care of his needs at home, he wouldn't have had to go looking for satisfaction elsewhere,' and statements putting me down. 'That Sawyer was such a disgrace to his father. He caused him to lose all pride in his family.'

We had to move in with my grandparents in Knoxville until mother got a job, waiting tables at the Cracker Barrel. She finally managed to get a small apartment for us. Both Melba and I took afternoon jobs to help us get by."

"Sawyer, now I think I have a better understanding of why you feel the way you do about the church and religious matters. I just want to remind you, though, in spite of what his people did or didn't do, Jesus never left you. He helped you survive abuse, poverty, and alcoholism to become a successful businessman."

Their visits continued with Sawyer receiving as much help as did Molly. He never failed to notice her benevolent attitude toward her sorry husband regardless of what disgraceful actions Jack took. When she got the word Jack was pursuing the divorce, Sawyer observed the true Christian position Molly assumed. Although he never conceded as much, his faith in Christian people renewed as he became aware of the many kindnesses Pleasant Valley members offered Molly.

One day Molly told him, "Sawyer, nothing would please me more than for you to give God and the church a second chance. All churches and Christians are not like those who let you down."

"Molly, if I ever change my mind and go to church, it will be because of you. You have shown me what a real Christian is like."

Benji Changes

Benji had always been even-tempered and had displayed a tremendous Christian attitude toward everyone. He changed.

Walking down Main Street one day, Benji overheard gossip. He recognized the two ladies from church. "There goes Benji. I'll bet a lot more went on in the Pate household than met the eye."

"Or less, especially in the bedroom. If Molly had done her wifely duties, our pastor might not have looked for satisfaction elsewhere."

"I know, but it may have just been an inborn character flaw. If that's the case, Benji may follow in his dad's footsteps some day."

Hearing these remarks made Benji's blood boil and tempted him to confront the gossips, but instead, he ducked his head and mulled over their words.

Others would ask questions as though they wanted to know details so they could comfort Benji, but he knew they were really being nosey. These offenses began stacking up in his heart like planks in the lumber yard.

"Why don't you watch where you're going?" he barked at Dog Hair one day when he barely bumped him in the crowded hall.

Dog Hair, not known for great patience, then gave him an intentional shove. "Take that you highfalutin used-to-be-friend." Only because the vice-principal came down the hall, a scuffle that was about to end in a full-fledged fight was diverted.

"What has gotten into you, Benji? Your teachers tell me you have transformed from the good-citizen boy you've always been into someone they don't even recognize—an ill-tempered, disrespectful punk. They all have cut you some slack because of your family problems, but I'm putting you on warning today. If your behavior doesn't improve immediately, you will be facing suspension."

His affable personality morphed to sullenness to the extent his closest friends lost patience with him. Tadpole vocalized displeasure first. "What in the h… has gotten into you, Benji? You're never any fun anymore. Every time we come over now, you treat us like strangers."

"You guys have no idea what I'm going through. Just leave me alone, and let me work through this the best I can."

The others cut him no slack whatsoever. "Boo hoo. Poor Benji is the only one who has ever had any problems," inserted Dog Hair with all the cynicism he could muster. "Your problem is you've always lived a charmed life, one with Ozzie-and-Harriet-type parents, one with no financial worries. You live in mansion, you have more friends than anyone I know, or at least you did 'til you started brushing off everybody. You're just getting a taste of problems. I've lived with them all my life.

"How would you like to come home every day to a mother like mine? My mom spends her days lying in a drunken stupor on our broken-down sofa. She looks like a witch with her uncombed hair sticking out in every direction, and she always smells like pee. Why do you think I never invite you guys in at my house? I don't think you could stomach it. You sure wouldn't find any cooked food there like you can at your house."

Tadpole joined in, "Have you ever had to search under every cushion in the house just to come up with lunch money? Have you ever had to lie and say 'I'm not hungry' or 'I don't want anything to eat' when we go to Sonic? Have you ever gone out the back door to keep from hearing your parents argue about where the month's money had gone? Have you ever studied by candle light for two weeks because your electricity had been cut off? I'll answer for you. *No.* You've always had it made. Now 'scuse me if I'm a little less sympathetic than you would like, but sooner or later, everyone has problems, so get used to them."

T-Winy felt uncomfortable with this attack on Benji. He certainly had had his share of problems but wasn't ready to unload them right then. He had nervously shifted his tall body's weight from one foot to the other and looked at his friends in disbelief. T-Winy usually was the least vocal of the group. He was the one who would laugh at the right time and occasionally offer a "yeah" or "nah" at the appropriate time in their conversations, but today, uncharacteristically, he joined in, not to berate Benji, but to defend him. "That's enough, you guys. Benji needs our encouragement instead of us needling him. Yeah, we've all got our own problems, but let's admit it. Maybe we haven't been publicly embarrassed like Benji has. Sometimes it's easier to never have had all this good stuff than it is to get used to it and then lose it." The others knew T-Winy was speaking a truth, one he knew all too well because he had lost it all when the rest of his family had been killed in an automobile accident when T-Winy was only six years old. Since that time he had gone from one foster home to the next. They knew some of the foster parents had simply used him for their own gain and that some had actually abused him. T-Winy never mentioned these things to the group, but they knew just as all the kids at school did. Word gets around in a small town.

The other two mumbled a bit more but stopped their attack on him. Benji merely agreed with the group. "You guys are right. I shouldn't complain, I guess." Although he agreed verbally, his demeanor was not changed then, nor did it improve in the days to come. It just became worse. Benji not only showed resentment toward those close to him, he also became aggressive with others. He had two altercations during basketball practice. His fuse was short these days. If he got knocked around more than he liked, his fists expressed his displeasure.

It didn't take much of this behavior before Coach called him aside. "Benji, I know you are hurting, but I'll not have you bringing this anger to the gym. One more outburst like this from you and you'll spend the rest of the season on the bench. Now shake it off, and get on with life. Besides, I've watched you; you've made a positive impact: you gave a Christian witness to the other guys and to me through your behavior. Are you going to destroy that with selfish self-pity?"

Benji dropped his head. He knew truth was all over Coach's words. Benji began a silent prayer. "Dear God, I guess I am mad at you for letting my dad destroy our family. I don't feel like praying, but you have assured us that when we can't pray, Jesus intercedes for us. Help me find my way back to you."

Although the change was not immediate, Molly, who had patiently waited for Benji to work through this stage of grief, noticed normalcy creeping back into his life. She had noticed he had cut her off for awhile and hadn't been as open with her as he had always been. But lately he had initiated more conversations. A few days after his coach had dressed him down, Benji came in the kitchen where his mom was cooking. He picked up an apple from the fruit bowl. Tossing it up and catching it, he said, "Mom, could I ask you to do something?"

"Sure, Benji. Just name it."

"Would you pray with me? I'm struggling, just as I know you are, but I can't seem to get through to God. I'm angry with Dad, with the church people, my friends, and, to be honest, even at you at times."

"Are you angry with me because of the divorce?"

"I guess, but I don't know. My thoughts are all confused. I really know it wasn't your fault, but sometimes I think you might have prevented it. That doesn't make sense, does it?"

"It makes perfect sense, and I have been angry too. I've asked myself many times how I could have done things differently. I think praying together about it will help us both." That they did. Answers didn't all come at once. Some never did. Instead, a peace bathed them like fresh rain.

Caitlin's Pain

Caitlin escaped the humiliation Benji endured because she lived out of town and didn't have to face the people who knew their story every day, but she had her own set of problems. Caitlin spent too many hours at home, just her and Emily. Bob's work took him out of town for days on end. Although she called her mother regularly to make sure she was okay, she no longer used Molly as a sounding board for her own problems. She felt it would be selfish of her to dump these on her mom. Her mom had enough to deal with right now. Not having an outlet to express her grief, Caitlin became more and more depressed. She had friends from her church in Atlanta but had not wanted them to know all the embarrassing details of her life.

Caitlin turned to medication to relieve her pain. She discovered quickly symptoms she could use to get the drugs she wanted. "What are you taking this early in the morning?" inquired Bob.

"Just something the doctor prescribed to calm my nerves. You just don't understand how I'm hurting."

"But you just took a handful of other pills last night that you said you got from the doctor. Don't you think you are getting too dependent on chemistry instead of God?"

This was just the first of many discussions the two had about this. The more they talked, the more heated their discussions became.

Emily, just as any baby does, sensed her mother's change. The teething process also made her uncomfortable. She reacted the only way a baby knows how; she started whining and crying incessantly. This only added to Caitlin's despair. By the time Bob would get back in town and home, Caitlin's resentment and anger would have reached its peak. She felt it totally unfair for him to go to all these interesting places and dine at great restaurants while she stayed cooped up in a small apartment and dealt with a crying baby. Unleashing all this on Bob as soon as he entered the house became routine. Although he tried to be sympathetic and understanding for a while, he soon became weary of being the supporter. When Bob would try to be affectionate, Caitlin would push him away. "All you want when you come home is for us to fall in bed. You don't know how tired I am taking care of your child all day. Men think sex is the answer for everything, and it's not."

"I don't think that at all, but I do miss our intimacy. I'm tired, too, after working and traveling, but I don't want to ignore our marriage." He was ready for the Caitlin he had married to return; he was ready for some affection for himself.

"You are just like my dad—like all men. You just focus on your own needs, neglecting to understand what I'm dealing with!"

Angered by the accusation, Bob realized he had to put some distance between them, or he would say too much. "I've got to pick up some things at the drugstore. I don't think you really want us to get into that discussion!"

One night Bob got his fill of being the scapegoat for Caitlin's problems. "Caitlin, I've tried all I know. I've sympathized; I've petted, I've tried to talk with you about your abuse of prescription drugs, and I've tried to be patient. I love you more than words can say, but I can't do this anymore. I'm leaving."

As he turned to go out the door, Caitlin hurled the can of beans she was about to open. Her aim was sure. Blood gushed from the cut on the back of Bob's head. "You just go on. Be like my sorry daddy. All you men are alike. You are all so self-centered. All you want is for your obedient wife to take care of the home front and service you with sex on-demand. You don't care about anyone else's needs." She sounded like a broken record, making the same accusations over again. As she heard herself, Caitlin knew she was being unreasonable and nagging, but she didn't know how to stop this downhill slide. Where was that faith she had relied on for so long? *If her dad could say one thing from the pulpit and then live another way, was there anything to this religious stuff?* She picked up the bottle of tranquilizers and took a couple.

Bob, not wanting to make their fight public by leaving the apartment with blood streaming from the gash, went to the bathroom to clean up and try to stop the bleeding from his scalp wound. He was both shocked and infuriated by his wife's unexpected physical attack. No longer did he want to argue with her because he knew it to be pointless; he just felt more justified in walking out. After changing out of his bloody clothes, he did just that.

There is a limit on pain and sorrow. After so much, it can't get any more intense. Caitlin lay dry-eyed in a state of shock across the bed, ignoring Emily's cry from the next room. She was faintly aware of the phone ringing on the nightstand next to her, but she chose to ignore it. She lay in this catatonic state for hours. Oblivious to knocks at the door and Emily's continued crying, Caitlin's only desire was to escape her miserable life. Zombie-like, she walked to the bathroom, poured an assortment of pills in her hand, popped them in her mouth, and swallowed them.

An hour after he left, Bob realized his mistake. Caitlin was suffering from her own kind of sickness now, and I'm just adding to the problem. He wanted to go back but wasn't sure how he should handle the situation when he did. He was afraid it would just bring on another of Caitlin's angry outbursts. Bob finally decided to call Molly even though he knew she had her own plateful of problems. He knew she would know how to help Caitlin and make Caitlin see she needed him back.

"Molly, I need you. Can you come to Atlanta tonight?" Bob then explained the ongoing problems he and Caitlin had been experiencing. "I haven't wanted to bother you with our problems, but I believe Caitlin is suffering from severe depression, and I can't help her. As a matter of fact, I added to the problems tonight by walking out. I've tried to call her repeatedly, but she won't answer the phone. I've even called our neighbor Vivian to go over to see if she's okay, and she doesn't answer the door. Vivian says she can hear Emily crying, but that's not unusual these days. You always seem to know how to handle things. Will you come?"

"Bob, I've got to work out a few things, but I'll be there as soon as I can. My car is in the shop, so I'll have to get transportation. Your job is to pray while I get to Atlanta. Keep trying to get through to Caitlin to make sure she's all right."

Just as she hung up the phone, it started ringing again. "Molly, this is Thad. I'm just calling for my regular Friday night refusal," he laughed.

In these past eight months since Jack left, Thad had called often. He gave the situation a decent time after her divorce was final before he asked Molly out. He had been the closest confidante Molly had. Most of their exchanges had been a few minutes of privacy in the medicine room. He had listened on Molly's bad days and always offered encouragement on the others. One day he asked if he could come over so they could continue a conversation they had started. "Sure, I'd be glad for you to," Molly had said after a brief hesitation.

That night they had talked at length, each remembering fond times they had spent with their mates. When Thad started to leave, he asked, "Molly, could I take you out to dinner Saturday night? I've enjoyed our time together tonight so much. I really get lonely sometimes, and I know you must."

"Thad, you are a great friend, and I don't know how I would have made it some days if I hadn't had you to unburden on, but I don't think I'm ready for that kind of relationship—one like a date—yet."

"I understand. But don't blame a guy for trying. I want us to continue being friends. You help me as much as I help you. I'll not pressure you, but be assured, I'll keep asking until you feel the time is right." His Friday night calls had become a joke between them. He always asked her out; she always kindly refused.

"Thad, I'm not refusing tonight. It's a God thing that you called when you did. I want us to go out, but not the way you think. Bob called, asking me to come to Atlanta to help him and Caitlin work out some things. He's worried about Caitlin. He thinks she's suffering from depression, and from what he told me, I think he's right. My car is in the shop, and I need you to drive me. Will you feel too put upon with this favor?"

"Molly, I would never feel put upon by you. In a hundred years, I could never repay you for all you did for me. Besides, I'll enjoy the drive with you. Be there in ten minutes."

Molly was waiting at the door when Thad drove up. "To be honest, I'm really worried about this situation. Bob walked out tonight in a fit of frustration. And now he can't get a response from Caitlin on the phone."

"She may need some medication to get through this bad streak, but I bet the two will already have their spat worked out by the time we get there." Thad tried to ease Molly's worries.

Molly agreed and relaxed for the rest of their journey. The two felt comfortable with each other and both experienced a special peace when they were together.

Things were far from peaceful in Atlanta, though. After talking with Molly, Bob did what she had instructed. He prayed harder than he ever had before. He continued calling home, letting the phone ring until the answering machine would pick up each time. He left several sincere apologies and urgent pleas for Caitlin to answer the phone. Two hours had passed when he went to the apartment and banged on the door. He had left his keys in the pocket of the bloody trousers he had taken off. Finally, he resorted to going to the landlady's apartment for the master key. He had not wanted her to know anything of their business because he knew she would spread it all over the building.

"Caitlin, Caitlin," he called out as he entered the apartment. Emily's crying had become screams by this time. He first went to check on her finding her lying entangled in the rails of the crib. Her diaper was soaked and smelly, and mucus and tears streaked her face from hours of crying. Not knowing how to prioritize what needed to be done, he grabbed the sobbing, wet child from the crib, all the while continuing to call out to Caitlin. He quickly made his way to the bedroom and found his wife unconscious, her hair matted with her own vomit. Panic-stricken, Bob felt for a pulse. His inexperienced hands found none. "Hurry, send an ambulance to the Park Place Apartments on Snelling Drive. Oh, apartment 915. Please hurry. My wife is unconscious and may be..." He couldn't make himself say the word.

"Bob, Bob," Molly called out. She and Thad were surprised to find the door to the apartment standing wide open.

"Molly! Come here quick! You've got to help her!" Bob was frantic. Thad and Molly exchanged troubled looks as they started to the bedroom.

Immediately Molly and Thad flew into action. After finding a weak, thready pulse on Caitlin's carotid artery, Molly started CPR. Her tears fell on Caitlin's ashen face all the while Thad scurried around picking up empty prescription and OTC bottles to assess what she had ingested. They all were aware of the approaching siren.

In minutes the paramedics arrived and relieved Molly. "I'm Dr. Thad Simmons, this is the patient's mother Molly Pate, and this is her husband Bob. It appears this twenty-five-year-old female has ingested unknown quantities of various OTC drugs, including Benadryl, aspirin, Sominex, Tylenol, as well as some of these prescription sleeping pills. She apparently ingested these sometime between—," interrupting himself, he turned to Bob for the time he left the apartment, "Seven p.m. and now." Apparently her system rejected this overload of chemicals, causing her to vomit up at least part of them.

Bob answered the questions about insurance and health history so the paramedics could pass it along to the hospital.

"Thanks, Dr. Simmons," one of the paramedics replied. "We will be taking her to Georgia Baptist Hospital over on Decatur Street."

Bob spoke up, "I know where it is. We will be right behind you."

"Bob, they have her somewhat stabilized for the moment. Before we go, we need to give this baby some attention. While I get her cleaned up, see if you have a neighbor you trust who could watch her while we go to the hospital," Molly instructed. "Come to Gram, you sweet thing. Let's see what we can do for you." In no time, Molly had Emily bathed, soothed, and checked out. She found some baby food and fed her while Bob was explaining, the best he could, the night's events to Vivian. Since he had already involved her earlier, she was the logical one to help out now. Emily had already calmed down and was chattering sleepily at her grandmother when Vivian came, ready to take over.

"Vivian, I warmed a bottle for you to give her. I think that will be all it will take to get her settled for the night. She is exhausted from crying so long. Her little legs are slightly bruised from the crib rails, but I believe both of you will get a good night's sleep."

"Don't worry about her, Mrs. Pate. I'll take good care of her. Please call me when you get to the hospital with a report on Caitlin. I don't think I could sleep a wink until I hear she's going to be okay."

"I'll do that. Thanks so much for coming over."

On the way to the hospital, Thad reminded Molly she should call Jack. "I don't think it would be a good idea for Caitlin to see him right now, but you're right. As her father, he should be informed about the situation." She dialed Darcy's number, knowing that's where she would find him.

"Darcy, I need to talk with Jack, please. There's a problem with Caitlin."

In just a minute, Jack answered. "Molly, what's the problem?" She heard the concern in his voice.

"Caitlin is being taken to Georgia Baptist. She has taken a handful of pills and is comatose."

"I'll be there as soon as I can," he began.

"No, Jack. I think that would be the worst thing you could do at the moment." She wanted to add, "Just pray for her," but she didn't have much confidence in his prayers at the moment. Instead, she said, "I'll keep you posted as soon as we know more."

Fortunately, Caitlin's involuntary defense mechanism saved her life. Although she was admitted for close observation, she awoke before morning. Still groggy and much embarrassed, she asked for some time alone with her mother. "Mom, I know I've really messed up, but I'm so miserable. My life has unraveled like a ball of yarn."

"Caitlin, I realize you feel rejected by your dad and by Bob, but I want to assure you, Bob loves you dearly. He tried to call and apologize for running out on you shortly after he left. Remember, he is just as ill-equipped to know how to help you as you are to handle what your dad has done." Molly assured her she would get the emotional and psychological help she needed. "You are never alone. Remember that, Dear. I'm as close as the phone, but your Heavenly Father is with you all the time. Regardless of how you feel humans have failed you, you can be confident He never will. He truly wants what is best for you. Bob is so worried about you. Do you feel like talking to him now?"

"Yes, I want to. I know I've hurt him, but I haven't meant to." That began a journey to wholeness.

The next day with Caitlin stabilized, Bob left the hospital long enough to find more permanent childcare arrangements for

Emily. He realized Caitlin would need help with her for a while even after she left the hospital the next day.

In the following weeks and after many counseling sessions, Bob and Caitlin learned to honestly express both hurts and desires. The psychiatrist drew out Caitlin's deep-seated insecurities. Caitlin finally made the phone call she knew she should but had dreaded. Jack had tried repeatedly to call his daughter during her recovery, but she refused to speak with him. He had become her dumping ground of blame. She finally realized before her healing was complete, she had to express her feelings toward dad, but she also knew she must forgive him. That she did.

Molly and Thad shared a strong comfort and connection as they drove home on Saturday. "I can't tell you how I appreciate your helping me and being with me through this ordeal, Thad. You knew just how to help and when to back away."

"Molly, you show such strength and efficiency in emergencies." Thad turned with a smile that transcended friendship and continued, "I was hardly needed, but it was so good to feel that I could be there for you."

Turning the conversation in another direction, Molly asked, "Do you really believe Caitlin will be okay after this?"

"Sure, she should be up and running at full speed in a few days."

"That's not what I mean. Do you think we will have a repeat of this type thing?"

"That's a definite no. Caitlin is not one of these chronic suicide-attempt people. Circumstances converged on her, causing frustration and despair. First was her dad's situation, then a crying baby, and finally, a husband who didn't know how to recognize or deal with her depression. She also could be experiencing some delayed postpartum depression. I talked with her psychiatrist at length. He's a good man—a Christian. He will help Caitlin dig deep and find some areas of hurt. He, then, will bring her from blame to forgiveness. That's a plus for having a Christian psychiatrist."

Molly surprised Thad by reaching over and holding his free hand just for a moment. "You bring me such comfort, I mean real comfort."

The Marriage

Both Darcy and Jack suffered their own humiliation in the days and months following his leaving Molly. For days, Jack refused to even talk with Darcy. She was the receptacle for all his blame. Not wanting to see or talk with anyone in Smytheville, Jack closed himself up in his boarding room. He left only long enough to drive to the next little community, avoiding contact with any Smytheville residents, to get some Pop Tarts from Quik Mart. He also bought a few cans of things that needed no preparation—Vienna sausage, sardines, crackers, and the like. He really had no appetite; he just needed survival food.

The guilt for his past actions hung over him like a dark cloud, but he wasn't ready to consciously admit fault or to show remorse. He constantly rationalized his actions to himself and played mind games, making himself the victim. Not only had he lost his family, for Benji and Caitlin wanted nothing to do with him, he also had lost the popularity and position that had given him his identity.

The realization of his financial situation began to sink in the day that Molly forwarded him the stack of monthly bills. After several months, he finally realized what his life had become without his huge salary padded with benefits. No longer did he draw his huge salary padded with his many benefits. How did Molly expect him to pay these? For years she had relieved him of the mundane task of paying the monthly bills. He never realized how many there were. In addition to these, his modest rent for his room would soon be due again. The cash he had brought with him was spent quickly. The last time he tried to get more, the ATM refused his card. He tried to charge some personal essentials on credit cards, and again his credit cards were denied.

Molly was showing tough love in regards to the finances. Corbin Hammer, the lawyer Molly and Jack had used when closing on the purchase of their home, spoke to Molly at church on her first Sunday back. At first, she thought he was offering his condolences, as had so many others that morning. Instead, he leaned over to her and said in a low voice, "Molly, you must come by my office tomorrow. There are some things you should do immediately."

She really didn't have the heart to do any legal business. Molly did as he instructed because she knew he wouldn't have mentioned it had it not been important. Corbin stressed to her that she must think with her head and not with her heart about finances. "Molly, I realize it isn't in your nature to be vindictive or mean, but regardless of your present grief and shock, you must do a few things to preserve the money available. Bills will keep coming in, just as they did when there were two incomes. You have a high school child whose expenses will only get greater in the days to come. Think about him if not about yourself. Until there can be a formal settlement, it is imperative you freeze any credit cards that have both your names on them and put a hold on your bank assets. Don't start trying to pay all the household bills out of your income. Jack has to know what a financial toll his escapades have taken."

Molly, for Benji's sake, followed Corbin's instructions to the letter. Jack's financial situation brought him to have a change of attitude toward Darcy quicker than anything else could have. Remembering she had received a nice settlement from Dr. Jenkins after her dreadful trauma at the hands of his son and his buddies, Jack suddenly had an epiphany: Darcy would help him out of this situation. *I'll call her as soon as she gets in from work,* Jack thought.

"Darcy, darling, I know I've been a real heel to you lately. I just couldn't answer your phone calls or talk to you since everything blew up at church. I've had to have some space to think through some things, but today, I realized just how much I've missed you, just how much I've needed you. I didn't think 5:30

p.m. would ever come so I could call you. I didn't want to call the office, so I waited until you got home."

"Oh, I've been home. You could have called any time."

"Didn't you go to work today?"

"Where have you been, Jack? Everybody in town knows Dr. Martin fired me. I haven't worked since we came back in town. He told me he had been tolerant and understanding with me through my affair with Perry Porter, but lately his phone had rung off the hook with patients calling to say they wouldn't be back to his office as long as I worked there. I really can't blame him. He has to think about his practice. He did give me three months' severance pay, which he really didn't have to do."

"What have you been doing since? Have you taken another job?

"I can't show my face on the streets of Smytheville without being verbally attacked by somebody. Even those who don't say anything to me act as though I have leprosy or some other horrible contagious disease. I've mostly stayed in. Jack, I've missed you so much."

"Darcy, I know I've treated you terribly lately, and I'm so sorry. You think I could come over tonight?"

"I wish you would. I've missed you, too. I felt like I was isolated on a deserted island through all this. I wish we could just get away from this miserable town."

"We'll talk about it when I get there."

When Jack left his boarding room that night, he didn't return until he went back to gather his few belongings a week later when he and Darcy set out for Nashville. The days they spent together at her bungalow eased both their misery. They soothed each other's guilt the only way they knew how. Although tongues wagged even harder at Jack's boldness in staying at her place day and night, Darcy and Jack didn't care anymore. They no longer had any reason to conceal their affair. Their known sins already had them marked as low-lives, and they couldn't do any more damage to their already ruined reputations.

But their boldness brought even worse shock and sorrow to the town. The citizens of Smytheville took this open adultery as the height of insults. Many reactions were voiced throughout the town.

"They just want to rub salt in our wounds."

"God will have to apologize to Sodom and Gomorrah if he doesn't strike them both dead."

"Where's the Ku Klux Klan when you need them?"

"I just hope certain body parts rot off."

After receiving nasty phone calls and some threatening letters, Darcy and Jack agreed they needed to go somewhere else and get a fresh start. Darcy called Dr. Martin one night and told him their plan. "We have no particular place in mind, but I thought you might have a colleague somewhere who might need a hygienist."

With that, he quickly made some calls, for he, too, was ready for them to leave town. He thought that might stop his patients' endless questions about her, which had been all they wanted to discuss with him. They weren't even subtle. They just wanted to know all he knew about Darcy and Jack.

Before long he found a buddy who needed someone to replace his hygienist who had taken a maternity leave and had hinted she might not come back to work after the baby came. "Darcy," Dr. Martin asked when he called to give her the news, "how would you like to go to Nashville? My friend Bob Shell needs some help. I've told him you would be a good employ. I told him you are tops in your field."

That sealed their decision. They had a destination, a new focus. Settling Jack's pressing debts presented no strain for Darcy. She had invested her settlement wisely, giving her a comfortable nest egg. She also planned to sell her bungalow in Smytheville, which would help with getting a place in Nashville. She already had several buyers in mind. Every few months since she had bought the place she had received offers. The cottage was in excellent condition and was the right size for anyone scaling down.

At some level, Darcy understood Jack might be using her for financial reasons, but she pushed back even the slightest thought of that into the recesses of her mind. Right now he showed her love and attention, more than he ever had. His promise of marriage after he got his divorce sealed her commitment to him. For Darcy, supporting him financially was an easy trade for his love for her. Both Darcy and Jack knew she couldn't continue paying both their bills for many months, but until Jack found a position somewhere, she could handle it.

"Darcy, I will find a good lawyer in Nashville and start divorce proceedings. I want to do my part for Benji, but with a shrewd attorney, I can get out from under some of this financial burden. When we meet with Molly, I know I can convince her to agree to pay her share of the household bills. I need to take care of this matter before I get a job and have a steady income. The judge will agree you can't get blood out of a turnip."

The week after Molly returned from Caitlin's, Jack called. "Molly, how's Caitlin? Why in the world did she do such a thing? Apparently she had no regard for anyone but herself. Doesn't she care about what happens to Emily or Bob or even how this upset you?" Jack's questions tumbled out, one after the other, not waiting for answers.

Listening to Jack's accusing tone stirred up ire in Molly, an unusual phenomenon. She wanted to unleash all her fury on him placing a load of the blame for Caitlin's emotional state on him, where it belonged. His questions magnified his chauvinistic attitude she had ignored for so long. Instead of attacking him verbally, she prayed silently, *Lord, help me through this moment. Help me to not hate this man. Give me your words to say and calmness to say them. Lord, as hard as it is for me to pray this right at this moment, I ask you to help Jack. Help me to remember I have already forgiven him, and I ask you to also.*

"Molly, are you there? I asked you questions."

"Jack, I heard you. Caitlin is going to be okay. She is going through some counseling. She isn't an emotionally strong person for some reason, and many things converged on her, making her load more than she could handle for the moment." Instead of saying all she wanted to, Molly asked of his health, "How are you, Jack? I heard you moved to Nashville. I hope you find what you want there. I really do."

Oblivious to the kindness she just offered, Jack got to the business he really called about. "Molly, my lawyer will be contacting you next week about our divorce and about arranging a time for a hearing."

Silence shouted from Molly's end of the line. She simply couldn't reply. She hung up the phone, crumbling under the inevitable. Since his leaving, a gradual awareness of who Jack really was had come over Molly. Her eyes opened to the fact she had been the giver in their relationship and Jack the taker. She had finally seen things for the way they were. Hurt by his past actions and this as well, she still didn't want a divorce; she didn't seek revenge. God could heal Jack and their marriage. "Nothing is impossible to God," Molly uttered, giving the whole situation over to God.

Over the next few months, Molly came to realize there was no need in fighting Jack. Corbin, her lawyer, Thad, and her children individually at different times gave her the same counsel: if he wants a divorce, there is no need in trying to stop it. Still not satisfied this was God's plan, Molly spent night after night praying and asking God's forgiveness for not being all to Jack she should have been and pleading for His holy guidance in what to do. Finally, God gave her a peace about it. It was almost as if He spoke to her in an audible voice. *Molly, if Jack chooses to put you away, that is his sin, not yours. Let him go to his own folly.*

With that confirmation, Molly relented. She signed the divorce papers in June, shortly after Benji graduated. Molly demanded very little in way of financial settlement for herself, but she took Corbin's advice and saw to it that Benji's future needs would be covered. Since he had been a member at Pleasant Valley, Corbin also knew of Jack's large annuity the church had paid into. "Molly, you must look ahead. You may not always be able to work yourself, so it would be wise to ask for a generous percentage of the annuity. Otherwise, Jack could draw it out to live on." Molly agreed with inner reservations.

Jack had taken a position with a large firm in Nashville, giving psychological tests to new applicants. He missed the praise and glory he enjoyed as pastor, and his earnings were far less than what he had received from Pleasant Valley. But at least he was bringing in a salary. This had helped to temporarily relieve some of the growing tension between him and Darcy.

Darcy managed money more frugally than Jack had ever had to. Many arguments had ensued over the past few months because of his careless spending on non-essentials. Darcy reminded him regularly that her settlement money had dwindled and her salary alone wouldn't continue to pay household bills along with his indebtedness.

Although the passion in their relationship had faded also, Jack needed Darcy for other reasons at this point. He couldn't take living alone again. When he was with Darcy, he could fight off the dragon of guilt for his deeds, but his sins confronted him like an opposing enemy any time he was alone.

Darcy began to hint at ultimatums if Jack didn't soon make their union official. In July the two stood before a judge at the courthouse and repeated their marriage vows. Because they both had new jobs, there was no time for an official honeymoon, nor was there much desire for one.

Because their egos needed the assurance they were happily married, they play-acted a marriage made in heaven. They not only wanted others to believe they had done the right thing, but they also needed to convince themselves. They were seen holding hands and looking starry-eyed at each other in public, but soon this mockery failed to convince even the two of them. Both Jack and Darcy were determined to make the marriage work at some level to save face with so many in Smytheville who were watching and hoping for it to fail.

After a couple of months in Nashville, Darcy had lived with Jack's private dark moods long enough that they were affecting her own. She longed for something to brighten their lives, something to make them the couple in private that they tried to portray in public, the couple they had been at the conference in Atlanta.

Darcy knew something wasn't right with her. Not only was she having emotional struggles, but she also was having bouts of nausea and dizziness. She finally sought out a walk-in clinic after work one day. In a few short minutes into her exam, the doctor had his diagnosis. "Mrs. Pate, nothing major is wrong with you, but you are two months pregnant."

"That can't be." Darcy's surprise was mixed with joy. "But I was told I probably wouldn't—couldn't ever have children."

"Whoever told you that was wrong. You are definitely pregnant."

Darcy's feet hardly touched the ground as she rushed into the parking lot to her car. Never had she been so elated. She could hardly wait to share this exciting news with Jack.

Darcy beamed as she came through the door. She expected Jack's reaction to match hers. She never dreamed how wrong she could be.

"Jack! Jack! I've got the best news I've ever had in my whole life!" she shouted as she entered the hallway.

Jack sat, staring blankly at a week-old newspaper, deep in his own thoughts and evidently uninterested with what she had to say. Jack muttered, "What could that be?" At the moment he was consumed by the darkness, which now marked all of his days.

"I just found out I'm *pregnant!*" With tears of happiness raining down her face, Darcy shouted the announcement with great glee. "I didn't think I could ever get pregnant after the injuries from the rape, but it has happened and—"

"You're what? How did you let this happen? Whose is it? What do you expect me to do about it?" Jack's red face and clenched jaw revealed his shock and anger.

"Jack, don't you see how perfect things will be. Of course it's yours. I haven't been with anyone else in a year. Don't you see what a difference this will make in our lives? You can close the door to this past life and start over completely.

The fact that he even had to ask if the baby was his made Jack's attitude vacillate like a floor fan even more. *Have I swapped a saint for a sinner?* The old faith which had guided Jack before Ego became his god nagged at him, magnifying his guilt. More than ever now, Jack regretted the choices he had made. He really didn't want to close that door. He didn't want this new family. He wished, as he had a million times since his fall, that he cold wake up from this bad dream and life would go on as it had with Molly, his real family, and the church. Instead, he was now stuck with a pregnant whore.

Darcy was not only disappointed, but she was crushed by Jack's reaction.

In the days that followed, Darcy's health began to deteriorate. She complained to Jack that she couldn't keep food down. She tired more easily than she ever had. Uncharacteristically for her, Darcy had to call in sick several times in one month. Her weight loss became evident. The uniforms that once formed beautifully around her nice figure now hung loose. One day Jack came home from work to find her lying unconscious on the kitchen floor. He called 911 and got her to the hospital.

Later, after the emergency room doctor examined her, he came out and said, "Mr. Pate, your wife is dehydrated, but we can easily remedy that with intravenous fluids." He gave Jack a list of foods that might be easier for Darcy to keep down and told him she would need to make an appointment soon with an obstetrician to be sure the baby was healthy and to give Darcy the vitamins she needed.

Even though Jack had seen to it that she got the emergency attention she needed, he showed little genuine concern for her; instead he reacted more as if it had been an inconvenience. Darcy's joy diminished as Jack continued to show such displeasure with her pregnancy. Jack had already experienced the child-rearing phase of life, although Molly had carried most of the burden, but he didn't look forward to going through it again. Darcy had been ecstatic at this news, but now her sickness and Jack's reaction had changed that.

The days following weren't much better for Darcy. Her morning sickness became noon sickness, nighttime sickness, and just total misery. She had to miss work more than she ever had. When she did go into the office, she often had to excuse herself in the middle of a case and go throw up. She no longer had the energy to shower on Jack—the love and attention he craved, nor was it his nature to offer support and care to Darcy through these rough days. Instead, he complained regularly about her declining libido. During her pregnancy, Darcy had to go to the hospital for fluids on a regular basis. Her obstetrician became increasingly concerned for both her and her unborn baby.

"Darcy, you may have to take a leave from your job. Your body is taking a beating during this pregnancy, and the baby isn't growing at the rate it should." This news stunned both Darcy and Jack. Darcy so hoped the baby would be healthy and would draw Jack back closer to her like he had been at the beginning of their relationship. Jack grew weary of his wife always being sick and also realized their financial situation would worsen if she didn't work. Unconsciously, he hoped she would lose the baby. That would solve many of their problems.

Soon Darcy did have to ask for a maternity leave, which didn't set well with her new employer. She just didn't have the strength to keep on, and she wanted to give her baby every opportunity for health and growth possible.

When she reached the seven month mark, Darcy's toxemia, as well as the incessant sickness, brought on a new crisis. Because of her snowballing health problems, the doctor called in both Darcy and Jack. "In these days of modern medicine, it is rare to reach this point. Usually we can handle prenatal problems in other ways, but from my examination of Darcy, I know neither she nor the baby can survive much longer. The baby has little chance of survival. We must intervene, now. Not only is the baby in distress, but the mother is also. We will plan to do a caesarean tomorrow. We simply can't wait any longer. Neither mother nor child will survive if we postpone this."

On the way home, Darcy was distraught, and Jack remained silent. He really didn't know what to do or say. Finally he mustered the words and reached over, patted Darcy's hand, and said, "You will be much better when all this is over."

Those weren't the words Darcy longed to hear. She wanted Jack to voice grief for the baby and some sympathy and concern for her condition. She wanted to lash out at him but lacked both the physical and emotional energy to do it. On that ride home, Darcy let herself admit that Jack Pate wasn't the person she thought he was; neither was he the person she wanted him to be. Where sickness and troubles bring many couples closer, they became a wedge between Jack and Darcy.

Just a mere glimpse was all Darcy was allowed the next morning, for her two-pound baby girl had to be whisked off to the neonatal intensive care ward. She heard no cry from her little form and saw just enough of her to see how blue she was. Jack stood by Darcy's side and held her hand. He had quickly diverted his eyes when the nurse had held up their baby for just that fleeting second. He wanted to continue thinking of the small piece of flesh as an "it" not as "her" or as "his baby." He could handle the situation better that way.

That morning when Darcy had been admitted, the pediatrician had encouraged them. "Many of these preemies survive even though the odds are against them." But when they saw him after he had examined the baby, his demeanor was very grave, and it was apparent he had lost any optimism. "It will take a super miracle from God if this baby makes it. Even if she does, she will have an uphill battle for years. Her lungs are underdeveloped as well as most of her other organs. I really can't give you much hope. I'm so sorry."

Tears ran like a fountain from the corners of Darcy's eyes. Jack stood dry-eyed and motionless, not knowing what to do. They lacked the ability or connection to share their grief, and there was no one else to share it with them. Finally, Darcy spoke what was on her mind. "Jack, this is God's punishment on us for what we've done. I thought our life together would be total bliss. Instead, we just seem to make each other miserable. God isn't going to let us ever be happy, is He?"

"Don't say things like that, Darcy. How can we know the mind of God? Things like this happen to people all the time. We are going to be happier after you are well. Just you wait and see." Jack couldn't face the possibility that they had made such a serious mistake. He also refused victory to the many who wanted their marriage to fail, but in his inner depths, he had to admit what Darcy was saying might be true.

Jack and Darcy left the hospital alone the next day. Their baby just didn't have the strength to survive. The odds were stacked too strong against her. In a couple of days when Darcy and Jack went to the cemetery for a private burial of their baby, Darcy grieved openly while Jack remained stoic and detached.

Darcy gave up any pretense of happiness with Jack. She wore her sorrow like a scarlet letter. She felt she had gotten what she deserved. Mechanically, Darcy went to work every day and then came home to bed. If Jack had not brought in food, there would have been no meals put on the table in their apartment. She had lost all interest in him or anything else. Strangely enough, her surrender to depression brought out a better side of Jack. Not wanting to admit to failure in their relationship, because he knew the townspeople and his family would have a lot of I-told-you-so comments and attitudes. At times Jack felt like a madman, his attitude changing from one of disgust and regrets to a soft place where he realized Darcy wasn't the problem; he was. It was as if God said to him, *"Yes, you have sinned and made bad choices, but don't compound them by being cruel to Darcy."* He realized it was time to man-up and make the present situation as good as he could. Jack's efforts for restoring their marriage doubled. He became more caring and understanding of Darcy. He insisted she eat, and he showed her the sympathy she had needed earlier. Though for Darcy, his efforts came too late; he simply wasn't present for her emotionally when she needed him most.

This mere existence continued for three months. Then one day, Darcy didn't come home after work. Jack frantically searched any place they had ever been in Nashville. No one had seen her. She didn't show up at work the next day nor any day after that. Darcy had simply disappeared.

Unlikely Helper

Sawyer was surprised with a call from Jack on the day following Darcy's disappearance. He gave him a brief history of what had gone on since their marriage. "I know you and Darcy had a thing going at one time. She always spoke highly of you. I was hoping you just might have an idea where she might have gone. She's not in Nashville, I'm sure. I've searched, and so have the police. I got them involved this early by lying and telling them she was dangerous and had a gun. I made them believe she had indicated she was going to kill me. Otherwise, I knew they would wait at least thirty-six hours to start their search."

"You know, Jack, I don't have a clue where she might be. Furthermore, if I did, you would be the last person I would tell. If she left you, it wasn't without good reason, I'm sure. Even if your story to the police was true, I believe she or anyone else would be justified in shooting you."

Again Jack took Sawyer off guard. "You are right, Sawyer. I didn't do right by her, I admit, but I do care for her and want to make sure she's okay. I understand your attitude toward me. It's justified, I assure you. I don't even like myself very much these days."

With that unexpected confession, Sawyer softened. "I'll check out a few places myself. If I find her, I'll let you know if she's okay, but that's all. Don't expect me to reveal her whereabouts if she doesn't want to see anybody. I'm doing this for Darcy, not for you."

Sawyer went by to tell Molly he would miss their meeting the next day and explained to her what Jack had told him. "Molly, I hate to admit it, but I think the skunk is finally showing some remorse."

"I sincerely hope so, but more than that, I hope you find Darcy. That girl has had more troubles in her life than anyone should have to endure."

"You continue surprising me with your attitude, Molly. Any other woman would want me to find her so she could claw out her eyes. Darcy always mentally glamorized the Florida beaches. She has never been there, but that may be where I will find her. Once we looked at some brochures together, and she told me she wanted to visit some of those places one day. I'll check out a few of those first."

"I'll pray for you and for Darcy. If anyone can find her, you can."

Sawyer knew Daytona had intrigued Darcy more than any of the other places. The second motel, one he remembered from the old brochure, was a winner. He knew she might have used an alias, so he showed the picture of her he had carried in his billfold for years. The desk clerk recognized it immediately and told him she was in unit seven. Sawyer knocked on the door several times with no response. Finally he called out. "Darcy, this is Sawyer. Open the door, please."

When she came to the door, Sawyer was taken aback by what he saw. Darcy looked emaciated, and her eyes were dark and sunken. "How did you find me, Sawyer? Is anyone with you?" She looked out the door suspiciously.

"I'm alone. I just want to make sure you are okay. Can I come in?"

She opened the door and turned back to the bed where she had been since she had checked in. She fell back on it and stared at the ceiling.

"Darcy, how long has it been since you've eaten anything?"

"I don't know. I'm not hungry."

"Well, I'm starved, and you're going to eat something if I have to force feed you. Go get a shower, and put on some clean clothes. We're going out to eat."

Darcy didn't have the energy to debate the matter. She did as he instructed. When she came out of the bathroom, there were minor improvements in her appearance. She wouldn't have opened the door earlier for anyone besides Sawyer, but she had always been able to trust him.

"What sounds good to you? What do you feel like you could eat, Darcy?"

"I really don't care. I'm not hungry. Whatever you want is fine."

"We're in Florida. Let's try some of the seafood they are famous for."

Darcy didn't comment; she continued staring straight ahead almost in catatonic state. Sawyer kept up small talk as though she was really interested in what he had to say. "I've always wanted to see Daytona. Do you remember when we used to look at the brochures and dream of coming here? Looks like we finally made it. I thought you might head this direction when I got word you had left. Darcy, in spite of the scoundrel he is, Jack really cares about you. He has called in all the big dogs to try to find you."

"If he cared so much, why couldn't he have shown it when it really mattered? I think he has just used me, as so many others have."

"Why don't you tell me what's gone on. I'm still a pretty good listener."

For the first time, Darcy showed some interest in conversation. Looking over at him, she said, "Sawyer, you've always been a good listener. You've listened to my sad stories for years. You may be the only person who has ever really cared about me. I guess I'm just reaping the oats I've sown. In reality, Jack has treated me no worse than I treated you. Before I tell you my latest tale of sorrow, I need to explain why I broke things off with you several years ago. I enjoyed being with you more than anyone I had ever been with. I'm aware you had desires as other men had, but after I told you my past history, you refused to make sexual advances. I appreciated your accepting me as a person, not simply as a sex object to take care of your needs. But when you proposed, I was stunned. I dreamed what it would be like to have a normal life— a loving husband, children, a little white cottage with tulips and roses, respect in the community. Then I had to admit it could never happen for me. First of all, I didn't deserve you—your kindness and acceptance, your love. I also thought I could never give you the children you so much deserved. I had to face the reality of my unworthiness."

Tears welled up in her eyes as she made her confession. "As with everything else I ever did, I messed that up by not giving you the explanation you deserved. I just broke off our relationship and left you to wonder."

"I understood more of that than you could realize. I just thought you might eventually come back to me if I didn't press you."

"Is that why you never married?"

"Oh, it may have had something to do with it, but not all. As I said, I waited on you awhile, and then days became months and months became years. I just got too comfortable in my bachelorhood, I guess. Tell me what happened between you and Jack."

"I guess our relationship was destined to fail from the beginning. What is it they say about ill-gotten gains? I just fell hard for the attention he gave me when he was listening so patiently to my life's troubles during our counseling sessions. He was so non-judgmental and so kind to me.

"After we married, all that good stuff disappeared. My unexpected pregnancy took its toll. Jack wasn't excited about fatherhood at this stage of life, and I felt so rotten throughout the ordeal. I wasn't very good wife material. Although I knew the timing was bad, I felt God had overlooked all my sins and was giving me a miracle child. The anticipation of that made all the sick days bearable. I have never been as devastated as I was when my baby died. Jack lacked the ability to be there emotionally for me. I'm sure he grieved in his own way, too, but it appeared to me that he was glad the baby didn't live. My postpartum depression, coupled with his lack of understanding at that point, was more than I could endure. I just left. I thought I would die if I didn't get away. I'm sure when this gets out in Smytheville there will be dancing in the streets. People there predicted our marriage could never last. I know Molly will rejoice. We did her so very wrong."

"It may surprise you to know Molly is as concerned about your safety and wellbeing as I am. She is truly remarkable. She forgave both you and Jack some time ago. She's the best Christian I've ever known. On second thought, she may be the only one I've ever known."

Sawyer pulled in at Captain Pete's Seafood Restaurant. "Let's continue this over some food. I'm starved."

Inside, Sawyer ordered for both of them. When Darcy said she would just take some soup, he ignored her and ordered the house seafood platters for both of them. "You've got to have some food. Besides, if I'm going to kill myself with cholesterol, I want company in my self-destruction."

Darcy laughed at that. "Sawyer, you were wrong about Molly being the best Christian. I think you may be."

With that remark, Sawyer's jaw dropped in disbelief. Then he began laughing.

"Why in the world did you say that? Didn't you know the good people of Smytheville have been trying to get me saved ever since I've lived there?"

"I know, but I know the real you. They assume you to be a heathen because of your attitude about organized religion, but I know where that attitude comes from. You don't have to wear a sign around your neck proclaiming your Christianity. You reveal it by the way you treat people, especially me."

"Now cut out that kind of talk. Let's eat." By that time the waiter had placed huge platters in front of each of them. One would have fed a family of ten.

Darcy laughed when she saw the copious amount of food he had ordered for her. Sawyer also saw the humor in the situation. Both dug in like ravenous dogs and finished off a sizable portion of what had been served. "I think I may throw up after eating so much. I haven't eaten that much in months."

"I must say, for a little girl who wasn't hungry, you sure ate more than a child's portion."

"Well, Mr. Thomas, you didn't do so bad yourself."

Why don't we try to walk some of this off? You want to stroll down the beach?" They both pulled their shoes off and started their moonlit trek.

After a few minutes of enjoying the sounds of the waves lapping the shore and squishing wet sand between their toes, Darcy broke the silence. "Sawyer, are you going to tell Jack where I am when you go back?"

"Not if you don't want me to."

They walked along in silence for several minutes before Sawyer continued. "Darcy, I'm no counselor, but as a friend, I want to give you a bit of advice. You can't keep running away from your problems. Jack doesn't deserve you, I'll admit, but I believe he, in his own way, does really love you. If you give up on your marriage now, you are going to feel like you've failed once again. I'd like to forget him and reclaim you for myself, but that wouldn't work because this issue would still be unresolved."

"I don't know how to make it work, Sawyer."

"Why don't you give God a chance to help you?"

As they stood on the shimmering moonlit beach, they stared into each other's eyes tempted to follow their mutual impulse to embrace, but they both resisted. Darcy broke their moment of temptation and said, "Sawyer Thomas, you never cease to amaze and surprise me. That would sound so churchy and fake from anyone else, but from you, it is genuine. I guess that has been my problem for too long. I've tried to solve my problems in my own power when I need to turn them over to a powerful God. To be honest, though, I feel so unworthy to ask anything of Him. I know he is angry with me for my many sins. I don't deserve to ask anything of Him."

"Darcy, you know what you've read on so many church signs—'Forgiveness is just a prayer away.' At least you've taken a step in the right direction. You admit you are a sinner. So many people from the holier-than-thou crowd never reach that point."

"You know what, Sawyer? I think you would make a good preacher."

"Perish the thought!"

"No, really, you sound different. What has changed you so?"

"I didn't realize I had changed." Thinking on it a minute, he added, "Maybe observing a real Christian like Molly has made me realize not all so-called Christian people are as sorry as my daddy was. Shortly after Jack left her, I started going to see Molly every week to try to help her, but instead, she has helped me. I've never seen anyone exhibit such strong faith in God and have such capabilities for forgiveness."

"Sawyer, you've given me the courage to go back and try to make things right with Jack. With the Lord's help, maybe we can find happiness again. When you go back, please let Jack know that I'm safe and will be returning in a few days. I just need to think through things awhile longer to be sure how I'm going to approach a new beginning."

Beginning Again

Jack was eager for Darcy's return. Her absence had given him time to reevaluate their relationship. Conviction had begun to surface. He realized that all his egotistical finger pointing and accusations had been misdirected. The fingers now seemed to point at him.

Not only did he feel great remorse for the way he had failed Darcy, but also his conscience burned about the way he had treated Molly. Realization of how their relationship had been dominated by his selfishness settled over him like a dark cloud. In contrast to his behavior, Molly's sweet spirit and Christian attitudes had stood tall as a tower throughout their years together.

His meditations took him back to Pleasant Valley Community where he had been the object of the members' complete trust and faith. They had held him in such high esteem and had followed his leadership, sometimes, to a fault, to the point they were vulnerable to his spiritual abuse. He recognized just how he had hurt so many by betraying their trust and by exploiting his position of power.

He also had to admit to himself how self-centered he had been in his and Darcy's relationship. Even though it was sin-flawed from the beginning, he had sinned even greater by taking such advantage of her mental and emotional state. He now saw clearly how he had made her the villain when she, so often, had been the victim. He felt like a lowly worm burdened with his weight of sin. Tears of regret and remorse flowed from his eyes this time. When he was in the strongest grip of despair, not knowing how to right his many wrongs, or even where to start, he caught a glimpse of the corner his old Bible sticking out from under a stack of papers.

Jack had not picked up his Bible in months. Maybe he knew it would only condemn him because of his sins. Now that he saw how wrong he had been, he picked it up, looking for answers to his dilemma. Immediately it opened to the Psalms, which he had read so many times before. Only now, David's confessions and pleas for forgiveness took on fresh meaning. "Against you, you only, have I sinned and done what is evil in your sight, so that you are proved right when you speak and justified when you judge."

David's confession in Psalm 51:3-5 jumped out at Jack. It was as though God was speaking to him, and it brought him to his senses. *I've got to admit to God that I sinned against him first before I can find my way through this maze of iniquities.*

Jack sat for hours diligently searching out all David's sins and confessions. When he read of God's forgiveness to David, tears dripped on the fine parchment pages on his lap. *If God forgave David, just maybe He'll forgive me.* First, Jack dropped to his knees. Then, feeling his complete unworthiness to approach the King of kings in prayer and supplication, he prostrated himself completely. Face down on the cold hardwood floor, Jack wept bitter tears, confessing his many sins as they came to his mind. They scrolled across like a video projected on a screen. Jack prayed the most fervent and sincere prayers of his life. He not only admitted his sins, but a great confession of his unworthiness followed. Admitting he was not deserving of God's mercy, he pleaded for His grace and for His forgiveness. Then he asked for God's guidance in the voyage ahead of him as he tried to right his many wrongs.

Jack convinced Sawyer to give him Darcy's phone number, so he could beg her to forgive him. He promised he wouldn't go where she was but rather allow her the choice to come back or not. "Darcy, my words can't express the sorrow I feel for my cruelty, my neglect, to you during the loss of our baby. But that is only the tip of the iceberg in my transgressions against you." After confessing his sins, one-by-one, he pleaded, "Even if you don't ever want to return to me, and I see why you wouldn't, I implore you to forgive me. I can't right wrongs, but I can apologize and ask for forgiveness. I knew you were first on my list."

Jack knew he must call Molly. "Molly, this is Jack."

"Oh, Jack, I was so glad to hear that Sawyer found Darcy safe. I know you must have been frantic."

"Your kindness and concerns are so undeserved. I called because I wanted you to be the first to know that I've repented to God for my many sins. I would like the opportunity to face my family now and ask their forgiveness. Do you think you could get Benji and Caitlin to come home so I could face all of you at the same time?"

"Jack, for your sake, I'm so glad you have reached this point. As a matter of fact, both Benji and Caitlin will be here this weekend. I will let them know that you want to come by."

"They probably won't want to even see me, and I couldn't blame them if they refuse to let me come. One other thing, though, could you contact Celeste Downs to see if she will join the meeting? I need to come clean about all my sins while I'm at it."

A Family Reunion

After a few days, Darcy returned as she had promised she would. Jack met her with genuine humbleness, reflected by his demeanor. "Darcy, I know I don't deserve you, or your forgiveness, but please don't ever leave me like that again. I worried so much about you, but all along, I knew you left because of the way I've treated you. I can assure you, things will be different from here on out."

He told her of his session with God and how he had entreated God to forgive his many sins and transgressions. "Darcy, I know I can't undo the many things I have done wrong, but at least, I want to start trying by asking for forgiveness from the many people who have suffered because of my sins. I am starting this weekend with my family. I plan to go to Smytheville Saturday and face them. I don't know what to expect, but I deserve anything they may want to lash out to me. I think, with God's help, I can take it."

"Jack, could I go along? I have wronged them also. I'd like to make my apologies for what I've done to them. You weren't in this by yourself, you know. I played my part in breaking up your home."

"Your being with me would mean so much. I just want you to know, neither our apologies, nor our presence—as far as that goes—may be graciously received. I guess if I were in my children's place, I would want to speak my piece to my wretched daddy instead of forgiving him. There's one other thing I must lay on the table and confess. You will also meet another daughter of mine there."

"What are you talking about? I didn't know you had another daughter."

Jack acknowledged his earlier affair with Gloria and told Darcy how Celeste had tracked him down. "I've really done her wrong for years by my failure to recognize her as mine. I really wasn't sure she was my daughter, but I had a pretty good idea she was. When I finally saw her, there was no doubt. When Gloria, Celeste's mother, told me she was pregnant, I accused her of being promiscuous when I was the one who had taken advantage of her when she was most vulnerable. You see, I've always been guilty of transferring my blame to someone else."

Darcy and Jack spent many hours in earnest prayer before the upcoming weekend. One-by-one they both confessed their sins to God, and one-by-one begged for forgiveness for them. They prayed He would prepare hearts for the meeting that weekend. "Give us the attitude and words needed in this situation, we pray, and then we turn the results over to you, dear Lord," Jack earnestly prayed.

Molly had waited until Benji and Caitlin came home on Friday evening before telling them about the upcoming gathering. Neither took the news kindly. "I don't want to be here if he is coming. You should have told me before I came home," Benji accused. "I could have stayed at the dorm and waited until another weekend to come home. You didn't shoot straight about this, Mother."

"I guess I didn't, Benji, but I felt we should do what's right in giving your dad a chance to apologize. Perhaps I deceived you, but if I had told you, you wouldn't have come home. I need you here."

"I totally agree with Benji, Mother," injected Caitlin. "You've never misled us before, but you simply conned us about this weekend. I think Bob, Emily, and I will just pack up and go back home."

"Please don't do that, Caitlin. I haven't seen you in weeks. I approached this situation all wrong by agreeing to this reunion for you, but I was caught off-guard by Jack's request; I didn't know what else to do. After all, I've prayed ever since he left that God would bring him to his senses and that he would repent before it was too late. I think you've probably prayed that also. Now, what else can we do but allow God to do His work?"

Both Caitlin and Benji sat silently with heads down for a while. Finally, Caitlin broke the silence. "Mom, I know you've never intentionally done anything wrong or dishonest in your life. I guess we owe it to you to give you some slack in this situation. I hate to admit it, but I know you're right about our prayers." She then turned to Benji and asked, "Do you think you're up to facing Dad?"

"Do I have to be nice to him if I do?" Benji asked, smiling sheepishly. "Not that I want to, but I'll stay and listen to what he has to say. I'm not saying I'm ready to forgive him, though, and I'm not sure what I might say to him," Benji conceded.

"I completely understand that sentiment, Benji. Many times I've played out this scenario in my mind. I've imagined just what I'd say to Dad if he ever reached this point. I've always wanted to hurt him the way he has hurt us, but I'm sure that's not the Christian spirit I should have," said Caitlin.

"Yeah, I know. I'd like to forget that I'm a Christian for about five minutes and give the man what he really deserves."

"Kids, if I've handled this all wrong, I ask you to forgive me, but I might as well tell you now there is one other piece to the pie. Your dad asked that Celeste be here also. He said she needs to be included in this meeting."

Caitlin had met Celeste for lunch in Atlanta several times after Celeste had made her pilgrimage to Smytheville. Shortly after her trip, Benji and Molly had discussed the fact that after seeing Celeste, there remained no doubt but what Benji and Caitlin shared some of the same genes with this young lady. Benji had told his mom that he would also like a chance to talk to her about their common lineage, so on one of their weekend trips to Atlanta to see Caitlin, the three of them met with Celeste. Since that time, they had gotten together on several other occasions. Both Benji and Caitlin were immediately drawn to Celeste. The three had developed an amiable rapport. At one point Celeste expressed regret that they had not had the opportunity to be together growing up. Benji told her, "Well, if you mean you missed having our dad around when you were younger, all I can say is you didn't miss much."

Suppressing a grin, Molly scolded, "Watch your tongue, Benji Pate."

"Face it, Mom. Facts are facts." They all chuckled at Benji's forthrightness about his dad.

Benji commented, "Well, at least we will have one family member at this grand reunion we'll enjoy." He had liked Celeste's relaxed but confident and persistent manner from the first day they had met.

With that, the tensions lightened. Benji always found a way to lighten the mood, even his own.

Early Saturday morning, Celeste arrived. Benji had met her at the door. "Well come in, Sis. Glad you are here to enjoy this monumental event with us," he said. He gave Celeste a bear hug and took her to the family room where Molly and Caitlin, still in their robes, sat in the floor playing with Emily. They both jumped up to greet Celeste when she came in. "I'm so glad you came, Celeste. Benji and Caitlin have already made me realize how difficult this meeting will be for all of you."

"Not really. You know I've wanted a chance to sit and talk with him for a long time. He's put my confronting him off so long now, I think I'll enjoy see him grovel," Celeste replied, "but I love any chance I get to be with the rest of you. When is the meeting to be?"

"Jack called earlier and said he and Darcy would be here after lunch tomorrow."

"Darcy?" the three shocked siblings questioned in unison.

"I didn't know she was coming either until he called. He said she wanted to ask our forgiveness also."

"And you are going to let her in this house, just like that?" asked Caitlin.

"What else can I do? Whatever they have done, let's not sin ourselves by denying them a chance to repent. This is difficult for me, also, you know. Even though I have forgiven both of them already in my heart, there were earlier times when I wanted to pull her hair out."

"Oh, well, doesn't this weekend get more interesting by the minute?" Benji said, rolling his eyes. Then he chortled as though he had told himself a joke. "I just got a mental image of that, Mom. I can just see you brawling with Darcy like two cats."

"Well, you know I never would have actually done that. I just had the devil-like urge to a few times."

The group all enjoyed imagining the gentle Molly in any kind of physical altercation. "Well if the urge strikes again tomorrow, Mom, just let me know. We will go out in the neighborhood and sell tickets. We could pay off a house mortgage with that." The others bent double laughing at Benji's comment.

With a wry smile, Molly said, "I can assure you that will never happen. The Lord and I settled my anger toward her a long time ago."

Molly's clan filled an entire pew the next day at Pleasant Valley. As soon as the morning service ended, they were surrounded with people greeting them. Molly simply introduced Celeste without explanation of how she was connected to the family. Many commented on her resemblance to Caitlin. Caitlin would just simply agree, "Yes, I guess we do look somewhat alike. I understand people often take on friends' characteristics." The family didn't feel this was neither the proper time nor place to tell all. As soon as they could make a graceful exit, they departed.

The doorbell rang promptly at two. Each of the family looked at each other. Finally Caitlin took a deep breath and said, "I'll get it. The sooner we get this over, the better."

All of the family stood shocked at the sight of Jack. He was hardly recognizable as the same man who walked out on them. He was thirty pounds lighter, his expensive suit and starched shirt had been replaced with a well-worn golf shirt. Now, much more white showed through his dark hair. A humbled, slumped shouldered figure had replaced the arrogant overconfident man they had known.

Although her change didn't affect the family in the same way, they could help but notice the altered appearance of Darcy. The strain of the last months had taken its toll on her. She looked like she had just been released from a prisoner of war camp. Her voluptuous figure had been transformed into this straggly shell of a woman with dark circles under her eyes. The Pate children felt unexpected pity for the two broken people standing before them instead of the resentment they had anticipated.

"Please come in," welcomed Caitlin with a stilted tone.

Jack had a great urge to reach out and hug his daughter, but he realized she wasn't ready for that. Instead, he said, "Caitlin, I've never before noticed what a beautiful young lady you've become."

Sarcasm still filled Caitlin's thoughts. *That might be because you have hardly noticed me at all before.*

Have you met Darcy?" Jack continued.

"Yes, we all know Darcy from the dentist's office. All except Celeste, that is. Come on in the family room, and I'll introduce her."

Simultaneously, the whole group stood when Darcy and Jack entered the room. "Darcy, this is our sister, Celeste. Celeste, this is Darcy," introduced Caitlin.

After perfunctory, awkward greetings, Molly suggested they all be seated. For several uncomfortable seconds of silence, Jack leaned forward, propped his arms on his thighs, clasped his hands, and stared at some invisible pattern on the carpet. Then he looked up and into the faces of his family. "I am very aware that words are inadequate at this point, but I'd like each of you to know I am aware I've done immeasurable hurt and harm to each of you. I'm unworthy to even be in your presence, and I know that. But I'm grateful you have given me this opportunity to acknowledge my sins to you face-to-face, as I already have to God, and to beg for your mercy and forgiveness." Nonstop Jack continued for the next hour. Beginning with Molly and ending with Celeste, he addressed each family member individually. He personalized his confessions, admitting the specific ways he had hurt each one. Darcy admitted her part in hurting the family and pleaded for their forgiveness also. Strangely enough, there were no dry eyes in the house.

An unusual silence from the others in the group had provided Jack with the unhindered time for confession. Then Molly spoke first. "Jack, I have already forgiven both you and Darcy, even before you've asked. I had to months ago to enable me to get past the bitterness that would have destroyed me if I hadn't. Even though I've already forgiven you, I appreciate your making your acknowledgements of your wrong doings. I've prayed that God would bring you to repentance so you could go on with your lives. I wish you no harm. I pray God will restore you as he has me."

Tears streamed down Benji's face. "Dad, 'God works in mysterious ways,' as you used to preach. I thought I would sock you right in the kisser when I faced you and then tell you just how sorry you are. Instead, all I feel for you now is pity. Through God's help, I think I can forgive you." At the same moment Benji and Jack stood and started toward each other. Jack opened his arms wide, and Benji fell into them. Jack lovingly embraced his son as he had never done before. The two held each other tightly and shook as they wept together. Jack was so aware of what he had missed for so many years because of his arrogance. Benji, too, silently wished he had known a dad this humble when he was younger.

The tearful offers of forgiveness came from Caitlin and Celeste also. When each of the family had said what they wanted to and needed to, Jack and Darcy stood to leave. The group said their good-byes as a great sense of peace filled each of their hearts.

After the door closed, Benji broke the solemnity of the moment. "I'm starved. Emotional events make me hungry. Is there more chocolate cake, Mom?"

"I think everything makes you hungry," commented Celeste.

The group filtered into the kitchen and sat around the table, eating cake and discussing the events of the day. By that time, Bob and Emily had awakened from their Sunday afternoon naps and joined them. The whole group broke into laughter when they noticed Emily in her high chair with chocolate caked smeared all over her sweet face.

Amazing Grace

On the drive back to Nashville, a joyful mood permeated the car. Jack and Darcy discussed how generously his family had offered forgiveness. "That truly had to be God's hand at work," commented Jack. "I'm not really surprised by Molly's Christian spirit. She has always exhibited such grace in all her ways, but I wasn't that sure about how the children would receive us. I realize how miserably I failed at fatherhood, even when I was there."

"Well, somebody certainly did right by them. Celeste, Caitlin, and Benji are all great young adults."

"Any good in them came from their mothers. Molly always covered for my shortcomings where they were concerned. God must have known Caitlin and Benji needed one good parent and gave them Molly. I also regret not accepting paternity for Celeste earlier. Gloria did a fine job parenting her without me, though. I'm really impressed at what a levelheaded young lady she has become. I can't believe how she so willingly pardoned me for neglecting and ignoring her for so long. All this forgiveness must be a God thing."

Both Darcy and Jack fell silent for a while, just basking in the relief they were experiencing. A great weight had been lifted. They both realized the process of forgiveness had just begun. Each of them had a list of people to contact to ask for pardon. They would begin as soon as they got home.

First, Jack merely started with a hum. Then he broke into the first verse of "Amazing Grace." Never had the words been so meaningful to him. Soon Darcy joined in. Jack recognized that was the first time they had ever sung together. Their realization and recognition of God's wonderful grace made for a precious worship service, for never had two people appreciated so much the undeserved favor of a Holy God and how it had paved the way for their steps to recovery.

"Darcy, I just had a strange thought. I probably would be a better preacher and pastor now than I ever was before because I would truly mean what I would say, but the irony is, I have forfeited my right to ever serve in that capacity again. Even though God has forgiven our sins, sin has a way of carrying with it its own form of punishment."

"God will still use you, Jack. Be patient, and He'll show you how."

He turned and looked at her with a new appreciation. He realized spiritual wisdom had just been spoken.

The next week brought freshness to their marriage. The sun seemed to shine brighter, the trees gleamed with color, and the very air seemed sweeter. All was not right with their world, but it was much better than it had been.

Jack could even go to his job of psychological testing in a better spirit. He resigned himself to the fact it wasn't really what he wanted to do, but it did bring in a salary. He remembered a sermon he had once heard: "Grow Where You're Planted." He resolved he would do just that.

The next Sunday Jack and Darcy attended a Baptist church near their home. It felt odd to Jack to sit near the back, listening to a sermon rather than being up front preaching one, but he was soon aware that God had brought him to this place for a reason. He needed to be on the receiving end for a while. Soon both Darcy and Jack found their niche in their new church. There was a Sunday school class for people like them. It was called "The Second Start" class and was made up of couples in their second marriages. They found others with whom they found a commonality.

After having attended Calvary Baptist for several Sundays, Jack made his way to the pastor's office. He felt the pastor should know his background. Again, Jack felt relief for having confessed his past to him. "I realize there are many jobs in church for which I have forfeited my credentials, but if you find some way that I can help you and serve the Lord in this church, please call me. I no longer have a need to be in the spotlight, but I do want to serve God as He would have me to."

Not many weeks passed until Dr. Abbott called. "Jack, were serious about helping out?"

"I've never been more serious."

"The deacons have decided our church needs to start a jail ministry. How do you feel about going down to our local jail each Sunday morning and conducting a Sunday school class?"

"I don't feel worthy to do that, but if you sense I could serve in that capacity, I'll give it a shot."

"Jack, remember you will just be a forgiven sinner talking to other sinners. Aren't all church leaders in that same boat?"

Jack took on his new mission with more sincerity and zeal than he had ever demonstrated before. He began by telling the inmates just what Dr. Abbott had said to him, "I'm just a forgiven sinner teaching you other sinners. I probably deserve to be behind bars more than some of you do." This new humbleness endeared Jack to those other men. They listened intently, and many made professions of faith themselves. "If a holy God could forgive Jack Pate, then he might forgive them, too," was their reasoning.

Jack wasn't the only one who found he could be used of God. Darcy found her role also. It merely took Dr. Abbott mentioning a rape crisis ministry for Darcy to experience an epiphany. She had never taken a position in church before because she felt so dirty and unworthy, but this is a place where she just might be able to help some young ladies from falling prey to the same self-destructive attitudes and actions she'd experienced.

Never had a person been so perfectly suited for a ministry than was Darcy for this one. God gifted Darcy with just the right words to help heal young women who had been violated. They listened to her when they turned off others because they knew she understood how they felt because she had also experienced sexual abuse.

God's amazing grace filled both Darcy and Jack with the sweet nectar of the Holy Spirit. God was truly giving them the unmerited gift of a second chance of happiness.

The Cleansing of Forgiveness

Back in Smytheville, Molly was enjoying life. Her spirits gleamed much brighter. The cleansing of forgiveness had washed away a great burden. Although she had already forgiven Jack and Darcy in her heart, even before they had asked, there was an intangible and unexplainable respite in knowing her children had met with their father and had also forgiven him. In conversations with them, they had assured her they also felt this relief.

Molly had called Sawyer shortly after Darcy and Jack had left that day. She felt he deserved to be one of the first to know the details of their meeting. After all, he had spent much time and energy getting them back together. She told him, "Sawyer, you can't believe what peace I feel today. I don't know when I've ever felt such serenity."

Strangely enough, through the vicarious experiences of Molly's family, Sawyer also seemed to feel closure on his own anger and resentment of his father. "Molly," began Sawyer, "I can never tell you how much you have helped me. I thought I was coming to see you each week to bring you comfort after Jack left, but strangely enough, instead I received help with my own bitterness.

I'm not saying I'm completely healed, but I think we both have reached the point where we no longer need our weekly counseling sessions. But I will still be seeing you each week."

"Oh, really? How's that?"

"I'll be seeing you at church. In the process of forgiving my father, I realize now that I was not only angry with hypocritical Christians, but I was also angry with my heavenly Father. Observing how your relationship with Him has enabled you to be so forgiving has shamed me. I want to mend my relationship with my heavenly Father. I plan to start by attending church again."

"I praise the Lord for bringing this good from an impossible situation," replied Molly, "just as he always does." You just can't imagine how glad I am to hear we will be worshiping together each Sunday. I want you to sit with Thad and me.

Sawyer, God isn't finished with you. He has already ministered to me through you, and I know he will use you to help others also."

By Monday morning, the kids had left and life was settling back into a normal routine. Molly then called Thad as she had promised him. She had told him before the family pow-wow that she wanted him to be in prayer for that situation. "Thad, I don't work tonight so I thought you might like to come over for dinner. I can give you a play-by-play account of the weekend."

"I'll be finished with rounds by seven, and I'm not on call tonight so that will be great. I can't wait to see you," Thad replied. "A day without you seems like a year."

Molly's glowing countenance astounded Thad when she met him at the door. She was more beautiful than he had ever seen her. She wore a new simple, but flattering, dress. Her hair had been combed back behind her ears revealing a smiling, peaceful face. An elegant candlelit table was set with her fine china and awaited them. Immediately, Thad sensed a, more than subtle, change in their relationship.

"Wow, what's the occasion?"

"I just thought we would celebrate a life-changing weekend."

Molly shared with Thad each word spoken over the weekend among her family and the tranquility she now experienced. "I can't tell you how different I feel now. I didn't realize that I was still carrying such a heavy burden until it was taken off my shoulders. Celeste, Benji, and Caitlin seem to feel this same liberation."

Automatically, Thad reached out and embraced Molly. She didn't push him away this time but gave in to the comfort of his arms. He knew not to press the situation any further, but he realized the pall of Jack's fall had been exorcised from their relationship.

Molly and Thad saw each other daily during the next few weeks. They seemed to be as giddy as teenagers and were always eager to be together. Thad discerned their time would come, that one day they would truly be a couple. He also knew he must remain patient and wait for Molly to come to the same realization. Although both physical and emotional desire for her was ever present in his mind, he would never do anything to make Molly feel dirty or feel as if she had sinned. He knew that would be detrimental, if not deadly, to their bond. He had waited this long for her; he could wait until she was ready.

The Accident

A month after Jack and Darcy's visit, Molly received a call from Jack. "Molly, I just want to thank you again for giving me a second chance on life by forgiving me and for arranging that wonderful meeting with my children. I recognize that I am truly the recipient of God's wonderful grace. There was a pause before he added, "And I want to tell you something I neglected to say so many times before. Molly, I love you and always will. You are the best person I've ever known. I know I've given up all rights to you, but you were always the best part of me. I just didn't recognize it when we were together." Tears welled up in Molly's eyes as Jack spoke, and her heart raced at his unexpected words. Then he added, "I truly hope someday you will find someone deserving of you who will give you the happiness you deserve. I wish nothing but the best for you."

"I think God is already working on that, Jack," answered Molly, "but the time isn't right now."

"It's not the same kind of love I have felt for you, Molly, but I have a growing love and appreciation for Darcy now. We are trying to get our lives on the right track by putting our focus on God, where it should be. I just wanted to update you on what Darcy and I are doing with this gift of a second opportunity in our relationship."

Jack related to Molly their involvement in their newfound ministries and told her how pleased they were to be doing something helpful to other people. He also informed her he had written a letter to the deacons of Pleasant Valley Community. "Molly, the deacons and church leaders have agreed to meet with Darcy and me next Sunday afternoon so we can voice our confessions and apologies to them face-to-face. We offered to go before the entire congregation to do this, but the deacons felt it would be more prudent for us to do it this way. They said healing had begun among the membership, and they felt their seeing us in church together would just open old wounds and renew resentments in many members."

"I think they are probably right, Jack," agreed Molly. "Some would not be ready to forgive you until they had their pound of flesh, but what you are doing will be a step in the right direction. I'm sure the deacons will spread the news of your apology throughout the membership. I'll pray for you as you talk with them. I know this must take great courage."

"Although this will be one of the hardest things I've ever done, second only to facing you and my children, but I realize God wants me to humble myself before these good people and apologize for the many ways I've hurt them. I know if you are praying for me, I will be able to go through with this."

"I'll talk with the children later tonight and will ask them to be in prayer for you also."

The next three days were the longest of Jack and Darcy's life. They truly learned what the Bible meant about "praying without ceasing." Praying was the only way they found to keep the jitters away.

Sunday morning Jack and Darcy prayed together once again before leaving their driveway heading for Smytheville. Never had the trees looked so green and the sky as blue. "God's in His heaven, and all's right with the world." Robert Browning's words came back to Jack and seemed almost fitting for the day.

They had been on the road about an hour when Darcy broke into song. "Wherever He leads, I'll go," she began softly. Jack gave her a loving smile and then joined in. The two had never before been at peace as they were now, even though they were facing a difficult mission, but one God was leading them to.

As they approached an intersection, Darcy looked at Jack and said, "You know something? I've loved you before, but I've never both loved and respected you as much as I do today."

He reached across the seat and squeezed her hand and she pressed his back. "I feel the same way about you, darling. I never believed God would allow us to be this happy."

The cacophonous sounds of crashing glass and crushing metal rudely interrupted their love fest. Neither of them saw the eighteen wheeler before it plowed into Darcy's door and rolled their car. When the car finally stopped rolling, Jack and Darcy's hands remained entwined; only now, fingers lay limp and still.

Jack was semi-conscious but felt anesthetized. He realized the air bags had deployed, but even after they started deflating, he realized he couldn't turn his head or body to see Darcy's condition. In fact, he couldn't move any part of his body. "Darcy, Darcy," he called out in a soft gurgle. She didn't respond. He tried several more times. Still nothing. Jack then gave in to the swirling sensation and closed his eyes.

Everything seemed so surreal. Once, he opened his eyes for just a moment and was aware of red and blue flashing lights, but the blare of sirens seemed to serve as a lullaby to soon send him back into a submissive sleep. A short time later, the sound of voices roused him.

"Sir, can you hear me? Blink your eyes if you hear me."

Although it took all the energy Jack could muster, he managed a couple of blinks.

"Sir, you are about to hear a loud crunching sound and a roar of a motor. We are using this equipment called the Jaws of Life to try and get you out of the car. Blink again if you understand."

Again, Jack tried to blink, but when his eyes closed, he no longer had the energy to open them. Somewhere in the recesses of his consciousness, he was aware of the noisy machinery. Then the clamor faded to nothingness.

Three days later, Jack heard something else. "Jack, Jack, wake up. Open your eyes. I know you can."

The voice was so familiar. There was a compelling magnetism to it. He wanted to open his eyes and tried, but his eyes just didn't seem to cooperate. They felt as though they had been glued together.

"Jack, this is Molly. Please try to wake up. You have to really try."

This time with great effort, he got his eyes opened to mere slits, just enough to see a fuzzy silhouette of Molly.

"That's it. You're getting them open now. Keep trying. Don't go back to sleep on me, you hear? Listen to me, and I will help you to get orient. You are in Erlanger Hospital in Chattanooga. You have been in a terrible accident and have some injuries, but you are going to make it. But you have to keep trying," urged Molly. "Don't give in to that desire to go back to sleep right now. You really need to get awake."

Molly? Darcy? Wasn't he with Darcy? Was this a dream? Strange, confused thoughts filled Jack's mind.

Molly had seen many horrifically injured patients before while on duty in the emergency room and had tended to their needs with professional efficiency. As a nurse she had always stayed objective so she could give her patients the best treatment possible. Objectivity was gone in this case though. This was Jack, the father of her children, the man she had loved since she was a teenager. Although she maintained an outward calm, she felt an inward panic not only for the immediate crisis but for his future—if he was to have one. She knew, if Jack, through some miracle managed to survive his multiple injuries, his life would forever be changed—for the worse, much worse. The doctors had already informed her that their initial examinations confirmed her fear. Jack was paralyzed from the neck down. Learning to live with this debilitating injury just might never be an issue though. He had other life threatening injuries—a head injury, a compound fractured leg, a damaged liver and spleen, plus a plethora of other more minor wounds. Her medical knowledge told her his most pressing issues would be dealt with first, and then each crisis would be handled in order, if he survived these initial critical days. The realization that Darcy was killed in the accident would still be another trauma for Jack to face in the days ahead.

As consciousness began returning, Jack struggled with something in his throat. He felt panic at his inability to free himself of this obstruction. Molly recognized the fright in his eyes and began explaining, "Jack, you have a tube down your throat that is helping you to breathe. Don't fight it. You are not choking, and it's doing the job it is intended to. Try not to be frightened. I'm right here with you and will know if anything is going wrong. Trust me, Jack, and trust God."

ICU rules didn't apply to Molly. In fact, the nursing staff welcomed her staying in the unit with him as much as possible. With her expertise, she relieved them of much of his care, and she welcomed the opportunity to do what she could.

Soon Jack drifted back to a drugged sleep. Molly took the opportunity to sit down and close her own eyes for a few minutes. The strain and loss of sleep had taken a toll on her. When she opened her eyes a few minutes later, Thad was standing over her.

"Hi, sweetie. How are you making it?"

"Thad, what are you doing here?"

"I had to come to see about you. I could hear the exhaustion in your voice when we talked on the phone. I told my secretary to cancel my appointments for today and tomorrow so I could help you out a bit."

"That's the nicest thing anyone has ever done for me, Thad. Just your being here gives me strength."

"Maybe so, but after we talk a bit, you're going to the motel room I've already rented and sleep some."

"Oh, I can't. I promised Jack I would stay and take care of him. When he awoke a few minutes ago, he was so frightened."

"Molly, I've already reviewed his chart. I know the severity of his injuries, and I think, just maybe, I would be qualified to see to his needs for a few hours."

Molly grinned at the absurdity of this situation. "Well, just maybe an MD would make a qualified sitter for a short period of time. I am exhausted, now that you've mentioned it. A nap might do me good."

"Not just a catnap either. I don't want to see you back at this hospital for twelve hours. Do you understand? I know you're concerned about Jack, but I'm concerned about you. I know Jack has no family left except for you and the kids, but I've talked to several people, and you aren't doing this alone. Benji, Caitlin, and Celeste are taking weekend shifts. Several of your Smytheville friends are also on the list to take shifts."

"Well, haven't you been the busy bee? You are the most thoughtful man I've ever known. But on another note, Thad, what is your assessment of Jack's prognosis?"

"I don't have to tell you, Molly, how grave his condition is. As a matter of fact, if I were in that same condition, I don't think I would want to survive."

"I'm afraid Jack will feel the same way, especially when he becomes aware Darcy didn't survive."

"Not only that, but can you imagine what it will do for a man's psyche to realize he is totally dependent on the very people he has hurt so deeply?"

"Thad, you know that will never even be a consideration in my care for him. He needs help, and I'm the one to do it."

"Rest assured, young lady, whatever lies ahead, you aren't facing it alone. But for right now, I want you out of here. Do you think we can trust this well-trained staff long enough for me to walk you out and get a taxi for you?" Thad teased with a grin

As Thad promised, support was plentiful in the weeks that followed. Molly couldn't believe the network of help Thad had arranged. Ironically, Jack's injuries proved to be the most healing balm for Pleasant Valley Community. Molly had laid the pattern. Her agape love toward Jack was the catalyst needed to propel the other church members into a frenzy of self-sacrificing support. They found the words from the prayer of St. Francis of Assisi, "For it is in giving that we receive. It is in pardoning that we are pardoned..." to be so true. Realizing Jack and Darcy met with this disaster on their way to ask their forgiveness gave added impetus to their desires to help care for Jack. This was as close to showing Christ-like agape love—in spite of love—as Molly and the others would ever come.

In spite of the great appreciation for other's assistance, Jack still felt a greater peace when Molly was at his bedside. Her voice did more to lower his blood pressure than the pills did. All he could do was look her in the eyes while tears trickled out the corners of his. She understood the sentiments he was communicating.

After several weeks of surgeries, therapy, and a series of other medical crises, Jack was MedFlighted to Smytheville Hospital where both Molly and Thad could more conveniently see after him. Molly resumed her shifts in the emergency room, but she found time to check on Jack several times a night. After many weeks more of rehabilitation, Jack's physical injuries were as healed as they were going to be. He still was reeling emotionally from Darcy's death and the fact he would require complete assistance for daily living for the remainder of his life.

He was about to be released from the hospital, but where was he to go? "There is no other place for him to go," Molly told Thad, "but my house."

She saw disappointment and dejection on Thad's face. "You know there are facilities equipped to care for quadriplegics, don't you? You also are aware cost is no object now that Jack has received a generous settlement from the trucking company."

"Yes, I know all of that, but I also know Jack still has a long way to go. I also know you were instrumental, and I thank you for foreseeing his future needs and insisting we employ a good lawyer to get the funds needed. I realize he can afford institutional care, but that's not what is best for him. He needs the support of family and friends close by. Without that, he will withdraw even more into his shell of depression."

"Molly, I'm being selfish in this, but I've waited patiently a long time for us to be together. I just don't know if I'm willing to go the long haul with this situation. If there was no other solution, it would be different, but you have already done far more than anyone could be expected to. Please give it up and let him go to Shepherds in Atlanta or some other appropriate establishment."

Unexpected tears erupted. Molly could not bear the thought of giving up Thad, but, at the same time, she was certain what her Christian duty was to Jack. She tried her best to explain this to Thad, but he was resolute in his decision to step out of her life if she insisted on bringing Jack to her house. He had waited long enough and had stayed by her side throughout the past months, but her taking Jack in on a permanent basis was too much. "I'm afraid there isn't room in your home or your life for both Jack and me. I love you and care for you, but I totally disagree with this move. It will take an unmerciful toll on you, and I refuse to be a part of it. All I can say is that if you insist on taking him into your home, our relationship will have to be on hold, at least for the time being."

Jack's Adjustments

Coming to terms with the trauma and aftermath of the accident was most difficult for Jack. As consciousness gradually returned, realization of his condition surfaced. Finally the medical staff weaned him off the breathing machine. Getting the tube out of his throat allowed him to ask the many questions that raced through his mind. Molly had tried to supply him with only the information she felt he could process day by day. She had said volumes to him by the things she didn't say.

Many doctors came by daily. Each would check responses in different parts of his body, only to find none. Jack had somehow hoped his paralysis was temporary. Just maybe getting off the breathing machine would allow him to move. As hard as he would try, his limbs wouldn't budge.

"Molly, give me the straight of what's going on with my body," Jack said in a husky whisper. Sadly enough, the only part of his body that seemed to be alive screamed with burning pain. His throat was raw from the many days of having a foreign object down it. "Molly, I can't move anything. Is this permanent?"

Before she gave a reply, Jack saw the answer in her face. "Jack, short of a miracle from God, the paralysis in your legs is permanent, but the doctors are hopeful you may get some restoration in your upper body. That's a wait and see situation. Your permanent injury is at the C-5, C-6 region. You have bruising to your spinal cord in other areas. You seem to be moving a finger occasionally. At the present time, we are just glad you are alive. That definitely is a miracle. You have been visiting death's door quite often since your accident. There've been times when I thought you would stay there." Jack had no control of the tears streaming off the sides of his face. He couldn't even wipe them away. He was totally helpless. Molly didn't try to stop the crying, for she felt it was an essential part of the grief process. Sometimes tears seemed to help wash away the grief.

"Why didn't you just let me die, Molly? I had rather have died than to be in this condition." Silence invaded the room for a while, and then he continued, "I don't mean for this to be a pity party for myself, but I detest the fact I will forever be a burden to others." Then he voiced the question he dreaded asking, for he, at some level, already knew the answer. "How about Darcy? Is she... is she here at this hospital or..." He couldn't finish the question. He simply couldn't say the words. The memory of holding her lifeless hand had played through his mind many times. He had wondered if his fear was true.

"Jack, do you remember anything about the accident?"

"Yes, some. I remember the horrendous crashing sounds. I remember Darcy squeezing my hand before the crash, and then it became lifeless in mine. Now I don't know if that was my loss of sensation or if it was hers. I couldn't turn to look at her. Tell me all. Tell me what happened."

"If you recall, you and Darcy were on your way to Smytheville to meet with the leaders of the church. I don't know why you were not on the interstate, but it seems you had taken an alternate route."

"I remember. The day was so beautiful, we decided to go the blue highways and enjoy the scenery. Molly, Darcy and I were so happy that day. We had even been singing together as we drove down the road. We felt like God was helping to put our lives back on track."

Molly continued, "The driver of tanker truck fell asleep and ran through the stop sign, hitting your car on the passenger side. Jack, Darcy experienced no pain. She never knew what happened. She was killed on impact. It was a miracle in itself that you survived. Your car looked like a can of sardines someone had stomped and then had opened with a knife. Not only did the truck roll your car, but it kept moving after that and ran up on it.

Apparently it was moving at a tremendous rate of speed when it hit you."

Jack pressed his eyes closed as if he could close out the reality of what Molly was telling him. He couldn't respond for quite some time. Molly let him have those minutes to process what she had just told him. He mentally rushed through the denial stage. *She can't be right. I'm really not permanently in this condition. Maybe Darcy's not really dead. Molly may just be telling me all this to hurt me like I've hurt her.* As soon as that thought passed through his consciousness, he knew how absurd it was, how absurd all his denial was. *No, I'm finally getting what I deserve. I'm experiencing the wrath of God.* In some peculiar way, that thought satisfied Jack. Maybe this was the price he would pay for God's absolution of his sin. Just as good children feel some sort of comfort in being punished for wrong doing, as though it assuages any guilt, so did Jack

When finally he spoke, his voice trembled. "I knew we didn't deserve the happiness we had begun enjoying. I deserve this, don't I? This is the ultimate price I must pay for my sin."

"No, Jack. This isn't some sort of punishment. It was one of life's accidents and nothing more. Don't make more of it than what is there. Don't you recall the many times you preached that Christ paid the debt for all our sins, a greater price than we could ever pay?"

Nothing Molly said changed Jack's mind. In some bizarre way, he felt like the other shoe had finally dropped. There was a strange fulfillment in believing he was enduring the punishment for his sins.

"What now? What will I do for the rest of my life? Where will I go when I leave the hospital?" The questions rolled like stones in an avalanche.

"Jack, we will all have to just take one day at a time, like we have been doing. Do you realize how God has provided so many friends to help care for you during the days since the accident?

Help has come from the most unexpected sources. The very people you were going to apologize to made many sacrifices to come to Chattanooga and sit with you. They even continued their vigil after we came to Smytheville. Do you think God will immediately cut off supplying His help? Keep this in mind God has provided and He will continue to provide."

"I don't want to be a burden to others and that is exactly what I'll be. How will I ever pay for all the care I've already had and for the care I'll require in the future?"

"Financial worry can easily be eliminated. The trucking company assumes all responsibility for the accident and wants to avoid a messy law suit and the bad press that would go with it. Besides that, the company doesn't have a leg to stand on. They had let this driver stay on the road many more hours than was allowed by law. With the help of Thad, we have employed a law firm, which has been dealing with this issue. There is a huge, more than ample settlement awaiting your signature. You will never have to worry about finances. As far as your being a burden, you won't be. I am taking you home with me. I will see to it that you get the best possible care. I have the medical expertise needed and the desire to do this.

"No, no, no. I won't let that happen. You don't deserve to be tied down with me," Jack violently and adamantly protested.

"Jack, when I am able to help anyone, I consider that I'm doing it for Jesus. You know the scripture, "When you do it unto the least of these, you've done it unto me."

"No, I just won't let you do this. Put me in a nursing home or some other institution. I couldn't bear the guilt of allowing you, the one I've hurt so deeply, to be saddled with my care."

"Listen to me, Jack. You still have many medical needs that will require trained professionals. You realize the insurance company limits the length of hospital stays. You simply will die if you go to a nursing home. Although your leg has healed some on the outside, there remains deep infection. It is still hot to the touch.

Not only that, but you will require special care at different levels. I want to do this. I hate to put it bluntly, but you really have no other viable choice."

Jack had no one else who could or would do for him what Molly would. More than the hopelessness that he felt because of his injuries, the depression he experienced because there was no other way for him to be cared for other than to be at Molly's mercy covered him like a shroud. He closed his eyes and cut off all communication for a while. *Maybe I can escape into sleep and just never wake up. I will merely will myself to die, or maybe I'll even kill myself.* He gave a sardonic inward laugh at that idea. *How could I do that? I can't even lift an arm. I am simply a prisoner to this situation.* Then he silently prayed most fervently, "God, if you won't remove this paralysis from my body, let me die or give me grace to endure it, please."

At Home with Molly

Rain poured from the sky and thunder roared. The black sky occasionally would be marked with streaks of lightning. Jack arrived at Molly's house during one of the many spring storms so common to the South. The ambulance's radio was tuned to the weather news. Jack heard that Smytheville was one of the many Georgia towns under a tornado watch until 6:00 p.m.

"Now wouldn't that be a hoot for me to have made it this far and then to get blown away by a tornado," Jack quipped to the attendant.

"Oh, I don't think that's likely. This looks like a pretty sturdy house," the driver said. Jack thought about the driver's comment and gave mental assent to it, except he wasn't thinking about the physical structure but rather his thoughts were of the strength Molly had always provided there. She had been the rock upon which their family had been founded and had relied on. She had been his emotional muscle through his many trials.

"Now, Mr. Pate, we are going to cover your head with this blanket to keep you dry until we can get into the house, added the attendant."

Not only must this scene have been strange for the neighbors watching, but it also felt very weird to Jack. "Surely I look like a corpse being taken into a house instead of out from one."

Molly met them at the door and directed them to the great room. There Jack saw more equipment than some rehab places owned. "Why are you setting me up here in the middle of the living area, Molly? I'll be in everyone's way here."

"Jack, this is the only room large enough for everything you'll need. Besides, the buzz of daily activity will be good for you. You won't get so lonesome in here."

The adjustments required for this new arrangement were almost insurmountable, both the physical and the emotional.

Molly explained she had employed sitters for the hours she would be at work and there would be a stream of other people involved in his care. "Jack, we have home health nurses who are scheduled to come by every day. I've asked them to schedule their hours here to coincide with my work schedule. That way you will have medical help throughout the day and night. Your physical therapist will also come after I leave for work."

The parade of people Molly had mentioned came as planned. Others also made constant paths to his bed side. Pleasant Valley church had never responded to anyone the way they had to Jack. Molly rarely had to worry about grocery shopping or cooking. Food was provided every day by someone. At least it took that much off her. The men's Sunday school class had their own schedule. Someone from that group visited Jack each day. On Fridays, the teacher came and taught Jack the lesson.

Molly remained bright and cheerful in spite of the telltale circles under her eyes and the sadness from deep within them that could not be concealed. She would work her night shift, come home and spend several hours doing the routine tasks required to keep Jack going. Although she had the same credentials as did the other nurses involved in his care, there was something humiliating about her taking care of his most personal needs. He wished many days she didn't have to do these for him, although they were necessary. She wasn't just a nurse; she was the one to who he had been married for many years.

Molly, after seeing to his needs, would stretch out on the sofa by his bed and sleep for a couple of hours at a time. She had trained herself to wake up at the slightest beep to monitor his machines and to turn him. She strived to keep away the much-dreaded and very threatening bed sores, which were a danger to all quads and paraplegics. She never got enough sleep, but she didn't complain.

Her children did, though. Jack overheard them have the same conversation every time they were home. "Mom, you can't keep on like this. It is killing you," said Caitlin.

"Mother, I've looked into this and found that there are some really good institutions that would care for Dad," Benji inserted.

"Children, I appreciate your concern, but I'm really making it fine. I don't think Jack would survive for very long in any other place. We fight medical problems daily. He runs a low-grade fever constantly because of the deep infection in his leg. There are weekly kidney flair-ups and other problems. I know to be alert to these and keep on top of threatening conditions. God is giving me strength for each day."

She never revealed to anyone the emptiness and loneliness she felt without Thad's presence. She realized a person must make choices in life, and some of them called for sacrifice. Her choice to give personal care for her ex-husband was costing her the companionship with Thad, which had become so very important to her.

Benji and Caitlin were concerned about other issues, also. Molly's entire life was consumed with Jack's care. Eventually they noticed that she and Thad weren't spending time together as they had before, although he did make necessary professional visits for Jack when needed. Finally, Caitlin inquired about him. "Where is Thad? I haven't seen him since Dad has been home. Are we just missing his visits or does he opt to stay away when our crew invades on weekends?"

"No, it's not that. He is just very busy with other things right now." Molly made excuses for him each time they asked.

Caitlin saw in her mother's eyes she wasn't telling all, but she didn't press the issue. Molly simply didn't have time for him with all her other responsibilities, surmised Caitlin. Little did she realize Molly's bringing Jack to her house had been the deal-breaker for Thad. He refused to stand by and watch Molly dedicate her entire life to Jack's care and destroy her own at the same time.

Caitlin and Benji, along with Celeste, showed up most weekends. They all encouraged Molly to get out of the house while they were there and let them help with his care. Molly would leave only long enough to make trips to the beauty shop and to get her car serviced. She never stayed away more than a couple of hours, though.

One weekend, Celeste brought an unexpected visitor with her—her mother. Gloria asked if she might have time alone with Jack. She had a very important matter to clear up. "Jack, in spite of my many years of anger and resentment toward you, I want you to know how sorry I am that this has happened to you. For years, I would have welcomed seeing you in this condition or worse, but not now—"

"Gloria, I deserve this and more for the way I treated you and for the many sins I've committed against others. I'm curious, though. What has changed your attitude toward me?"

"I've observed the way Celeste has responded, and she has related to me how your family has forgiven you. I decided if they could forgive, so could I. In doing so, a great yoke has been removed from my life that has weighted me down for years. I've stopped drinking, and my entire outlook toward you, as well as other things, has changed."

"This is better than a dose of medicine for me, Gloria. I have felt so responsible for destroying your life all these years."

"Well, in spite of all the bad stuff, you did give me one great gift—Celeste. She has been the light of my life and my very reason for living. By the way, she absolutely adores the rest of your family. They have made her feel a part of it. More than once, she has told me how wonderful Molly is. After one of her early visits here, she came home totally amazed. She said, 'Mother, the best way I can describe Molly is that she lives out Christian love. I've never seen anyone who has been hurt so deeply with such an ability to offer complete forgiveness.'"

"That is a perfect summation of Molly," concurred Jack.

Later that night, the family gathered around the table for supper. Again, the church ladies had outdone themselves in providing a feast. Knowing Molly's family gathered in on weekends and that she was off work for a couple of days, they didn't want her to spend all her time in the kitchen. While they were eating and enjoying conversation, the doorbell rang. "I'll get it," volunteered Benji.

The rest of the group heard him pleasantly greet Sawyer. The kids felt like he was just part of the family. Benji insisted he come in and eat with them.

Molly told him how nice it was to see him again. He regularly stopped by to check on Jack and to brighten his day. Molly introduced him to Gloria. "Sawyer, I want you to meet Celeste's mom, Gloria. Gloria, this is Sawyer Thomas, a dear family friend."

"So nice to meet you, Gloria." Sawyer stuck out his hand to her.

"I'm glad to know you. I've often heard Celeste speak of you." Sawyer got a plate from the cabinet and pulled a chair up to the table.

"I'm glad you invited me to eat with you, Benji. I'm starved."

Gloria observed how comfortable Sawyer seemed with the family. She also noticed his handsome build and was embarrasses by the sexual attraction she felt. He made quite a striking image. The attraction was mutual. Gloria's appearance had drastically improved since she had gotten off the booze. The sheen had returned to her thick auburn hair. That, as well as her nice build, had not gone unnoticed by Sawyer. More than once that evening, they caught each other staring. Then they would quickly avert their eyes.

About nine o'clock, Gloria asked Celeste if she could borrow her car. "I'm a little tired. I think I will check in down at the Holiday Inn and go to bed."

"It won't be necessary to use her car, Gloria. I'm about to leave and will be going right by there. I'd be happy to drop you off," Sawyer quickly offered. For some reason, he wanted to steal a few more minutes in this woman's presences."

"How nice of you! I'll get my bag out of Celeste's car, and we can be on our way."

"Gloria, I would ask you to stay here, but all of our bedrooms are taken. Anyway, you probably will get more sleep there than you would in this buzz of activity."

Gloria appreciated Molly's sentiment. It just reinforced what she had already learned about her. *What other woman in the entire world would even entertain the idea of having her husband's former lover sleep under her roof,* mused Gloria. Molly was the most gracious, forgiving person Gloria had ever known.

"Are you up to getting some ice cream before I take you to the motel?" Sawyer asked after they got in his car.

Gloria was stuffed from the larger-than-normal supper she had eaten, but she wasn't about to say that. She was eager to spend more time with this man. "Sure, butter pecan is my favorite. I can never turn it down."

Sawyer drove to the edge of town to a family-owned ice cream parlor, which was a Smytheville landmark. The two went in, and in less than an hour had heard each other's life history in brief. Later Sawyer drove under the Holiday Inn portico. He didn't care who saw him this time or what the town gossips might think. He grinned to himself as he imagined the tales that might be spread. As with other gossip, he was totally impervious to it. As a matter of fact, he had always gained a weird pleasure in keeping the busy-bodies in town guessing. More than once had he let them make fools of themselves by toting rumors, only for them to be proven wrong later. He picked up Gloria's bag and saw to it she got checked in properly. Gloria reached for her bag and said, "Sawyer, I feel I've known you forever. This has been such a special treat. I hope I'll see you tomorrow before I go home."

"I've got an idea. Why don't I pick you up in the morning and take you to church with me?" suggested Sawyer.

"I'd love that, but I'm not sure I brought the appropriate clothes for church."

"What you have on would be fine. We are very casual at Pleasant Valley."

Gloria assumed an out-of-character-for-her shy expression for a moment and then added, "I have to confess something, Sawyer. I haven't been inside a church in years."

"Well, there's no time like the present to get started back, so I'll accept no excuse," he jibed. "I'll pick you up at 10:30 a.m."

The weekend had been a special beginning for a wonderful relationship for the two. Sawyer made a date to come to Atlanta the next Friday night to see Gloria. It was a rarity for him to become smitten by a woman so quickly, but he felt an unfamiliar attraction to Gloria. He examined his feelings and tried to determine what the magnetism was. Although she definitely had been a victim of Jack's philandering, for years she had proven to be self-sufficient in her role as a single mom. Sawyer realized he had always been drawn to the injured or the underdog, but this time, it was more than sympathy he felt. As a matter of fact, Gloria exuded a "don't feel sorry for me" attitude, "I've made it just fine without a man" tone. No, it definitely wasn't pity; there was so much more at play here. The only thing he knew was that he was drawn to her like fish to water, and he was certain they would spend more time together. He would see to that.

By Monday morning, Molly was completely exhausted from the busy weekend and from trying to get the house back in order. After her crew left, the house looked like a storm had blown through. She couldn't keep from feeling somewhat despondent after everyone had gone home, and her weekly routine started anew. Although she was aware there was no time left in her life for a relationship, she thought constantly about Thad and what a void was left without him. She coped the best she could and didn't reveal to anyone how she missed him, especially not to Jack. He already felt guilty enough having her care for him.

Without even getting a nap during the day, Molly went in for her second shift in the ER. Professional contact with Thad was unavoidable. For a while after he had given her an ultimatum about her taking in Jack, he would look at her with longing eyes when they met at the hospital. She realized he was suffering as much as she was, but she saw no other solution to the present situation. She had to do right by Jack in his helpless condition.

Molly was now experiencing a new emotion where Thad was concerned: jealousy. A few days before, as Molly had driven into the hospital employees' parking lot, she had seen the new nurse supervisor get into Thad's midnight blue BMW convertible with him. Thad let the top back, and the two of them left, laughing and smiling as the wind whipped through their hair. Molly felt sudden pangs of envy, but she understood why Thad would be attracted to this woman. Her long, pale-blonde hair framed a perky, young face. She had to be young enough to be Thad's daughter.

On several other occasions, Molly spotted the two together, laughing and talking. Once Molly saw Thad reach over and pat her hand in a loving gesture. There had been very few people Molly had ever met who she simply disliked, but this woman was one of them.

She had been introduced to her when Tanya Townsend assumed her new position at Smytheville Regional. Nurse Townsend, fresh from the university where she had graduated with honors and had been acclaimed the new Florence Nightingale, came in with new ideas and new ways of doing things. Molly had never minded change. As a matter of fact, she had always prided herself in staying current with the new trends. But Molly never liked a condescending manner in anyone, and that was the image Nurse Townsend conveyed. The hospital grapevine had been abuzz since she had run rough shod over each department, one by one. "She may have plenty of head knowledge, but she doesn't have a clue about the realities of hospital life," said one of the veteran nurses. "She will be the undoing of this hospital."

Townsend had insisted on all chart forms being updated. Accountability and documentation had been her platform. Her new methods called for much repetition in documentation. She insisted that computer records had to corroborate with handwritten duplicates to the letter. Then she had nurses sign off on what others on their shift had done to verify the records were accurate. Trust was not in her vocabulary. She conveyed disrespect and doubt even to nurses who had proven track records. What she asked nurses to do required precious time away from their main focus: patient care. Her demands were totally unrealistic.

Molly expected her invading and revamping of the ER. One night shortly after Molly had come on duty, the unit clerk said under her breath, "Here comes the bulldozer." Molly looked up to see Nurse Townsend marching through the door with her entourage. She had her personal secretary taking notes on insufficiencies at every station and also had a nerdy-looking guy recording her dictated observations on his hand-held computer. Without speaking to anyone in the cordial way other supervisors always had, she picked up every active chart and one-by-one critiqued it. She told her computer guy to verify that the current computer records agreed with the written ones. Well, they didn't because the ER had been busy all night, and no one had had time to catch up the computer records. These very efficient nurses had always seen their paper work was in order before they left the hospital, even if it meant staying an hour after they were off the clock, but they also had the reputation of putting patient care before record-keeping. Nurse Townsend took this as an opportunity to berate Molly on the spot. She didn't care that patients' families were overhearing her. "This is the most inept excuse for documentation I've ever see. I'll not have this sloppiness. Someone's head will roll if ever I catch things in this condition again." With a nod of the head, she indicated she meant Molly.

Dr. Nixon, one of the local surgeons overheard the exchange. "Ms. Townsend, would you step in here just a moment." His tone left no room for doubt about what he was about to do. "Molly Pate has run a superb ER since she came to work here many years ago and, because of family responsibilities, had turned down, more than once, the position of nurse supervisor. I'll not have you reprimanding her in front of patients and their families. This is not even good PR for our hospital. Just so there will be no doubt in your professional cap, I am the chairman of the board here, and you will be on your way to the unemployment office if this ever happens again."

"But I was hired to make this hospital run more efficiently and bring its records up to date with the new laws and standards , and I'm just doing my job," inserted Townsend as soon as Dr. Nixon paused for a minute.

"Yes, you were, but this is not the way to go about it. I would strongly suggest you and your associates take your mission elsewhere, maybe to a department that really is in need of revamping, but leave Molly Tate and this ER alone. Do you completely understand me?"

"Yes, Sir," Townsend answered in an insolent tone. She slung the chart she was holding across the counter, turned her nose a little higher, and marched out with her two associates behind her.

As soon as the door closed behind her, and Dr. Nixon emerged from the record alcove, he met with smiles and a round of applause of all the ER staffers except Molly. She had busied herself in a patient's room to avoid facing Dr. Nixon. Although she was appreciative his support of her, which had been overheard by all, she was also embarrassed by the whole encounter.

Townsend had followed Dr. Nixon's instructions, but it had made her resentful of Molly. She had been overheard by another department when she referred to Molly as the "untouchable." When their paths crossed in the cafeteria, Nurse Townsend made a production of busying herself with some other matter.

It gnawed at Molly to have anyone be antagonistic toward her, but she realized there was nothing she could do to change the situation. What puzzled her was the fact that Thad seemed so attracted to this dislikeable person. He had always been so level-headed and had been resistant to flirts.

This Monday night Molly arrived at the hospital to find the ER extremely active. Staying busy served as a welcome diversion for Molly. It helped her fight off the blues, which so often came after the children left, and as long as she was involved in the care of sick patients, she had no time to ponder what was going on with Townsend and Thad.

She was in treatment room three, taking vitals of a man who had come in with chest pains. The unit clerk stepped to the curtain and said, "Mrs. Pate, there's a call on line two for you. It's the sitter. She said she would hold until you could get to the phone."

Molly finished her task and rushed to see what the problem was. She knew there had to be one for the sitter to call her at work. "This is Molly. What's wrong?"

"I thought I should call. Mr. Jack is burning up with a fever. He seems to be delusional."

"Have you checked his temp?"

"Yes, it's 103.8." Although Jack ran a low-grade fever most of the time, this was definitely a crisis.

"I'll be there as soon as the supervisor gets someone down here to take my place. In the meantime, bathe him with cold water. You can even fill some plastic bags with ice and pack those around him. It's important not to let his temperature keep rising."

Thad was coming in as Molly was rushing out. He had been called to check on one of his patients. "Where are you going? I know your shift's not over."

"It's Jack. The sitter called and his temp is soaring. I've got to go see what I can do."

"You are always on-call where he's concerned, aren't you? I really don't see how you keep the pace you do," Thad responded with a note of resignation.

"You're one to talk. It looks like you're burning the midnight oil pretty often around this hospital." Molly couldn't help wondering if it were patient's emergencies or if it was Nurse Townsend that was bringing Thad to the hospital at unusual hours.

This had been one of the more personal exchanges Thad and Molly had had in quite some time. Even though they pretended nothing was amiss when they saw each other at church or at the hospital, their conversations had stayed impersonal or professional.

"I don't have anything better to do," Thad said with a smile. "I've got to check on a patient here, and then I'll run by and see about Jack if you want me to."

"That would be great if you would. I don't know what the problem might be this time. It may be another kidney infection, or it could be that leg again. It has healed on the outside, but it keeps some heat from a deep infection."

"I should be there within the hour," said Thad. "You will know what to do until I get there."

Molly welcomed his medical assessment of this new situation, but secretly, she was also relieved to know Thad would be involved in this rather than zipping down the road with that new interest of his.

When Molly arrived home, she found the sitter in a dither. She had done everything as Molly had instructed her to do over the phone, but Jack was hallucinating. On quick examination, Molly realized he was in serious trouble. She checked his catheter and noticed the red-tinged urine. "It looks like another kidney or bladder problem," Molly said aloud as much to herself as to the sitter. She continued her assessment. "I don't know if I should give him the antibiotic I have on-hand or if we need to try another one this time."

"Mrs. Pate, I just don't see how you keep going," inserted Mrs. Brown, the night sitter. "It seems you are on-call with him twenty-four seven."

"Mrs. Brown, I do it with the help of the Lord. He seems to give me the strength for each day." Molly was forever mindful to give God the glory for her strength in this situation.

"I'm not talking just about the physical strength. His care consumes your life. How do you cope with that? No one should be this devoted and burdened with an ex-husband."

"I don't view it as a burden. I see it as an opportunity to minister unto my Lord. Jesus teaches, 'When you do it unto one of the least of these, you've done it unto me,'" Molly responded with a smile.

"I know, but even Jesus and his disciples found opportunities to rest." Mrs. Brown's response surprised Molly. She thought about what she had said but quickly dismissed it. There simply was no break in the care Jack required.

Jack vacillated between delirium and moments of lucidity. Surprising both the ladies, Jack inserted in a weak voice, "Molly has always given of herself without a thought of what was best for her."

"I didn't realize you were awake, Mr. Pate," said Mrs. Brown.

Ignoring her comment, Jack spoke what was on his mind while he could. "Molly, I'm really sick this time, aren't I?" Not waiting for Molly to confirm what he already knew, he continued, "Molly, regardless of what happens, I know I haven't said it often enough, but thank you for all you do for me. I'm aware it can't be easy, but I've never heard you complain, not even once. You must be an angel God has sent me. I am so undeserving of your mercies and of His."

Jack wept for the next few minutes before lapsing into hallucinations again. "Do you hear that beautiful music? How sweet it is! Look, look over there! There she is. Mom, Mom, Mom!" Finally he quieted.

"I wonder what he sees and hears when he gets like this," questioned the sitter. "Earlier he was calling Darcy. He told her how beautiful their baby was she was holding."

"I think he must get glimpses of heaven and the people who are there," answered Molly. "I've seen him like this a few other times, but I wonder how many more crises his body can take. The ravages of infections and these high fevers must take an enormous toll on his body. I believe in his mind he's longing for heaven. You know, often Christian people do that near the end."

Soon, Thad arrived as he had promised. After examining him, he said to Molly, "He probably needs to go back to the hospital. It's evident he has a kidney infection, but his leg is also redder and angrier than it has been. We need to do some cultures and get him on intravenous antibiotics. The Wyeth drug rep introduced a new one to me just this week. Maybe it's time to try a new one on him."

Just as he finished saying that, Jack aroused again and surprised them all with his next comment. "Thad, will you promise me something?"

Thad had long since learned not to make an indefinite promise to any patient, so he asked, "Jack, what would that be?"

"If I recover from this bout, please don't let Molly bring me back here. I want her to have a life. Thad, will you take care of her? She deserves a good man like you."

Looking into Molly's eyes, Thad answered, "I'll do my very best on both accounts, Jack. But right now, let's see what we can do to get rid of this infection. I've called the ambulance to transport you to the hospital."

Molly couldn't take this discussion, so she left the room. She was deep in thought when Thad walked into the kitchen. She had already turned her back to try to hide her tears. He walked over, put his arm around her shoulders, and said, "You heard Jack's wishes. I hope you will abide by them this time. I really would like to take care of you for the rest of your life."

Molly was perplexed by his comment after what her observations with him and Tanya had indicated. Of all things, she didn't believe Thad to be fickle.

"I thought I had missed that opportunity already."

Thad questioned, "Why would you say that?"

"I understood why you gave me the ultimatum, and why you had decided to close this chapter and move on to another."

"I'm not sure what you're talking about. Yes, I refused, and still will to stand by and watch you give up a life of your own to care for Jack when there are good alternatives. I can't stand to watch you sacrifice your life for his. In spite of that, I refuse to close the possibility of having a life with you at some point in time."

For the first time ever, Molly let jealousy show its ugly head. "Come on, Thad. I've seen you with Tanya Townsend and the way you look at each other. I don't blame you for wanting someone younger and prettier, but she is more the age of my children. I'll have to say, I'm sorry she's the one who got her hooks in you."

At the absurdity of that, Thad laughed. "Why, Molly, is that jealousy in you I'm hearing?"

His reaction only served to anger Molly. Fortunately, she didn't have to offer a reply because the ambulance attendants were at the door. She welcomed any excuse to end this conversation. Thad's explanation that Tanya was his professionally-struggling goddaughter would have to wait for a more opportune time.

Thad quickly assumed his professional persona again and gave orders for the attendants to take with them to the hospital. "I'll be there in a few minutes to finish the admission procedure, but these orders will give the staff something to start on."

Before walking out, he turned to Molly. "Young lady, we aren't finished with this conversation, but it will wait until we get Jack settled in the hospital." Then he walked to his car and left.

Molly was speechless. She was stunned by the day's events and with her fruitless conversation with Thad. *I know what I've been witnessing between them. I know I'm not mistaken about this, but why did he act so strange about their relationship when I mentioned it. He even laughed at me.* With that thought, her resentment resurfaced. Anger was an emotion as out of character for Molly as was jealousy. Why was she experiencing both of them at the same time? She decided the devil was hard at work on her.

It's Over

She closed the house and followed Thad to the hospital. For the next few days, Jack's condition was so fragile that there was no opportunity to continue her personal discussion with Thad. Circumstances kept their conversations on a professional level.

On Jack's third day in the hospital, Thad asked for her to step outside the door so he could talk to her privately. "Molly, have you considered calling in the family? I'm sure you're aware that Jack's condition is only deteriorating. The different antibiotics we have tried don't seem to be working this time. He has multiple infections—his leg, his kidneys, and now his lungs. Chest X-rays show he has some pneumonia. Besides that, you look as though you could use some relief. Have you even been home since we admitted him?"

"Yes, someone from church comes every day for me to go home to bathe and change clothes, but thanks for your concern." Her tone remained cool. "I felt certain he had some pneumonia because his breathing is more labored, and he seems to be slipping deeper into a coma. We have been through so many hills and valleys with his problems. I've made it a practice to avoid disturbing the children unnecessarily. They don't need to miss work and school every time he has a medical emergency. Do you think I would be safe in waiting until weekend to get them here?"

"Molly, you know as well as I do that these things are not absolutely predictable. He may last weeks, or he could go tonight. There's still the possibility he will rally once again and show improvement. I'm just saying, in my best medical opinion, I am afraid he isn't going to survive this go around. Why don't you go ahead and alert them about his fragile condition so they can be ready to come at any time," Thad suggested.

After Thad left, Molly sat down in the bedside chair where she had spent most of the last few days. Her thoughts rambled.

Am I doing all I can to help Jack, or do I unconsciously wish him dead because I'm so bone-weary? Is Thad the right one to be treating him? Can he possibly be totally objective? Maybe he doesn't want him to survive. Oh, that's the most preposterous thought I've ever entertained. His interest for me has been supplanted by that "young thing." Molly shook her head to clear it from the strange and ridiculous thoughts.

As soon as she closed this self-discussion, the door opened. In walked the new supervisor. Molly stiffened at her presence. "I am just making rounds and am stopping by to see if everything is okay here or if you need something," Tanya said in her most professional comportment.

"We're well taken care of here. Thank you," replied Molly, echoing Tanya's tone. Remembering to put in a good word in for the nursing staff, who had been daily harangued by Tanya Townsend, Molly added, "The nurses in this unit have anticipated our every need and have been wonderful."

"By the way, do you have any idea when you might return to work? Your many absences have worked a hardship on the rest of the ER staff."

Molly felt the fire rising to her face soliciting her tart reply. "No, Ms. Townsend, I don't know when I will return. As you can well see, my ex-husband is gravely ill, and I will attend to him as long as necessary. If my absences are causing a problem, I will be glad to render my resignation." Knowing the answer before she asked, Molly added, "Why? Are the others in the ER complaining?"

Realizing Molly's resignation would present an even greater problem, and having observed the close bond that existed among the staff, Nurse Townsend quickly softened and altered her position. "Oh, no. No one has complained. I've just observed the scheduling strain. I didn't mean that I wanted your resignation. I didn't mean to pressure you unduly."

Nurse Townsend quickly made her exit and documented her visit to room 318 on her clipboard, wrote herself a reminder to put a note in Molly's personnel file indicating their conversation, and then stopped outside the door and duplicated the report on the wall-mounted computer. Then she walked to the nurses' station and began her vigil of combing the charts, one-by-one. As she rounded the corner, she found Thad dictating his morning's chartings. Molly spotted the two of them there when she left Jack's room to go call Caitlin, Benji, and Celeste. Seeing the two of them in very private conversation erased any doubt Molly might have entertained about their relationship. She had been in hospital settings enough to distinguish medical consultations between doctors and nurses from their intimate personal conversations. She also noted the unprofessional way Townsend massaged Thad's neck.

Molly despised this new emotional warfare within her. *Why should I even care what he does privately or who he chooses to spend time with? After all, I had my chance with him and gave up our relationship to care for Jack. I know I can't expect Thad to sit around twiddling his thumbs forever. Still, she is the wrong one for him, I just know it.*

Thad glanced up to see Molly as she quickly averted her stare and walked on by. Her head held high and her lips pursed tightly revealed her seething resentment. He couldn't help but be amused by this uncharacteristic jealousy in Molly, but at the same time, he felt a satisfying assurance that she cared for him enough to react this way.

While Molly was still dialing Caitlin's number, she heard a code blue called for room 318. Immediately, medical personnel converged on his room. She knew what it meant because she had been a first responder many times before. She dropped the phone and ran back to his room and wasn't surprised to find Thad already there. He called a halt to the emergency procedures. "Stop immediately. We have a no resuscitation order on this patient"

Thad announced. He already had his stethoscope to Jack's chest when Molly stepped in. She stood quietly while he finished the final assessment. When he looked into Jack's eyes, he found the pupils fixed, dull, and non-responsive. "Time of death, 9:08 p.m.," Thad dictated.

"Oh, Thad, are we doing the right thing by stopping the resuscitation?" Molly cried.

"Molly, you were present, as was I, when Jack made clear his desires in this matter. We must comply with his wishes. You've done all you could do—more than anyone could expect."

He opened his arms to comfort her, and she gladly surrendered herself to them. Even though she was no longer Jack's wife, and in spite of all that had transpired in their relationship, Molly felt an emptiness at the finality represented by the sheet being drawn over his face. There was an eerie, unexplainable void. After all, she had invested most of her life in caring for this man. She had, for many years, found her identity in being Jack's wife and her children's mother. What was next?

"It's over," whispered Thad as he led her to the private room the staff knew as the grief alcove. His statement held many layers of meaning for both of them.

The Funeral

Molly couldn't believe the many tasks associated with death and a funeral. Notifying Caitlin, Benji, and Celeste was first on her list. Their forgiveness of their father proved to be a double-edged sword for them.

Receiving news of his death would have been, at one time, a welcomed relief; now relief was replaced with sorrow for a plethora of reasons. All three of them had invested time into his care, not only trying to be of help to Molly, but also to show evidence of their forgiveness. During their visits, each sibling had had their own private conversations with Jack. These had provided closure to mountains of resentment toward him. Now, they loved Jack in unique ways. Both Benji and Caitlin appreciated the change in their father. Celeste found his charismatic personality to be endearing, just as so many of his former church members had and as Gloria had when she first met him. It was no mystery to Celeste why her mother had been drawn to him.

The siblings had enjoyed a new camaraderie as they met on weekends to help with Jack. They feared this newfound bond would wane when they no longer had this common mission. Celeste felt she had the most to lose. She had never before had the joy of family like she had experienced the last few months. Gloria had been good to her, but even with her mother's love, she had felt a void in not having a father or brothers and sisters. Benji and Caitlin had filled that emptiness. She wondered if, after the funeral, she could find reason to come back to Smytheville to visit Molly or if Molly would even want her to. Celeste's walk with the Lord had become more intimate as she had observed Molly's many expressions of faith. She couldn't believe how graciously she had accepted her as part of the family. As soon as she received word of Jack's death, she made arrangements to be off work for an indefinite period. She would stay in Smytheville as long as necessary to help Molly with the many details.

Benji lacked one exam being finished with the term when his call came. "Mom, I'm scheduled to take my zoology exam tomorrow, but Dr. Stinson will understand, I know, and will let me make it up when I return to school next term. He may even give me a take-home exam. He's a pretty understanding guy. I'll call him now."

It didn't take much packing and preparation for Benji; he just loaded up and drove home in record time. He felt urgency in being there to help Molly with whatever she had to do and to also provide moral support for her. In less than two hours, he stood by his mom's side.

Perhaps Benji had felt the strongest hostility toward his father earlier. He not only had been offended by his father's lack of attention to him, but also Benji's male protective instinct toward his mom had made him not just resent but literally hate his dad for treating her badly. Crossing that hurdle to reach a point of forgiveness had been a monumental feat, one only achieved through the grace of God. *Strange*, thought Benji, *how my dad had to be flat on his back and totally helpless before we really discovered each other. He had finally become my pal. I found I could tell him some stuff that a boy can't tell his mom. He had even given me some good advice about my relationship with girls. I remember his cautioning me not to date a girl I wouldn't want to marry. "Marry a girl who mirrors your mom's Christian spirit if you can find one," he counseled. He also told me to always show respect to the opposite sex. He confessed he had made many mistakes in that department and didn't want me to repeat them.*

Benji's rush of emotions caught him off guard. He found he couldn't hold back the tears when he made necessary phone calls for his mom to inform people of Jack's passing. Benji hadn't shed tears since he was a small child, but his father's death triggered this emotion more than he ever dreamed it would. The events of the past months had brought maturity to Benji. He had learned to take responsibility and to take charge.

He showed Molly the list of people he had already called and the ones he planned to call. "Mom, have I thought of everyone?"

Molly was astonished at the comprehensiveness of his list. "Benji, you have even thought of things and people I hadn't. I had forgotten about checking with the cemetery about opening the grave. I don't know what I would do without you."

Benji grinned and replied, "Well, I certainly hope you don't plan to try. I expect to be around for a while longer." Then he added in a more serious tone, "But we really don't know when our time here on earth will be over, do we?"

"That's right, son. That's why we need to do as much good for others as we can while we are still here," Molly answered.

"Mom, I didn't realize it would be this difficult to face Dad's death, and I don't mean this disrespectful toward him, but as hard as it is to lose him, I just don't think I could bear it if I lost you."

"Benji, I hope I'll be around to see you married and with kids, but rest assured, you will never really lose me. I will always be a part of you whether I am in this world or the next."

"If, it's all the same to you, Mom, I need you in this one for a long time to come." Benji took his mother and pulled her close. They embraced each other and wept.

After a couple of minutes, Molly broke the tender moment and told Benji, "Caitlin, Emily, and Bob will be arriving about ten tonight. Caitlin had to wait until Bob got home from work for them to leave. I can't wait to see that Emily. She is growing into such a sassy little girl, but I love her more than life."

"You should," said Benji. "She has begun to look just like you." Then he added tenderly, "And that's not a bad thing. I guess I'm getting all gushy for some reason today, but I haven't said this often enough. I love you so much, Mom. Besides that, I think you are beautiful. I don't think I've ever even put into words how I appreciate the way you have remained so strong and faithful for us. You are the best person I've ever known."

"Oh, Benji, you have told me volumes before without having to put things in words. I love you, and I thank you for always being such a good son. You've made parenting an easy job."

"Now don't go that far. I've never known you to lie before, Mom, and this is no time to start," Benji laughed. "Don't you remember the time when I was four that you had to call the firemen to get me off the roof?"

Molly smiled. "I still don't know how you got up there."

"I climbed that tree growing next to the house and crawled up on the roof. I wanted to see if I could find Santa's tracks. Then when I looked down, I was petrified and couldn't move. I stayed up there about an hour before you found me. It seemed, at the time, an eternity."

Caitlin received the news of her father's passing somewhat differently. Caitlin felt ashamed because the news came as a relief for her. Although she had gained a new and improved image of her dad since the accident, that didn't alleviate the strain she had been under. Of course, she never complained to her mom because she understood Molly had been under such a much greater burden. She was also realistic in believing that her dad didn't want to continue living in his miserable condition.

The trips home every weekend had taken a toll on Caitlin. Just the packing was a chore because it took so much for every trip—clothes, toys, and other baby paraphernalia and things to keep Emily content on the ride to Smytheville. These had necessitated her being away from Bob on the weekends that he couldn't come along. Although their relationship had been much better since they had gone through counseling, she had to fight the inclination to wonder if he was seeing someone else while she was in Smytheville, helping out with her dad. *Maybe life will get back to normal after this,* she thought. *Maybe mother can even have a life. She certainly deserves it. She has been such a martyr.*

On the drive to Smytheville with Emily asleep in her car seat, Caitlin shared some of these thoughts about her dad with Bob. "Bob, do you think I'm selfish and awful because I feel this way?"

"No, I don't, darling. You are simply being honest. If we really believe what we Christians say we do about death and eternal life, why shouldn't we celebrate instead of mourning when someone dies? The ones who die are simply getting a promotion."

"Bob, I've got another confession to make. I've thought about it a lot, and I just don't think I could do what my mother has. If you had ever treated me like my dad did my mom, I'm not sure I could forgive you like she has him, much less take care of you as an invalid."

"Caitlin, don't beat yourself up with thoughts like that. None of us know what we could or would do until the situation arises. First of all, I hope you know by now, I would never treat you the way your dad did your mom. Another thing I've discovered is God gives us grace for the moment, just as he has supplied it for your mom and for you."

Molly heard the car door close and ran out to meet them. She hugged both Caitlin and Bob and told them how glad she was they made it safely. Seeing Emily always brought joy to Molly. Emily was just waking up. "Come to Gram, sweetie. We will go in the house and get you something to drink while Mommy and Daddy unload the car." Emily always eagerly went to her grandmother's arms. "Gram, cookie, too?" asked Emily.

"Sure, you can have a cookie if Mommy says it's okay." Emily knew right where the cookie jar was. She squirmed out of Molly's arms and ran to that cabinet, opened the door, and helped herself to the sugar cookies Molly kept there for her. Molly then put her in the highchair she kept sitting in her kitchen for her. While

Emily sat eating her cookie and drinking apple juice from her special cup, Molly embraced Caitlin again. "You children are so very important to me. Do you realize that? I think times like this make people not only focus on what they have lost, but also on what they still have."

"That is so true, Mom. I think I love Bob and Emily more, if that's possible, than I did before you called. And Mom," she added, "my love for you grows every day." She reached out, and the two women held each other close.

Bob came in the kitchen after he had taken their luggage upstairs and said, "Now what was that I heard about some cookies and something to drink?" Molly then busied herself getting snacks and drinks.

"When you finish here and Benji gets back from his errands, we need to sit down and discuss funeral plans. Celeste has already gotten in. She went with Benji to the florist to arrange for the floral casket spray.

As the family planned the service, Benji took the lead as he had done since he had gotten home. Each sibling offered input. They agreed the service should be upbeat and celebratory in nature, but none of them desired to make Jack more than he was. They concurred all comments should be genuine, and if possible, helpful to others. "Perhaps, if anything, the message should be that God is good and offers forgiveness to His children when they stray," offered Celeste.

Caitlin nodded and said, "I totally agree with that."

"You have such great spiritual insight, Celeste," Molly said.

"Any spiritual understanding I have must be attributed to you, Molly. You've taught me so much by example."

The family awoke on Friday morning to a beautiful sunny day. Molly had a full night's sleep, the first in months. The mood around the house echoed peaceful acceptance. Janice Baugh had come to care for Emily while the family attended the funeral. Janice always seemed to know what to do to help without even asking. Gerald, of course, would attend the funeral. Molly, at Benji's suggestion, had asked him to be a pallbearer.

The service was held at Pleasant Valley church. The family pew was filled with a handsome group. On the front pew sat Molly, Benji, Caitlin, Bob, and Celeste. Directly behind them were Gloria and Sawyer. Molly had insisted on their sitting with the family.

The music was upbeat. "Amazing Grace," "To God Be the Glory," and "How Great Thy Art" were sung by the entire congregation in a spirit of worship. The family joining in for these hymns served as a testimony of God's provision for them through their trials. Benji presented the eulogy before Pastor Tim brought the message.

"All have sinned and come short of the glory of God," Benji began in a strong confident voice. "My dad was no exception to this. His sins have been made very public, so that is no new revelation to people here. Sin hurts. The people closest to the sinner and the ones who love him most are hurt the greatest. Many of you have experienced hurt and disappointment because of Jack Pate's sin. None have hurt more than his own family. Today I'm not here to condemn the man who was my earthly father, but to praise our heavenly Father for his agape love toward each of us and for His great capacity for forgiveness. I rejoice to say my dad genuinely repented, and God willingly and gladly forgave him. What else could his own family do then but to forgive him also? Each of us in our own way and in our own time have come to terms with Dad and have also forgiven him. I ask you, if you have not reached that point of forgiveness, that you will today. I am a walking testimony of what a relief it is to forgive and unburden one's self of bitterness and resentment because, as most of you know, I wore those emotions as a badge for quite some time.

"One other thing—I would remind you that you are also part of the 'all' in 'All have sinned.' Some of you need to do the very same thing Jack Pate did, and that is to fall on your face, confess your sins to a loving Father, and ask for forgiveness. Yes, my dad did some bad things, but he also did much good. Thanks be to God, since He forgave him, all He remembers is the good. May each of us do the same."

As Benji returned to his seat, something very unfuneral-like happened. The congregation began standing, one by one, and gave him a standing ovation. In so doing, they not only showed approval of what Benji had said, but some did it as an outward profession of their faith in God. Grown men wept in repentance for their sins. Several of the good 'ol boys were among them.

A spirit of celebration permeated the house as friends gathered after the funeral for a feast, which had been prepared by the church ladies. Many had come from Jack's former church. Some people had to introduce themselves. Benji and Caitlin didn't remember many of them, and Celeste had never even met most of them.

"I don't mean to dampen this time of celebration in any way by getting too serious, but I feel I must say this," inserted Gloria. "I want all of you to know, I've been so moved by the way all of you have responded to Jack in his last months and how you have handled his death. It is so, so…Christian-like. I will never be the same after sharing this experience with you. And I won't view death as the Grim Reaper anymore."

Thad and Tanya

When Thad said good-bye to Molly at the hospital, he realized it would be days before he would see her again but didn't feel it was the time to tell her that. First of all, Thad just didn't do funerals. He could handle the goriest situations while patients were alive, but once the sheet was pulled over their heads, he was finished. Funerals only served as reminders of his medical inadequacies in preserving human life. If he could no longer be of medical help, he just didn't want to be there. Thad thought funerals were an inane, outdated, useless custom anyway.

Thad realized Molly would have many people around to help her through the tedium of the next few days. He could be with her after things settled back to normal. He decided there was no reason for him to cancel his plans to go to Charleston to visit Tanya's parents.

On the following Monday, Molly decided to return to work, although she had lost her enthusiasm about her job since Nurse Townsend had come on the scene. She had seriously considered leaving the hospital and relocating. There was little to hold her in Smytheville now. Thad had made it quite evident he was through with her by his absence at the funeral and by keeping his distance for the days surrounding it.

Her coworkers greeted her when she came in. Evelyn, her nurse friend closest to her, met her with a hug. "You just can't believe how glad I am to see your face. We've missed you. I saw you from a distance at the funeral but didn't get a chance to talk to you. I had to rush home and get ready to come in to work. I'm so sorry you have had such a rough and tiring time lately, but to be truthful, I'm glad this whole ordeal is over for you. No one else I know would have done what you have in caring for your ex."

"Evelyn, I'd like to say I'm glad to be back, but if I did, I would be untruthful. I don't know what it is, but I just can't get excited about coming to work like I used to."

"You know as well as I do. We all feel the same way. Nurse Townsend has sucked all the joy out of the hospital."

"True, but that's not all of it. This is for your ears only, but seeing Thad with her just tears me apart. You know I've never been a jealous person, but this woman brings out the absolute worst in me."

Evelyn considered for a minute whether she should tell Molly or not. Then she thought it would be better to come from her than from the others in the department. "Molly, I've got to tell you something you're not going to want to hear, but if I don't, you'll hear the others gossiping about it."

"Well, tell me. The suspense is bound to be worse than the message."

"You are going to catch on after a while that both Dr. Simmons and Nurse Townsend aren't here. Joanne, the first shift unit clerk, saw them speeding off together in Dr. Simmons's convertible as she came in. She said suitcases were visible in the backseat. When I asked around about Nurse Townsend's absence, I was told she is off for a few days for a trip to Charleston. That's got everyone here abuzz with gossip."

Molly's heart felt as though it would break. Her eyes reddened as she fought back tears. "Well, that settles it."

"Settles what, Molly?"

"I've been considering relocating, and this confirms that I should. I'll just go ahead and turn in my notice tomorrow."

"You can't do that. It's too soon to make important life-changing decisions. The experts say you shouldn't make any major adjustments for at least a year after a mates' death." Then she corrected herself, "But I don't know if that would apply to an ex-husband's death or not. Still, I don't want you to leave. I would miss you too much. Your presence makes all of us act more civilly to each other around here."

"I'll miss you, too, but I can't say I'll miss this hospital anymore. By the way, when are the two lovebirds due back?"

"I heard she would be back ransacking departments on Thursday. We all will enjoy a brief reprieve from her scrutiny, but nobody here likes the idea that a good man like Simmons has taken up with her. It makes absolutely no sense."

"Well, this may be the shortest notice in history, but I will be sure to be gone by the time they get back. There's no need in causing myself more suffering by seeing them."

"Where will you go?" asked the bewildered Evelyn.

"I'm really not sure, but I think I will get a condo at the beach for a while. I think the sand and sun would help me relax. I don't have to be in a hurry about going back to work. One good thing that has come from Jack's death is the fact that I will be financially comfortable. The lawyer called the day after Jack died to tell me I was the beneficiary for Jack's sizable settlement. Jack had instructed him to notify me of that as soon as he died. Of course it will be awhile before the money is actually in my account, but Jack wanted me to know I could count on getting it. There is enough that I can share with the children and still do what I want to for the rest of my life."

"If anyone deserves good fortune, it's you. I hope you get tanned and rested and then meet a handsome young man who treats you like you deserve. I don't know what we will do without you here at the hospital, but I certainly don't blame you for wanting to get out of here. I would too if I could."

"Meeting a man is the last thing on my mind. I think I'm finished with ever thinking about another relationship, but getting tanned and rested sounds wonderful right now. The more I consider going, the more confident I am that I want to do that and soon."

Before Molly left the hospital the next morning, she laid her letter of resignation on the desk of the director of personnel. Although she was despondent about Thad's behavior, she felt free and unencumbered as she drove away from the hospital. *I'll get over him. I just know I will. But I do love that man. I wonder if all men have this wandering spirit or if it is just the fact I can't keep one interested. I know Thad was true to Margaret all those years, so it's probably just me. This whole scenario is so unbelievable. This fling with Tanya Townsend is just so completely out of character for him. I don't know what to do about the situation, but I'll just turn it over to the Lord.*

Beach

Two days later, the white sand warmed Molly's feet as she strolled down the tranquil gulf beach. An early morning salty breeze wafted the cobwebs from her mind. She had never felt so totally unencumbered and liberated in her entire life.

Once Molly made up her mind to do something, she acted on it. So it was with closing up the house and finding a place at the beach. She picked Gulf Shores, Alabama, for her destination. It was known for its family atmosphere and gorgeous white sand beaches. She knew a couple at Pleasant Valley church who owned a vacation condo there and who could direct her to a suitable place. When she called to inquire, they told her about a condo complex down West Beach, which was out of the main tourist traffic. "The place is quiet and well-maintained. The swaying palms and fragrant oleanders make the place seem like a tropical paradise," her friend reported.

It sounded perfect, so Molly wasted no time in leasing a two-bedroom condo overlooking the beach. She made the perfunctory calls to her children to inform them of her decision to resign from her job and to get out of the house for a while. They agreed this sounded like an ideal plan. If anyone needed a break from the world, it was their mom. She told them the place she had leased was large enough for them to come for a visit. Instinctively, both of them knew their mother didn't need visitors, at least not for a few weeks.

Molly spent her first two days experiencing her new freedom by walking the beach, swimming, reading, and taking an occasional nap. She spent the late afternoons and early evenings sitting on her balcony, letting her heart match the rhythm of the waves hitting the shore while enjoying the sun setting over the gulf. The sun was a huge ball of fire getting increasingly larger until it dropped off the horizon, leaving ribbons of pink and orange in the distant sky. Her communion with God during these times renewed and restored her spirit and soul. She reflected on how God had brought her through so many valleys and how he had given her the strength to cross the hurdles she had faced. She had no regrets for she was satisfied what she had done for Jack in his last days was in keeping with God's will. Occasionally during these afternoon meditations, she would spontaneously break into praise choruses. On her third morning there, she started singing, "God is so good, God is so good, God is so good to me." This was her sincere expression of accumulated thanks.

She went inside and was pouring her coffee and getting a bowl of cereal while watching *Fox News* on the small kitchen television. The ringing of the phone startled her because it had remained silent since she had been there. She hadn't even bothered to check to see if the office had turned it on because she had appreciated this time without interruptions.

"Hello," she answered tentatively because she assumed the call was intended for the previous occupants.

"Molly, where in the world are you? I've just about gone crazy trying to find you since I got back into town."

Just the sound Thad's voice made Molly's heart flutter, but his message infuriated her. "Why would you be so frantic about finding me now? I haven't heard from you since Jack died." The curtness of her voice transmitted her pent up anger.

Ignoring what she said and sensing what she must be thinking, Thad replied, "Molly, we need to talk. I know I have some explaining to do. Things aren't like you think they are with Tanya and me, but I want to talk with you face to face about the situation. Will you trust me on that until we can get together?"

"I can't imagine any explanation but the obvious one when you left town with her," Molly replied.

"Molly, please believe me when I tell you things are simply platonic between Tanya and me. I want to come down there as soon as I leave the office Friday. I've been swamped since I got back. When I returned to the hospital, I was told you had resigned. I wore out your home phone, trying to call you. I even went by and banged on the door until a neighbor told me you had closed the house down and had gone to the beach for a while. I then called Benji to find you. I had to persuade him to give me your phone number. He finally told me you were in Gulf Shores but said if you wanted me to know exactly where, you would have to tell me. He said, 'I'm not telling anyone where she is. The woman needs a well-deserved rest, and I'm not sure she even wants to see you right now. Although she didn't mention it to any of us, it was evident she kept expecting you to show up at the funeral or at least afterward. I think it was Sawyer who finally put all our questions into words, but you know how Mom is. She just brushed it off by saying you were probably tied up at the office.'

"Benji is so very protective of you. Please say I can come and explain things to you. You are the most important person in the world to me. Never forget that."

Molly was stunned, but Thad's tender tone softened her anger somewhat. "My better judgment says I should just forget the past and go on with my life, but I suppose I should give you a chance to tell me what's going on."

"That's what I wanted to hear. It will be midnight or after before I can get there Friday. Do you know a place close by where I might get a room?"

Molly hesitated for a minute and then said, "I have an extra bedroom here at my condo. It will be too late to try to check into a motel, so you can use it if you would like."

Knowing the offer was strictly for a place to sleep, and in spite of her cool tone, Thad was still elated with that much concession from Molly. Just maybe that meant she was open to his justifications for his actions. "Molly, I am truly sorry I couldn't be there for you at the funeral. I'll try to clarify everything when

I get there. Please stay safe. Lock your doors, and don't talk to strangers."

His paternal cautions brought a tinge of a smile to Molly's face. Although for the next few days, she tried to think of what reasons he might proffer for his past actions, she simply couldn't think of any scenario but the obvious one, although his words resounded in her mind, "Just trust me."

The tranquility of her seclusion evolved into loneliness after Thad's call. She felt like a young girl waiting for her first date. Restlessness replaced relaxation because of her eagerness to see Thad again.

Although she had passed up even going to a restaurant since she had been there, she decided she would forgo her usual sandwich or salad that night and pass the time by eating out. She drove to Hazel's, a popular seafood restaurant on the strip. The awkwardness of asking for a table for one reinforced her desire to have a life companion. Her singleness amid the couples and families seated there stood out like elephant ears. *Maybe the freedom of the single life isn't all it was cracked up to be. I really didn't realize how much I've missed Thad until he called. Should I receive him with open arms and be gullible as I was with Jack, or do I make him convince me of his innocence with Tanya?*

Molly sat at the table mentally playing out possible ways to react when he arrived.

The waitress interrupted her reverie when she delivered enough seafood to feed a family. The stares and smiles of onlookers in the restaurant, who seemed curious as to whether a little lady like Molly could actually eat that much food, embarrassed her. When she ordered the Captain Dave's seafood platter, she had no idea how gigantic it would be. "Enjoy." Molly chowed down on the savory shrimp and succulent oysters, leaving the fries on her plate. When she had eaten her fill, she asked for a take-home box. "This is enough food to feed me for a week," she told the waitress.

"I know. I should have warned you about how much came on that plate, but I thought you might just be one of those ladies with a huge appetite. I've seen a few who could eat the whole thing."

Just half-way listening to a local radio station as she returned to the condo, the announcer gained her full attention when he reported a tropical storm moving in the direction of Gulf Shores. *That's totally unbelievable. Never have I seen skies so clear. Oh, well, the weathermen usually make way too much of any blip on the radar. Even if it does become a reality, it shouldn't be here for several days. I've always believed one shouldn't borrow troubles from the future; dealing with today's provides enough challenge for me.*

When Molly returned to the condo, it was still too early to go to bed, so she decided to sit on the balcony and try to finish her novel. After a while, she realized she had read the same paragraph three times. Her mind wasn't focused on fiction; the reality of Thad's call provided enough adventure and tension. She put the book on the vinyl side table, leaned her head back, closed her eyes, and imagined what life would be like if they were to actually marry someday. The sound of the pounding surf became a lullaby. Soon she drifted off to sleep.

Thad was holding her in a passionate embrace. Their lips melded as though they were one. Desire to be even closer, to truly be one in the absolute sense, made Molly dizzy. Thad's gentle touch and kind words soothed Molly's soul. Never had she felt such euphoria. Could this moment be frozen in time?

A clap of thunder startled Molly, bringing her out of her dream. She realized she should go inside to get out of the reach of any lightning. Sadness at the loss of the sensations she had just experienced crept in. *Oh, so much for that. I knew it seemed too good to be true, and I guess it was.*

Molly slept fitfully that night. Every time she awoke, Thad was on her mind. She knew he would be there the next night. She felt like a child waiting for Santa Claus. Plans for the next day replaced any hope of more sleep. *I think I'll call the all-inclusive spa I saw advertised in the local paper. I've never allowed myself the luxury of being pampered, but now I can well afford it. I'll let the hair stylist give me a new look. I could use some help with makeup also. Then I need to go to the grocery store and bring in something more substantial than ham sandwiches. If Thad isn't coming in until midnight or later, he'll probably be starved when he arrives.*

She got up at five. A morning jog on the beach would be refreshing, she decided. As light was breaking, she headed east on her run. She ran in the water's edge where the surf had firmed up the sand. It was a glorious day. Molly felt as if God had created all the beauty and serenity of that place just for her. The wet sand shimmered in the morning light, and the wide expanse of the white-capping gulf confirmed God's love for her.

When she returned to the condo, she made toast and coffee. Her morning devotion time was special as she asked the Holy Spirit to join her at the breakfast table. Her prayer recounted all the ways God had blessed her. Her supplications echoed as pleas for Thad's safety in travel and for His blessings on their reuniting.

By ten, Molly arrived at the spa. Looking at the services listed on the sign behind the receptionist, she told her, "I'll take 'The Works.'" 'The Works' was their advertised all-inclusive package—full-body massage, hair care, makeup, manicure, pedicure, and the list went on and on. Molly felt extravagant, but her giddy mood assured her she was worth it today.

By noon, Molly was just to the halfway mark of her day's indulgence. A waiter dressed in a white dinner jacket and tuxedo slacks served her a gourmet salad lunch. He offered champagne, but, instead, Molly opted for the non-alcoholic sparkling grape juice. By the time he set the orchid-garnished plate on the glass-topped table and left the beautifully decorated small private room, Molly was diving in like a starved animal. The night of tossing and turning, along with her morning exercise, had given

Molly a ravenous appetite. Just as the masseuse was finishing her hypnotic massage, she asked "Are you ready for your bikini wax, Ma'am?"

"My what?" Although Molly knew what a bikini wax was, just the idea of her having one shocked and overwhelmed her. "I think I'll pass on that."

"That is totally up to you, but it is included in your package."

Why in the world would I even want one? I don't want some stranger messing with me down there. These people will think me totally unsophisticated for refusing, but that just takes this event too far for me.

"I think I will opt out on that service. If it's all the same to you, I will move on to the hair stylist." Molly smiled at the mental image of herself getting a bikini wax.

At four that afternoon, a revitalized, modernized Molly walked to her car. Molly had always been attractive in a sweet preacher's wife manner, but today she had been transformed into a beautiful, sophisticated, youthful Molly. Even the dark circles of fatigue had disappeared. She had spent the day away from *Fox News*, or any television for that matter. The Isis Spa played only peaceful music, keeping away all stressful distractions. Molly needed no weather report to inform her that the tropical storm was fast approaching. The sky was dark, threaded by continual patterns of lightning. Thunder roared in the distance. Molly drove faster than usual trying to get home and inside before the rain set in. She had no more than stepped inside her door when sheets of rain poured from the sky. The surf bellowed angrily.

The serenity of the day was replaced with concern for Thad. Realizing he would be driving into the storm, Molly turned on the TV to get the latest updates. Every local station was abuzz with warnings. A voluntary evacuation alert streamed across the bottom of the screen. Molly's uneasiness wasn't for herself, but her apprehensions were for Thad's safety.

Molly immediately dialed the number. "Dr. Simmons's office. Teresa speaking." Molly recognized the friendly receptionist's voice.

"Teresa, this is Molly Pate. Thad hasn't left the office yet, has he?"

"I'm afraid he has, Molly. He left early, about 2:30 p.m., and had me to cancel his appointments through Tuesday. He was unusually mysterious about where he was headed. Normally, he leaves a detailed itinerary with me, but not this time. If you have an emergency, I can put you through to Dr. Gravely. He's taking his calls."

"No, that's okay. I'll just try to reach him on his cell phone. This is not a medical problem."

She felt urgency in stopping him before he got too far. Thad answered on the third ring. "Thad Simmons speaking."

"Thad, I'm so glad I got through to you. I was afraid you might be in one of the cell dead spots. Where are you?"

"I'm about an hour and a half out of Smytheville. Why?" Thad recognized agitation in Molly's voice.

"Have you been listening to the weather reports?"

"No, I've been in the office since early this morning, and now I'm motoring along listening to my Neil Diamond CD. Why? What's up?"

"A tropical storm, that's what. It is fast approaching Gulf Shores. The weather alert suggests people who are in trailers or unsafe wooden structures should evacuate. You should turn around and go back. I feel safe in this large, sturdy condo, but you're traveling into this storm doesn't make sense."

"Just call me the mailman. Neither rain, snow, nor will dark of night keep me from my appointed rounds."

His jovial mood amplified her desire to see him, but still she didn't want him driving into danger. "Thad, I'm not even sure if you can get through. Water may be over the roads by the time you get here. I've never seen rain so heavy."

"I'll walk or swim if I have to. I want to be with you. I've waited long enough."

Thad was not to be deterred, and Molly had mixed feelings about his determination. On one hand, she was elated he wanted to see her so badly; on the other, she knew the drive would be treacherous at best, or, even worse, the highway might be blocked, or he might wreck because of the storm.

"If you are determined to be so foolish as to try to get here, promise me you will be careful. I'm really worried about your doing this."

"Hmmm, let me see. Aren't you the young lady who once told me, 'Worry is sin because it shows a lack of faith in God'?"

"I just hate it when my own words come back to bite me like that," Molly teased. "All right, I will just say I'm concerned."

The rain volume and the wind speed picked up with each mile. Thad hated to admit it, but the closer he drove to Gulf Shores, the more he doubted his decision to travel directly into the storm. The north bound lanes of US 231 were packed with evacuees trying to get to higher ground. The good thing about that was Thad had the south bound lanes to himself; the bad thing was, he had no tail lights to follow and guide him through the torrential rain. At times the roaring of the tires indicated he was at the edge of the highway. Visibility was at zero. He gripped the steering wheel and sat on the edge of the seat, straining to find the white lines.

At last the lighted intersection near the I-10 ramp helped to orient Thad. Just as he turned to get on the ramp, he saw blue lights ahead. He felt disheartened to see the orange barrels blocking the road. When he stopped at the barrier, a state trooper got out of his car and fought the wind to get to Thad's car. "I'm sorry, sir, but the road is closed. It's too dangerous to go any further south."

Thad resorted to a tactic he had never implemented before. Using his doctor title and credentials to further his cause seemed excusable in this situation. He lied. "Officer, I realize the danger, but I'm on an emergency call. My patient can't get out, and it is imperative that I try to get to her."

The officer tried to dissuade him for a few minutes but finally relented. "Sir, I understand your calling to care for the sick, but I'm afraid you are the one who will need a doctor before the night is over if you persist in going on. I won't stop you, though, if you feel you must."

Thad sighed with relief when the officer pulled back the blockade to let him pass. The drive just became more difficult though. By the time Thad reached the beach, waves were washing over the road. Only by main strength did Thad hold the car on the highway. Thad prayed aloud, "Dear God, I know I got myself into this mess, but I beg you to help me through it." Several times, Thad realized he had absolutely no control of the car. Only the water and God had control. What should have been a six-hour trip had taken ten.

As he neared West Beach, Thad was aware he wouldn't be able to see the Condo's sign nor the street markers. For the first time in hours, he took one hand off the wheel to push the redial button on his phone. "Molly, I'm on the beach road, but I need your help."

"Oh, Thad, I'm so glad to hear your voice. I've been frantic with worry. I mean, concern. I don't see how you've made it this far."

"Molly, I don't need to talk long. I need both hands to control this car, but tell me how far it is to the condo from the intersection of state road 59 and the beach road. If I know the distance, I can find you by using my odometer. It's raining so hard and the wind is blowing so much water across the road, there's no chance I'll be able to see the condo."

"It is exactly 8.4 miles from there to Sand Castle Condos."

"Thanks. That will help greatly. I'll be there soon."

"Soon" meant thirty minutes creeping through the deluge. Finally, Thad had driven the 8.4 miles. He was able to get glimpses of a white rock path and turned in on faith that was the driveway.

Minutes later Thad rapped on the door. When Molly opened it, she saw Thad standing there looking like a weary wet dog, but he had never looked better to her. All questions about how she should receive him were instantly erased. Her dream came true, but in a twisted way. She opened her arms and pulled him close. Contrary to her dream, she was the one initiating the intimate kiss.

After Thad had a warm bath and had put on dry clothes, he devoured the lasagna and French bread she sat before him. The two spent the remainder of the night cuddled on the sofa, holding each other tightly as though the storm might try to separate them. The furor of the storm on the outside raged in marked contrast to the warm bliss Thad and Molly enjoyed inside.

Thad's explanation of his relationship with Tanya—that she is his goddaughter and her father, his college roommate—seemed totally unimportant to Molly now. He insisted on giving her a full explanation, including the fact that Tanya, although smart, was lacking in social skills and, that as a favor to her dad, he was trying to mentor her. Thad wanted nothing to tarnish their relationship. She listened but really didn't care. Thad had beaten all odds against his getting there, but with God's help and his heroic efforts, he was with her now and was safe.

The Wedding

Molly and Thad awakened to the morning sunlight shining through the sliding glass door. Just as God had shown His might through the storm of the previous night, even greater, He revealed His love through the beauty of this new day. They were still huddled on the sofa like two innocent puppies.

Molly stretched and yawned, and then she suggested, "Let's go for a walk on the beach if you're up to it."

"What do you mean, if I'm up to it? I'm up to climbing Mount Everest as long as I'm with you."

Even with his tousled morning hair, Molly melted at his broad grin and handsome presence. Love beamed from his eyes as he gazed at her.

They changed into their swimsuits, brushed their teeth, and headed out to face a new day. After strolling in the hot morning sun for a while, Thad challenged, "The last one in is a rotten egg."

With that, the two ran through the surf like kids. They swam, jumped waves, and then chased each other along the water's edge. "I'm going in to cook breakfast. I'm starved," Molly yelled over the sound of the crashing waves.

"I'm right behind you." Thad couldn't bear to let Molly out of his sight.

After showering and dressing, they ate a breakfast hearty enough for lumberjacks. "I don't think I told you last night, Molly, but you have never looked so beautiful. Something has taken fifteen years off your appearance. What's your secret? Did you find a fountain of youth here or some magic elixir?"

"Getting several full nights' sleep hasn't hurt anything, but to tell the truth, I pampered myself with a day at the spa. I got a new hairstyle and some help with my makeup in with the package. I feel guilty about spending so much just on myself."

"Trust me, it wasn't just for you. I'm thoroughly enjoying the results. Besides that, I hope for the remainder of your days, I can pamper you even more."

Their joy and exuberance found no stopping place. The two explored and enjoyed everything Gulf Shores had to offer in the way of entertainment, from deep sea fishing trips to hot air balloon rides. They even reverted to their youth and went to the amusement park and rode the Ferris wheel and rollercoaster one night, ignoring the pointing and giggling of the teenagers who found this strange behavior for middle-aged adults. Molly was the first to admit fatigue. "All of this fun is about to kill me," she joked.

"Me too," confessed Thad, "but I'll tell you part of the motive in my madness. I have to keep you out of the condo and keep us both totally exhausted to maintain a gentlemanlike behavior toward you. To be honest, I just don't know how much longer I can hold out."

Molly was ashamed to admit it, but temptation had been knocking at her door also. "That doesn't look as though it will be an issue for either of us much longer if you still insist you have to go back to work tomorrow," she replied.

"Ah, you would have to remind me. For our last night's fling, I want to make it a good one. What is your all-time favorite restaurant here?"

Without a moment's hesitation, Molly answered, "Bayside Grill in Orange Beach. They have the best coconut shrimp I've ever tasted. They make this special dipping sauce for it that is good enough to drink"

"Bayside Grill it is then. I hope it isn't a coat-and-tie place, because I didn't bring dress clothes."

"I don't know of a place at the beach where casual dress isn't acceptable. I plan to wear a sundress myself."

When they arrived, they stood out as the most striking couple in the place—Molly dressed in her new, pink, gauzy sundress and Thad in khakis and a golf shirt. Thad had called ahead and made reservations earlier that afternoon. The receptionist had asked if he would be interested in a two-hour sunset cruise after dinner. "The days are long now, and you can eat at seven and still make the sunset. The ship embarks from the dock outside the restaurant."

"That's a great idea," he told her, "just right for what I have planned."

The dinner lived up to Molly's commendation. When they finished off the last of the shrimp, the waiter brought a tray of scrumptious desserts. "What will it be?" Thad asked after the waiter recited the choices.

"I wish I had room for one of each," answered Molly, "but I'm stuffed."

"This is a night of indulgence. Let's splurge and stuff some more. I'll order something different from your choice, and we can share."

"Do you really like fat women?" Molly asked with a grin.

"If it is you, the answer is yes. I like you any way I can get you, but I think you would have to eat an entire tray of these desserts every night for a month to put on even three pounds. You are blessed with great metabolism."

Molly debated whether to choose the key lime or the bourbon pecan pie. "Okay then. Here goes. I'll take the key lime pie."

"I'll take the bourbon pecan then," said Thad.

After they had finished feasting on the desserts and drinking their fill of coffee, Thad suggested, "Let's take a walk out on the pier. We need to kill a few minutes."

"Why?" asked Molly.

"I've made reservations for us on the sunset cruise."

"I've always wanted to do that," Molly commented with the gusto of a child.

Soon the ship pulled in and the passengers from the early cruise disembarked. Thad and Molly were some of the first passengers to board for the next one. Thad led her to the bow of the upper deck. "I think this will be the place for the best view," he said.

He was right. Never had there been a more beautiful sunset. Molly watched in awe as the sun glistened on the water, making each ripple sparkle like diamonds. The buzz of the excited passengers quieted as the huge orange ball neared the water. The surf mirrored the blaze of the sun, giving the impression the whole world around them was caught up in its fire. Never had Molly looked so beautiful. The glow of the sunset reflected on her face as the ocean breeze swept her hair back from her face. The pink sundress contoured her slight frame and accented her tanned skin. Thad knew this was the right moment.

"Do you see how gigantic the sun is, Molly? That merely starts to measure my love for you. Do you see the wide expanse of the gulf? That's how far my love will last." Taking her hands in his, he asked, "Molly Pate, will you marry me? Will you entrust the rest of your life to me, so I can care for you and dedicate my life to making you happy? Will you let me be part of your children's and grandchildren's lives? Will you accept this ring as a token of my love for you and as a symbol of my never-ending devotion to you?"

Molly was staring into Thad's most beautiful blue-gray eyes, which revealed nothing but love, truth, and honesty. Without even stopping to weigh all the pros and cons, as she usually did with any decision, she whispered in perfect awe, "Yes, yes, yes."

The couple was unaware of the audience observing this moment until applause echoed throughout the deck. The celebration was in part for the glorious sunset the passengers had just witnessed, but even more. It was for the romance of the moment, represented by Molly and Thad's engagement.

Molly had packed up and had driven back to Smytheville just behind Thad the following morning. She couldn't bear the thought of being away from him, even for a few days at a time. The beach had served its purpose. Seclusion no longer held appeal for her. Now she was ready to go home. Besides, both of them were eager to announce their engagement.

They felt it only proper to tell the family first. For the occasion, they planned a party and invited Benji and his girlfriend Meagan; Caitlin, Bob, and Emily; Gloria and Celeste—who Molly treated as one of her own; and of course, Sawyer, their adopted family member. Wanting to get through the necessary preliminaries as fast as possible, the party was scheduled for the very next weekend. Because of the time element, they chose to invite by phone rather than by formal written invitations. They planned to keep the whole wedding affair as simple as possible. They didn't even attempt to hide the excitement in their voices, so all of the invitees had some idea what was behind the invitation.

Thad insisted Molly not tire herself out cooking for the group, so he reserved the private dining hall at Jilli's, Smytheville's most elegant restaurant, for the gathering. After a superb meal, Thad stood to make the announcement. He pulled Molly to her feet to stand beside him. "Caitlin, Benji, Celeste, first of all, I want to ask you if I might have your mom's hand in marriage. I promise to love and care for her for our remaining days."

The two girls whispered something in Benji's ears. He stood and announced, "Well, it looks like I'm it. Caitlin and Celeste have asked me to serve as the family's mouthpiece." Then with great enthusiasm he startled everyone with an ear-splitting "Yes, yes, yes! Praise the Lord, yes! All we want to know is why has this taken so long?" Then in mock seriousness he added, "Wait just a minute. You're not pregnant are you, Mom? This isn't a shotgun wedding, is it?" The crowd roared with laughter, and a spontaneous thunderous applause began. The entire group stood in a mutual show of agreement and approval.

Although Molly and Thad had agreed to make the wedding a small family affair, Molly's children simply wouldn't hear of that. Caitlin spoke up first. "Mother, Pleasant Valley Church has been every step of the way with us throughout our troubles. They have offered support for a long time now. I believe it would do those fine people an injustice to exclude them. They are eager to celebrate with you two. I know you don't want to bother with the details for a formal church wedding, but if you will allow us, Benji, Celeste, and I want to take care of everything. All you and Thad will have to do is show up, say your vows, and leave on a honeymoon. Will you permit us to do this for you?" Benji and Celeste stood by nodding in agreement. Molly looked at Thad with question mark eyes, and he nodded his consent and added, "I think Caitlin is right. There are many people in Smytheville who would like to celebrate this occasion with us."

With only a month to plan for such an event, Caitlin called in all the troops—both friends and family. She discovered the town buzzed with excitement about this marriage, and people were eager to volunteer help. Smytheville's best caterer took charge of the food. She had been a member at Pleasant Valley for years and felt she hadn't been available to help Molly the way some of the other ladies had, so she jumped at the opportunity to make up for it now. Eighty-year-old Sadie Ferguson called Caitlin to say she had a brother who was a florist in Hawaii. "With your permission, I will have him ship in tropical flowers—orchids, bird of paradise, and the like—and I will take care of the arrangements. You know, I grew up in a flower shop, so I still remember how to do some unique arrangements."

Within the week, so many had offered their services that all "The Three Musketeers" had left to do was address and send out invitations. Even Gloria was caught up in the excitement. "Molly, I would like to take you shopping in Atlanta and help you find a dress, if I may."

Molly was thrilled with Gloria's offer because she knew she had classy taste and would steer her in the right direction. That she did. Whenever Molly would try to settle on something inexpensive, Gloria wouldn't hear of it. "No, you aren't going to buy your wedding dress off the clearance rack. Nothing but the best will do for this occasion. Molly was totally exhausted after a day of trying on dresses, but the efforts paid off. Molly, herself, was shocked at how flattering her dress was. It was the palest sea foam green imaginable and flowed down every curve of her body like condensation running down the outside of a glass.

"You'll knock 'em dead, Molly. That's the perfect choice." Gloria wouldn't even let Molly see the price tag. You can afford it. Don't worry about the cost," she said. Molly drove back to Smytheville with a carload of clothes, shoes, and other accessories. Gloria wouldn't let her stop until her trousseau was complete.

The morning of August 9th, Molly woke up early and lay in bed trying to imagine how life would be for her as Mrs. Thad Simmons. She felt at perfect peace. She reflected on her marriage to Jack and was satisfied she had been a good wife to him. Also, she had done what she knew God wanted her to in taking care of Jack until the end. Then some insecurity about how Thad might perceive her middle-age body sneaked in. Molly had never had a lover other than Jack, and during their years together, he had never failed to point out her inadequacies in bed and in her body. His eyes were always drawn to her motherly abdomen pooch. He had complained she wasn't adventurous enough in bed, and she had no idea what he meant by that.

Then Molly determined to block out all negative thoughts. She had entirely too much to rejoice in. Her children had grown into responsible, independent adults. She no longer had financial worries, and she felt great comfort in knowing she had God's approval for this marriage to this kind, wonderful man.

A rap at the door brought her out of her cogitations. "Mom, we've cooked breakfast for you. Can we come in?"

"Sure, baby, but you shouldn't have. I was about to get up and go to the kitchen."

"No, stay put. You deserve breakfast in bed today. This will be a busy one, and we want you fresh for the wedding," Celeste added. The children had completely taken over the wedding plans; now they were taking over all of her decisions, but she really liked their pampering.

Benji opened the door, and Caitlin brought in the tray. Celeste spread a towel over the bedding for Caitlin to place the tray on. Molly loved the way the three had joined forces to make this day special and to show their unwavering support.

"How can I ever repay you children for all you've done for us?"

Benji put a finger to his mouth and said, "Hmm, let me see. Oh, could it possibly be that we are just trying to start repaying you for all you've done for us. Now that's enough of that nonsense, and I'll not listen to any more of that 'repaying' business." Benji became more serious for a minute and added, "If you hadn't allowed us to do some of these things, you would have stolen our blessing, Mom."

Molly ate the hearty breakfast and then bounced up to shower and finish packing her suitcase. All Thad had told her was to pack for a warm climate. He wouldn't reveal their honeymoon locale because he wanted it to be a surprise. Molly felt giddy like a school girl. Her heart raced with excitement. She wouldn't give her headache a second thought even though one had nagged at her for several days. With all the buzz of activity, she was sure it was due to tension. *This, too, shall pass*, she reminded herself. She had never been a complainer before and certainly wouldn't start now although she was marrying a doctor. The last thing he wants in a wife is another patient. *Nothing would mar this day.*

Thad and Molly both had begged off for the customary two-hour photo shoot before the wedding. "All that would do is tire out us, as well as all of you," they had expressed to the children. "We had rather the photographer get some candid shots before the wedding and at the reception. That way we can arrive at church just before the two o'clock hour," Molly added.

Molly was stunned as she arrived in the limousine Thad had sent for her. The parking lot was overflowing. She couldn't believe this many people would show up for their wedding. An open invitation had been placed in the church bulletin, and hundreds had been mailed to Molly and Thad's friends. It was evident most had accepted the invitation.

Mrs. Sadie had come through royally. The sanctuary had been transformed into a tropical paradise, fitting for the king of Siam. The wedding party had gathered in the foyer, except for Thad. He was holding to tradition and avoiding seeing his bride until she walked down the aisle. Molly had asked Caitlin to be her matron of honor and Emily to be the flower girl. Celeste and Janice Baugh, her long-time friend, were her other two attendants. Benji was going to walk Molly down the aisle and give her away. Thad had selected his partner, Dr. Joe Cross, to be his best man. He turned over the selection of ushers to Benji, so he had enlisted his old high school buddies, Tadpole, T-winy, and Dog Hair. Molly was surprised at how beautiful the group was. The female attendants wore teal green silk sheaths, a color just a few shades deeper than Molly's sea foam. The guys, decked out in tuxedos, would have given Tom Cruise and Brad Pitt a run for their money. Little Emily rushed to her grandmother as soon as Molly entered. She put her arms around Molly's legs and squeezed her tightly. "Gram, you look bu-ti-ful."

"So do you, Miss Priss," replied Molly.

Gloria, who was running the show as the wedding director, pulled Emily away. "You mustn't wrinkle Gram's pretty dress. Besides, I need you to take your basket and be ready to strew petals down the aisle like we practiced." That was all it took to loosen Emily's grip.

When the wedding march finally began, and Molly started her stroll down the aisle, Thad was overcome with emotion when he saw this beautiful woman who was about to be his wife, walking down the aisle, her eyes meeting his. Thad had never been known for being emotional, but unexpected tears of joy streamed down his face.

When they faced each other at the altar and held hands, Thad leaned over and whispered, "You are the most gorgeous thing I've ever laid eyes on." This did much to bolster Molly's confidence.

She uttered softly, "I love you so much, Thad."

The minister cleared his throat and lightened the mood when he teased, "If I could interrupt you lovebirds, we'll get this wedding underway." This brought a chuckle from the entire congregation.

After the birdseed was thrown, Thad and Molly entered the waiting limousine and were whisked away. They were hardly out of view of the church when they celebrated their union with a passionate embrace. "Mrs. Simmons, would you join me for two weeks in Bermuda? I've got plans for you."

"Dr. Simmons, I'd join you for not only for two weeks in Bermuda, but I plan to join you for a journey of a lifetime."

CPSIA information can be obtained
at www.ICGtesting.com
Printed in the USA
LVOW04s0915130716

495507LV00004B/12/P

9 781622 955398